BRIDE OF GLASS

CANDACE ROBINSON

For Mom
Thanks for showing me the way

PROLOGUE

After the Awakening - The Bride

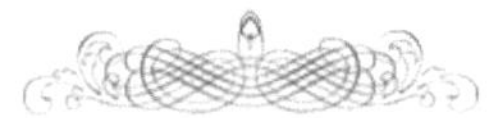

The electrical current beaded and trickled from the Bride's hands, rolling down her fingertips like whips. They popped with each thrust. One after another, she hurled a long charge toward the civilians in her path. She did it without a thought, without remorse or guilt for what she had done. *And why should I?* The mortals became glass the instant her power touched their frail skin.

Bride watched as their souls abandoned their glass bodies. For every final breath that left their lungs, she felt fulfilled—her appetite sated.

The knocking inside her head had quieted. At first, it was incessant, pounding like a drum as though something was begging to be awakened. She couldn't make it go away, so she drowned it out.

The more Bride crushed, the quieter it became—she needed to destroy. She *wanted* to destroy. Nothing else mattered, not even the others who had followed her out from behind the doors of the Glass Vault.

Nothing.

Except, *him*. He was right beside her—the one she was endlessly drawn to. Together they could be anything—together they could create true havoc. The moment Bride opened her eyes, she had wanted his heart to be hers. His heart sat in his chest without any real force, but it was *hers*. It would always be hers.

Vale.

That was his name. His *true* name. Yet, something continuously beat at the back of her mind, wanting her to remember there was more than that—there was more to him.

"Again!" Vale yelled, his eyes hard and focused.

A white flash of light, her light, struck an entire row of brick homes, bathing them in momentary daylight. The blow was powerful enough to freeze every living soul within the houses' walls. She could feel her electricity snaking its way through each mortal's veins, their every cell heating like desert sand, until their bodies became glass, petrified in their last moments of fear, their souls drawn away to the Glass Vault. Trapped forever.

Bride looked back at Vale. His blond hair stood on end, a lovely mess of curls, from her electricity. He was wickedly beautiful, like a lonely bright star illuminating the night sky, searching for its partner. The friction of her power receded back into her bones until there wasn't a single spark flickering. A wrongness stirred within her. He noticed the shift and his green eyes found her.

Beyond his penetrating emerald gaze, a nightmare was lurking. A nightmare Bride wanted to be a part of. Stalking toward her, he backed her up against a tree. The bark dug into her flesh, and she savored the sting. No matter what happened to her, she couldn't die. Vale treated her differently than the others—she was his Bride.

"Can you keep going?" he asked softly, his lips dangerously close to capturing hers.

She couldn't tell him no. She didn't want to tell him no.

She would *never* tell him no.

"Continue," he pleaded as his head nestled in the crook of her neck.

The knocking in her skull had ceased. Bride lifted Vale's head from her shoulder and gazed one more time into his emerald eyes, a devious smile spreading across her lips. That was the only answer he needed, the only one he would ever need with her. Then his mouth claimed hers in a fierce and devilish kiss, their lips slanting over one another's, their tongues entwining, tasting, devouring. And she relished his kiss—she always did.

Vale's hands roamed over the curves of her body, cupping her backside when she pulled him closer. His hard length pressed against her, making her anticipation for what was to come rise even more. The electricity sparked again in Bride's veins as her power resurfaced.

For him, she would always continue.

ONE

The Awakening - The Bride

Her eyelids flew open, no longer consumed by darkness. She looked around wildly as her vision cleared, and a pair of emerald irises met hers. A young man with golden hair leaned over her, his face mere inches from hers. His bright, dancing gaze tamed her in place. She couldn't remove her eyes from those two beautiful specks of green light. He smiled down at her with a hint of allure, danger.

She *liked* it.

"Welcome to the new world, Bride. I am Vale, and you are going to be the most magnificent creature the world has ever seen."

Bride opened her mouth to speak, but a sharp pain in her chest halted her. An ache around her heart stirred, a craving for chaos and destruction. It sat in the deepest part of her soul, begging to be filled, yet she didn't move.

"Vale." The name, his name, rolled across her tongue like wildfire. She treasured it.

"Are you ready?" The ache in her chest rose with his

question. She knew what he was asking her.

Vale pulled her up to a sitting position. Bride's legs, ready to move, dangled over the metal edge of a cool silver table. A white gown, like a waterfall made of silk, spilled down her body to her ankles. She didn't remember wearing this—then again, she couldn't remember how she had gotten here. With a growing curiosity, she held out her hands in front of her, and a spark popped from the tips of her fingers. A buzzing sensation pulsed through her entire body. Bride focused on it, concentrating on the electricity and gathering it into her palms.

As she thrust her hand forward, a bolt of electricity shot out from her palms, slamming against the wall, shattering like glitter. She smiled to herself with gratification when the bright light created a deafening pop.

"I am ready," Bride said, determination filling her with a will to do whatever he wanted.

Vale nodded and clapped his hands loudly in front of his chest. One minute she was seated on the table, and the next she stood on the floor with glass objects surrounding her. Glass machinery was positioned directly above her. She lowered her head and scanned the area until she found Vale in the middle of the room.

He wore a white shirt of the same material as her dress, ruffles positioned down the center of his chest. His face beamed with malice, and she wanted to be a part of whatever gave him that pleasure.

With inhuman speed, Vale moved to where she stood and held a hand out to her. "Lead us," he instructed.

Bride shook the stiffness from her arms and took hold of his hand. The warmth of his fingertips awakened something positively wicked inside of her. She couldn't help but feel enkindled by his attention and soft touch.

Lifting the skirt of her dress, Bride rigidly stepped down from her box with Vale's aid. Like her, other lovely creatures were leaving their own confinements.

Bride fixed her gaze on Vale as he led her to a hallway. Together, they walked, and they walked, and while they did, a slight sense of familiarity rushed through her, as though she had been down these halls before. Ornate wallpaper lined the walls, and crystal chandeliers hung from above.

Vale came to a stop as they reached the end of the hall, a door standing between them and what waited outside. He pointed to the golden handle and bowed low, waiting for her to make the first move. She pressed forward, throwing open the door in one swift movement, and stepped out into the darkness which called to her very heart. This was what she thirsted for.

With a glance over her shoulder, Bride stared at the others behind her, all of whom had followed her into the darkness. She scanned the crowd, her gaze stilling on a young woman wearing a blue patch over her left eye. A crazed smile was spread across the woman's face—she wanted the same thing as Bride. Something then tugged at Bride, telling her to go after the woman, to chase her down, or cry out for her. But then, unintentionally, a small crackle of light slipped from her palm, striking the ground at the woman's feet.

Bride refocused, the moment forgotten.

As she turned her head back around, Bride searched for Vale, finding him farther up ahead, his eyes narrowed at the other immortals. She caught up with him in a matter of moments, then he placed his hand against her lower back as he spoke to the others.

"This was your home." Vale flicked his hand back at the building. "Within the Glass Vault you have become immortal. Those who you use your power on will become glass, and their souls transported back here. We need as many as we can get for now, but I want them all. You will obey my rules or there will be many ways to be punished. We are going to take everyone. Follow her." He motioned at her. "The Bride will lead us on our path to elimination, and then we will separate to finish."

"I will help lead," a voice called from the crowd.

Furrowing her brow, Bride whirled around to a young woman walking toward them. Her thick red hair cascaded down her shoulders and her silky blue dress swished as she moved.

"Do not belittle me, Red," Vale growled. "You will have much to answer for if you dare speak out again."

She lifted her chin in defiance, slowly approaching Bride, the woman's brown irises boring into hers. "Do you remember me?"

Bride didn't answer.

The woman bared her teeth as she grinned. "My name is Fannie."

Bride studied the immortal, finding nothing familiar about her. The electricity crackled in her palms once more, and she drew up her hand to strike the woman in her pretty face.

Vale was faster, though. He grabbed the back of Fannie's neck and squeezed it. Fannie's grin twisted into a grimace, and Bride smiled.

"I'm warning you. If you oppose the Bride or me, I will end you in seconds. Do you understand?"

Fannie remained quiet, her face pale.

"I said, *do you understand*?" He shook her back and forth like a little doll. One that Bride would make broken.

"Yes, Master," Fannie grunted.

Vale tossed her to the side and she stumbled backward, catching herself before crashing to the ground. He turned his back on her again and faced Bride.

"Don't forget what your father would do if something happens to me," Fannie said, her lip curled into a snarl.

Vale flexed his beautiful hands and balled them into tight fists. He then jolted toward her, slapping Fannie across the face. A thunderous sound clapped as Fannie's head was thrown to the side. With a vicious smile, she slowly brought her face back to him but remained silent.

"Do not mention my father again," Vale ground out.

He settled his gaze back on Bride, and his furious expression turned to one of delectation. "Begin."

Without hesitation, Bride moved forward. She could feel the immortals' eyes on her back as she took her first steps onto a paved road full of sky-scraping trees. Into the night they followed, driven by the need to destroy. Destroy. *Destroy.*

When the first civilian came into Bride's view, she didn't hesitate. She lit up with white crackling light and hurled her first bolt of electricity at the young male. A rush of satisfaction stormed through her as his skin ignited and froze into glass. He didn't even have a chance to scream. His soul would now be at the Glass Vault for Vale to do with as he chose.

The world spun for a moment, a dazed feeling washing over her. But then her body relaxed, and she wanted to do *more*, to taste that darkness again.

After the first soul was claimed, the immortals trailing after her responded in a monstrous uproar. Fueled by their desire, and hers, for more, Bride led them down streets, cutting off electricity, phone lines, and lighting the world up with her power. The more civilians she turned to glass, no matter how thrilled she was, the more she needed to continue. She *ached* for it.

By morning, the civilians in town had become more aware of what was happening, and chaos ensued. They tried to pack their families into cars and flee, but they were too slow. Guns were fired, knives thrown, gasoline and matches attempted to strike, but nothing from humanity could stop an immortal.

After several days, the immortals separated in their own directions, leaving only Bride, Vale, and Fannie. Bride wanted

Fannie to leave—she yearned to have Vale to herself—but the woman remained.

"Can we rest?" Bride asked, her lids fluttering from lack of sleep. Unlike the slap he would have given to Fannie, Vale lifted her chin with a gentle touch.

"Try," he whispered, his emerald gaze locked onto hers. She knew he trusted her and believed in her strength.

Because Bride believed in him too, she held her palms up in front of her and willed the spark to life. A tiny flicker popped, then the light snuffed out.

"I can't." She furrowed her brow, growing frustrated with herself. But he only nodded, while Fannie clenched her jaw and gave her a dark look, dripping with hatred.

They trekked to the nearest house, a two-story with a wide porch and white-washed wooden balcony. Vale charged to the porch and kicked the door open, breaking the deadbolt. A heat flowed through her body at his raw strength and inhuman speed and went straight to her center. She wanted him then and there, flesh to flesh.

Screaming went off inside her, and she shook her head to clear it.

Setting the odd feeling aside, she followed Vale down a narrow hallway to a living room. She took a deep breath and inhaled jasmine and refocused once more. A spark of energy popped in her hands when she found an old couple huddled on the floor behind the couch, their bodies trembling, their eyes open wide in horror.

"Please leave us be," the old man begged.

He gripped his wife's wrinkled hand tightly. Beads of perspiration dotted his sun-spotted forehead. The man pulled his wife closer into his side to shield her as best he could. Bride wasn't the least bit moved by the gesture—she wanted to feel her power again and destroy.

She lifted her hands, willing enough energy to create a spark, then unleashed a bright bolt that illuminated the room.

It hit the woman first, and the man released a choking sob as he held his wife's glass body. Bride listened to his beautiful cries a moment longer before taking him next. A sense of fulfillment rushed over her as the couple cradled each other in their glass positions.

"I will be back shortly." Vale nodded his approval and left the room.

Bride sank into the cushions of an old floral couch while the statues of glass hovered behind. Fannie lingered in the room, watching Bride the entire time. The blue skirts of her dress swished as she approached and lowered herself beside Bride. She propped her elbow on the back of the couch and gazed at the side of Bride's face.

Bride chose to ignore her and examined the many-framed photos of loved ones hung across the wall. It was far more interesting than engaging in a staring war with the one immortal she wanted dead.

"You know," Fannie drawled, "you are only his marionette. Eventually, he will cut your strings and toss you aside. Then there will be a new one to take your place that he will latch the threads onto."

Her words burned, and for a moment, she wondered if he really would do that to her. Toss her aside for someone else? Vale called her his Bride—*the* Bride—and he wanted her to lead, not Fannie. She shoved the words away as if they meant nothing because Fannie was *nothing*.

"You wish," Bride said and continued to stare straight ahead without blinking.

In an instant, Fannie pressed a knife into Bride's throat. Her head pushed back against the couch as the blade bit into her flesh.

"You may be immortal, but that doesn't mean I can't have a little fun with you." She inched the blade closer to the scar at Bride's throat. "Maybe I'll just peel off your skin, bit by tiny bit. I'll begin with this soft little nose of yours. Maybe slice it off?"

Fannie grabbed Bride's nose with her free hand and squeezed, pinching it to the right. Anger brewed within her, creating a storm of wild fury. Bride's fingernails dug into the skirt of her silk dress to keep her power from unleashing.

"And what would Vale do if you delivered on your threat?" Bride asked.

Fannie threw her head back and laughed hysterically. "Vale? What is the worst he can do? Shove me back in my cage or send me back to the Underworld? His father would destroy him. He already has."

Bride frowned—her last words hadn't made sense. "What do you mean by that? How has his father destroyed him?"

Fannie released Bride's nose, but the cold steel remained pressed against her throat. "Tut-tut-tut. Enough talk for now." She pulled the knife away and slipped it back into her dress. "But maybe you're not so special after all, are you, *Bride*?"

Bride brushed her fingertips across her throat, and her nostrils flared. The blade might have been gone, but her anger demanded to be free. She balled her hand into a fist and threw a flash of electricity at Fannie's chest. The immortal flew off the couch and slammed against the sheetrock, her body knocking down a shelf of figurines from the wall. As she crashed to the floor, surrounded by shattered ceramic, Fannie cackled with laughter.

"Silly girl, you can't turn immortals into glass." She stood with her spine pulled taut, her hand rubbing at her chest. "Still, it hurts like fire to the skin."

"Good." Bride smiled, threatening her with another small current in her palm.

Fannie watched the energy in Bride's hand spark to life, seeming hesitant. "Believe what you want, but you truly are only temporary. Have fun with him while it lasts, *little puppet*." With a smirk as though nothing happened, Fannie swayed her hips and sat on the couch. If Bride could sew

Fannie's eyes and mouth shut, she would use the immortal's red hair as the thread.

The front door squeaked open as Vale returned.

"The street is clear for now. We will begin again in the morning after you have time to rest." His eyes and words were for Bride only. The fact he didn't acknowledge Fannie made her chest swell with pride.

"Where should we sleep?" Fannie asked, as though she would be the one riding Vale into bliss tonight.

"*You* can choose wherever you wish to sleep," Vale snapped at her. "Let us find somewhere upstairs." He held his open palm out to Bride, and she took his perfect hand, tightening her fingers around his warmth.

"But—" Fannie stopped short, halted by the hard, icy look in his stare. The immortal could pretend she wasn't afraid of him all she wanted, but she was. Fannie's gaze shifted to Bride, murderous.

"I am going to take a shower. Join me?" Vale's face softened as he asked Bride. His eyes mirrored the same emotion that danced in hers—he wanted her as much as she wanted him.

Bride's lips tilted upward and she grasped him through his pants, his hard length ready for her. "Yes."

A low groan escaped his throat as she gripped him harder before releasing him. With that final exchange, Bride led him up the stairs to create a storm of their own.

TWO

Before-Josselyn Shaw

Fuck this place, Josselyn thought as she toted a six-pack of beer from the rundown gas station in her shitty town. Tonight was different than any other night—she was going to drown her sorrows away, alone in her apartment.

Josselyn's "best friend" Emma had stood her up earlier, even though Emma had known how much Josselyn needed her. Josselyn's ex-boyfriend broke up with her the night before because he said they were *too different*. Yeah, but not too different to have sex with her before he'd told her that. *Fucking asshole.*

Screw him and screw Emma. She didn't need anyone except herself and the beautiful pack of beer hanging in her hand. The clinking of the bottles was practically chanting her name, so she pulled one out before climbing into the driver's seat.

The engine purred to life after she used her keychain to pop the lid on the beer. She knew she shouldn't be drinking, but she didn't give one single shit. Josselyn brought the tip to her mouth and took a swig, humming along with the car as the coolness slid down her throat and drifted to her stomach.

"Where to now, Josselyn?" she asked herself, peering out the window at the little bit of daylight that was left.

"Time to get this party started," she answered, revving the car and swerving violently from the parking lot.

Josselyn continued taking swigs from her beer as she turned left on Oak Street, almost finished with beer number one, when she slammed hard on the brakes. A building, a rather *big* building rising high from the shadows of tall trees, had caught her attention. The structure had never been anywhere on Oak Street before, and it was out of place in a town like hers.

She shouldn't be buzzing from her first beer already. At least, she didn't think she should be—drinking had never been her thing, until tonight. Reckless just so happened to be her new middle name.

Josselyn put the car in park and stepped out, bringing her almost full pack of beer with her. She cracked open another bottle and took a long drink as she approached the building.

It wasn't the aged stones around the base of the building or lack of windows that drew her focus, but rather the door. It was large enough for an elephant to fit through.

"Okay, that's an enormous door," Josselyn said. She nearly dropped her beer when it suddenly flew open, her heart pounding.

A young blond guy emerged from inside, halting when his green gaze settled on hers.

"Need something?" he asked as he pulled the door shut behind him.

"Um, no?" Josselyn furrowed her brow. "Well, maybe. Has this place always been here?"

Though she'd only taken this route a couple times, she had never noticed a building at any point. It was quite possible she couldn't remember or just hadn't paid much attention. *I would've remembered a building like this though, right?* There would've been people talking about something like this coming to Deer Park.

The guy's gaze stayed locked on hers, and a smile tugged at his lips. "Yeah, we recently cut the trees surrounding the building to make it noticeable for customers."

Josselyn's eyes darted back and forth between the guy and the stone of the building, curiosity blooming inside her. "What is it?"

"It's a museum with glass statues displayed in different artistic ways. We are currently closed, but you can check it out if you want." The blond guy pointed toward the door with a large grin spread across his face.

Maybe it was the beer, but Josselyn felt her curiosity grow into excitement at seeing something so unique. She definitely wanted to go inside and take a look. Running her hand through her short blonde hair, she said, "If it's okay with you, I will."

The guy opened the door for Josselyn, ushering her in with a wave of his hand. Butterflies danced in her stomach when she took her first steps forward. The idea of being alone inside a museum was both creepy and electrifying.

"Take your time," he purred after her as the door closed. Josselyn stared at the wood and golden knob, not knowing what to think.

"What a weirdo." Slowly, she turned around and peered down a long hallway. Clutching the bottles close to her side, she took another deep drink of the bottle in her other hand.

She walked down the long entrance, which led to another hall, which led to another before she froze. Displays were everywhere, aligned in a circular fashion from her left, looping all the way around to her right.

"Now the party can officially start."

Josselyn stepped to her right, passing several fairy-tale displays where the statues weren't in a very fairytale-like state. She stopped in front of one with a large bridge—three grotesque trolls sat underneath it, and a goat broken into small glass pieces rested on top of the arch. The precision in the glasswork was almost life-like. She shivered, the scene leaving her impressed and shaken at the same time.

The second beer bottle emptied, and she cracked open number three as she passed by the next display. She stopped in front of it, surprised by the description: *Jack the Ripper*. The longer she looked at it, the colder she became, so she hurried on.

The next glass scene displayed a large sign with the words *Sleepy Hollow* written across it. *I love that movie and book.*

She was about to take a drink when something tugged at her legs. Frowning, she looked down, but nothing was there. Just as she chalked it up to her imagination, it pulled at her again—harder this time, and strong enough to knock the beers out of her hands. They crashed to the marble floor, shattering on impact. Her heart slammed inside her chest, and her body trembled as she glanced around the empty room.

The invisible wind pulled one more time and her feet dragged across the floor while she screamed. Josselyn then smacked to the marble, falling into the cool liquid and shards of broken beer bottles. She screamed louder and clawed at nothing, crying out for help. With one final pull, she was yanked into the display.

Once the tugging stopped and the wind dissipated, Josselyn jumped to her feet and hauled ass. She didn't get far as she struck a wall and fell back, landing on the ground with a hard slam. Josselyn rubbed the sore spots on her ass when she realized it wasn't a wall she'd hit. There wasn't anything there to block her way, yet she couldn't walk through it. Instead of something solid, she stared out at grass and trees. She shouldn't have been seeing grass and trees—she should've been seeing displays and glass statues.

"Where the fuck am I?" she shouted, running as hard as she could at the invisible barrier. It shot her backward. With each try, she rebounded harder.

Josselyn fell once again and rolled onto all fours with a deep breath. Blonde hair spilled over her shoulders and she pushed it away, annoyed. One tendril continued to dangle in her face. A horrified scream escaped her when she realized her blonde hair was no longer short. It was now long and curled, the way it used to look when she was younger. *This has to all be a dream.* Josselyn sat back on her heels, and peered down at her lap—her T-shirt and jeans had been replaced with an old-fashioned gray dress that had seen better days. Her hands shook and her voice was trapped in her throat as panic took up the space within her.

Josselyn stood on wobbly legs, the dress swaying against her body and bare feet. She gripped the fabric of the dress until the skin on her knuckles turned pure ivory. Trees and bushes surrounded her with only one direct path ahead. It was in the opposite direction from where she'd fallen. Josselyn didn't know what to do until she took a deep breath and decided to run for the path laid out in front of her.

She trampled through bushes and branches, stopping only for a second to see the same Sleepy Hollow sign from the display. The wind blew at her hair, cold against her warm back. *This was impossible.* A fog settled around her, and she took off running again, jogging into a town with rows of rotted houses lined on either side of the field. Her heart pounded harder. She didn't stop, didn't think, she just ran.

As Josselyn finally came to a halt, the wind paused and the world became silent. The hairs on her arms stood on end at the eeriness of it all. She didn't know where to go, what direction to take, but then she didn't need to know—a graveyard rested before her. Littered in front of every headstone sat a severed head, their blank dead eyes seeming to be focused directly on her. They were everywhere. No bodies, just bloodied, abandoned heads. She gasped loudly and covered her mouth.

The ground beneath her feet shook with a deep vibrato.

Pound, pound-pound, pound. The sound of it was deafening in the silence of the graveyard, yet it only grew louder. Josselyn couldn't move, couldn't think, as the first living thing she'd seen, since the guy at the museum, barreled through the fog.

A man on a horse approached. She was about to yell for help when her mouth fell open. To her immediate horror, he had no head. No *fucking* head at all. Josselyn closed her eyes tightly and swallowed hard. If this was, without a doubt, *the* Sleepy Hollow, then that could only mean the man on the mount was the Headless Horseman.

"This can't be happening. It's only a dream." The beat of hooves on dirt came closer, each step louder, and she begged herself to wake up. For one split second, a searing pain tore at her throat, then it faded away as quickly as it had come.

Katrina awoke in a wooden chair in her sitting room. "What was I doing again? Oh yes, I need to start cooking. I must finish everything before the Headless Horseman returns, when I will have to fall silent again."

THREE

Maisie

An eye for an eye.

That was something Maisie no longer believed after the shenanigans she had to face once she'd been set free from the Glass Vault. She'd managed to avoid the other immortals ever since they'd all gone their separate ways.

Maisie had followed Perrie pretty much the entire time without her notice, while pretending like she was wreaking havoc on Earth, as August, no wait—Quinsey, no wait—Vale barked out his demands. She should've been shocked by the whole Vale-being-some-type-of-demon thing, but after dying and coming back to life so many times, nothing could surprise her these days.

Then she'd lost them.

Now, today of all days, Maisie stumbled upon Josselyn Shaw, AKA Katrina Van Tassel. She barely gave Maisie more than a side-glance, yet Maisie knew the immortal was watching her since she hadn't joined in on Josselyn's turning people to glass excursion. Freezing people into glass wasn't

Maisie's idea of arts and crafts, but then a young man with black hair passed them. Josselyn reached out and touched him, just barely, but it was enough.

The guy's body stilled, his eyes wide open in shock as his skin turned into a clear glass. He looked just the same as the ones that had once been inside the museum's displays, minus his glass being clear instead of having color. His neck cracked, and his head slowly slid off his shoulders to the ground, causing a *clink-clink* ripple effect. *Hmm, that's the tenth time she's done that in a row, and the heads never break.* Maisie's main thought was, *Why do the heads fall off her statues if she isn't the Headless Horseman?*

"Darn, that was to be mine," Maisie yelled, shaking her fist in the air, pretending as though she wanted to help destroy these lives. "I'll get the next one."

"Not if I get to them first." Josselyn grinned wide, her long blonde hair sashaying with the wind.

"I think it's easier for you to see them since I only have one eye." Before, Maisie wore patches to show that people with one eye could liven up their look. But now that she did only have one, it wasn't so bad since she was already used to the patch.

Josselyn ignored the comment and strolled away.

What? Maisie had *only* been giving her a true statement. *Okay, what do I do now?*

Maisie followed behind Josselyn and contemplated how to get Perrie out of this huge mess. Weeks ago, after a couple of days out of the Glass Vault, Maisie was able to pull herself out of her locked-and-lost-in-her-own-head stupor. That meant there *must* be a way to do the same for Perrie.

When she and the immortals first walked out of the museum, Maisie was hidden, safely tucked away somewhere in her own brain. It was like an out of body experience—she'd been shut off from everything, while Crazy Maisie, as she now liked to call her, had full control.

Crazy Maisie had been insane—constantly skipping up to civilians, talking gibberish, grabbing onto their clothing and singing to them until their flesh turned to glass. She knew Snow White liked to sing for no reason, but that was ridiculous.

Somehow, like always before, she traveled her way back to the surface and kicked Crazy Maisie aside to wherever she'd come from. At least Maisie's eighteenth birthday hadn't been totally wretched that day. And since then, there'd been no sign of the lunatic.

Everyone in town was gone—her parents, her uncle, schoolmates. Maisie had cried silently on the inside because she'd missed them so much, but she had to cut it off. It was already done.

She couldn't stop it when the immortals had gone down her and Perrie's old street because she'd still been Crazy Maisie. Perrie had been farther behind, down the road, while Maisie had skipped up to her old house to sing her own family into glass. But when she'd gotten there, some little, creepy immortal kid had already done the job.

Once freed, after being locked away behind Crazy Maisie, the memories hit. A part of her had felt content that she hadn't turned her family to glass. In a weird way, she was thankful her parents and uncle were together when they'd turned. It helped to know they weren't alone in that moment, and Maisie was eighty-nine percent sure Perrie would agree.

She *had* to find her cousin.

Maisie blinked and realized she was no longer walking—she'd completely lost sight of Josselyn. A relieved sigh escaped her at being alone again. Then the ground trembled beneath her feet, her teeth clattering together as the shaking became stronger. The only thing to do was pluck up a glass head laying unbroken on the cement—the warmth penetrated her hands. One would think the glass would be cool to the touch, but it wasn't.

With its already-frozen mouth open in horror, Maisie sang to the severed head, "Little head, you must forever remain glass." The ground rumbled harder. She froze in place, trying to sing another melody as a giant troll from the Glass Vault pounded his way across the street. "Glass is the only way to be in order to help us conquer the lands."

The troll didn't give Maisie one look as his matted hair blew off crumbs of filth with the breeze. She tried hard not to stare at his long length in between his legs flapping about. If the other immortals had to wear clothing matching their display scenes, then couldn't the trolls at least be covered in a loincloth or something? She shivered in revulsion, then gently rested the glass head back on the ground.

Maisie blew out a breath. "That was close."

"Maisie?" a deep voice asked.

She jerked upward and whirled around to find herself face-to-face with another immortal.

"Who is Maisie? My name is Snow," she said, attempting to get back into character, role play, or whatever this was.

Entering Crazy Maisie mode, she lifted her head to give a delighted and creepy smile, baring all her teeth. Despite the ripped black T-shirt and new scars, Maisie would recognize this guy anywhere.

Neven.

"Hello, um, Frankenstein's Monster," Maisie sang. "How are you on your mission to end it all?" She didn't even stutter when she met his light brown eyes.

Neven palmed his forehead with his scarred-up hand and shook his head. A vibration started from the tip of his scalp and ran through to his toes, shaking his entire body.

"Are you okay?" Maisie reached out to touch his arm but ripped it back.

Then it broke out. A laugh. A hard rumble of laughter escaped his mouth. She darted her eye side to side to plot her best escape. But she didn't have any blasted time. He grabbed her by the shoulders, holding her firmly in place.

"Cut the shit, Maisie." Neven's laughter stopped, his brow furrowed. "I know you're *you*. I've been following you around for a while now, not sure what state of mind you were in at first. I just didn't want to say anything until I was sure. That thing you just did with the head was a little overdone, though." His gaze peered over at where she'd safely set the head next to its body.

"So, you are you?" Hope, relief, and happiness all played tug-of-war inside her head.

Neven smiled sheepishly and ran a hand through his shaggy black hair. "Yeah, I've been me since we stepped out the door. As for everyone else, seems like they're all lost in their own little world."

Oh, thank goodness for that! Excitement bloomed in her chest, so much so that Maisie could wrap him up in a hug, but she held back. There was no way of knowing who, or *what*, else might be creeping about, so it would be better to leave things as they were.

She nodded and silently agreed with herself.

"We can't stay out in the open like this. Let's find somewhere and go," Neven said, searching up and down the cracked and broken street.

Placing her fingers to her temples, she thought back to what she'd passed by earlier. Then it came to her. "I know a place. Follow farther behind me and look grim."

His face was already set in his normally non-smiley face.

"Okay, that's perfect."

Neven's one un-scarred eyebrow popped up. "This is my normal face, Maisie."

"It's *perfect*." She grinned.

Neven staggered behind Maisie as she led the way. The place wasn't too far back, but she did remember a barbershop on the strip, sitting alone beside a few abandoned buildings. She doubted anyone had lingered in that area for long, so it was her best idea.

The shop's red, white, and blue pole, no longer spinning, slipped into view. Thin mini blinds covered the cracked windows, and a small white and black sign on the door read: *Open*.

So that means it should already be unlocked. Gripping the handle, Maisie pushed open the glass door and peered inside.

Immediately, she took a step back, slamming her head against Neven's solid chest.

"What is it?" He slid past her and stepped inside.

"Nothing," she said to his back. "Only three glass statues over there."

Neven shook his head, and Maisie knew he was rolling those brown eyes of his. Chewing on her thumbnail, she followed him inside.

The shop was small with only two seats and mirrors, 1950s barbershop photos lining the walls, and an old black and white checkered tile made up the floor. Maisie headed to the back to confirm there were no signs of immortal life. Nothing was there except a closet-sized bathroom and one person break room.

"Nobody's here," she said, plopping down on one of the two barber chairs. This was the first time in a while since she'd been able to sit down, and the pleather red seats were unbelievably comfy. Neven dragged the other chair closer to hers and took a seat.

While studying the small room, she noticed the phone on the wall, but it wouldn't dial out if she tried. After weeks of immortal destruction, phone lines, car engines, electricity—it was all gone. Who would she call anyway? *It would go over really well when I say there's a demon out loose on the street with immortals tearing down the city with different powers.* It sounded like a pretty good movie, though—she shrugged to herself.

Her gaze stayed locked on Neven, a scowl planted on his

face as he sulked. "Mopiness isn't going to do anything, Neven."

He shot her a glare from beneath long lashes. "Well, it's not like I'm going to go back out there and pretend to murder people, Mais. I'm just … thinking."

"You know, you could've just said you were thinking."

He rolled his eyes and shook his head. "I'm trying to figure out what we can do, but I can't think of anything we can do on our own."

"I can't think of anything either." She tapped her chin several times. "Although, I thought it'd be possible to snap people out of their trances at one point, but I doubt that would have gone over well. I'm sure someone would've run off and tattled to Vale."

Neven ground his teeth. "When I find him, I'm going to kick August's ass *hard.*"

"You mean Vale," Maisie pointed out.

"Whatever. Same difference. Vale is going to be sent back to hell."

"Hey, you know that almost rhymes."

"You know people are dead, right? Everyone is gone. My *mom* is gone." Tears beaded at his eyes, and Maisie's heart thumped a slower tune. She kind of felt bad for making light of everything, but there was nothing else she could do in this apocalyptic situation.

Maisie knew how close he'd been to his mom, how hard it must be to lose her so soon after his dad died. She hadn't talked to Neven because she thought he'd cheated on Perrie. Even then, it was hard for her because she'd cared about him so much. But Perrie was her best friend and her cousin—how could she not have taken her side?

If only Maisie could read Perrie's mind to locate her. There was the one time when they'd been twelve and performed a blood oath by pricking their fingers to become official sisters versus cousins. They'd touched the small tips of their fingers together since they hadn't been ready to go gashing their palms. If only that connection could lead Maisie to her...

Maisie now knew it wasn't Neven who'd cheated on Perrie. But she didn't know the whole story either, only that Vale was responsible. Even without her pencil and notepad, she was able to put two and two together once she'd left Crazy Maisie behind.

Neven wouldn't look up as he hung his head, grieving for his mom. Maisie bit the inside of her cheek and traded her seat for his lap. She leaned to the side so she could wrap her arms around him as best she could.

"I'm sorry, Neven," she started, lying her head against his warm chest and inhaling his familiar minty scent. "I shouldn't have stopped talking to you, but after everything that happened, I couldn't help but feel betrayed, too. I know now it wasn't you, and I'm sorry I didn't figure it out sooner."

He lifted his long arms and circled them around her, sobbing softly as he rested the side of his face against the top of her head. Maisie had never told Perrie how much she missed him because she knew it would hurt her, but she did. She missed his laughter, his rare smiles that would pop up throughout the day, and his friendship. But Perrie's was more important to her. It wasn't like Perrie had forbidden her from talking to him or anything, but Maisie couldn't, not after finding out what she'd thought he'd done. What *they* had thought he'd done.

Neven's sobs finally slowed and he lifted his head away from hers. Maisie peered up, studying his face for a brief moment, reassured by his calm. She then hopped off his lap and straightened the skirt of her dress. "Are you okay now?"

Pursing his lips, Neven closed his eyes and shook his head. But then he started laughing while rubbing at his temple with the back of his hand. "I don't think I'll ever be okay, Mais, but you made the day a whole lot more interesting."

She gave him a soft smile, glad she could semi-cheer him

up. Now he could help her release more immortals from their mental prisons. "You know what we have to do now, right?"

"What's that?" He looked her straight in the eye and arched a brow.

"We have to get Perrie back."

FOUR

Before-Vale

The day Perrie Madeline poked Vale in the chest with her makeshift weapon he knew he had to have her. The very moment her cello bow had connected with his chest, a gateway inside of him opened. It may have been an obsession, but the shining light within her had a subtle potential for darkness that matched his own. He had felt his Bride resting inside of her, dormant—he could make her his equal when she rose. She needed him, and he needed her.

Before Perrie, anyone else would have suited him fine. He would have chosen a mortal who was easier to manipulate, someone with inherent darkness, but it had to be Perrie. No one else made his fingers yearn for the cool metal of a scalpel more than her. It was her throat he ached with longing to cut into—the day her light had called to his darkness.

Vale had slowly slinked his way in, careful not to be too quick about his work. Besides, she was too wrapped up with Neven Lee and that needed to be handled *delicately*. Neven could never have satisfied her in the long run, and Vale had to show her he was the only one who could.

As Vale walked out from the Glass Vault, followed by the redhead, he could not care less about anything except Perrie. The redhead trailing behind him was a means to an end, and her attempt to woo him by tugging the front of her shirt lower was pathetic. He did not care to know her true name because she meant nothing to him, so he only referred to her as Red. His father, on the other hand, seemed to believe otherwise about her.

Red slid her hand down Vale's arm, and he withdrew it from her grasp. The immortal huffed, seeming perturbed by his rejection. She was a touchy one. It was true in the past he may have enjoyed their plotting and fucks, but she never mattered. There was one plot, one focus, and it all revolved around Perrie Madeline.

He felt it every time he saw her, that little glow of light waiting to be snuffed out—for him to eclipse it. But he could wait. The Glass Vault still needed to be filled. The process had been slow, but when the time was right, the pace would pick up. By the time the Glass Vault was stocked with his army of immortals, he planned to have Perrie sitting on the edge of his blade.

"What do you think of the new additions?" Red asked, a smile slowly spreading across her face. She wanted Vale's approval like the little servant she forgot she was. He never gave it, knowing she had a hidden agenda—most likely with his father.

"They work." Vale had built the outside structure, an architectural masterpiece, while Red came up with the ideas for inside it. Her past-life experiences contributed to much of the décor. She had felt the need to include real-life horror, historical aberrations of past events, and altered human fairy tales as grotesque curiosities. By turning modern horror films into panicked chaos of unpredictability, Red had wanted to transcend human entertainment. Vale did not care. He only needed the souls.

"Follow me," he demanded.

This was the first and only time he would let her out of her cage. Unlike the other immortals, she had a little more freedom to roam around. She could go up and down the halls of the museum or walk between the trees outside the building, but she was prohibited from going farther than the tree line. Vale made sure of that.

"So, you appreciate the fact I added the trolls?"

"I said they work, did I not?" Vale came to an abrupt halt, glaring at Red. "Why are you asking me this again?"

"But you said nothing else." Red rubbed her palms together, and all Vale could focus on was how filthy her nails were. He shuddered.

"I said they *work*." Vale clenched his teeth so hard his jaw throbbed. He was not fond of pointless drawn-out conversations—he already knew she wanted to have several displays that used the corrupt souls and the hellish beasts from the Underworld.

Despite his harsh tone, Red beamed, appearing genuinely pleased by his answer. His fingers itched for a blade to use on her, but she was needed for his plan.

It was time to make his move, and his play was Neven Lee. Vale had been stalking his home for weeks, which meant he knew Neven's schedule inside and out. He studied Neven's behaviors, his habits and ticks.

Neven's two-story house was a familiar sight as they made their way to the end of the long drive. If his timing was correct, and it always was, then Neven would be heading out for a jog. The sound of the front door cracking open confirmed his precision and also caught Red off guard. Vale shoved her to the side of the house, and her body crashed into the brick with a loud smack. He smirked at that.

Vale easily scooted beside her, watching around the side as Neven closed the door behind him and descended the porch steps. It took a special concoction to put Neven out for half a day, but he managed to slip a little into his drink at lunch the day before. Vale was especially careful on the dosage as too much could have killed Neven instantly. A small dose, like the one in his soda, was potent enough to give Neven a sense of "food poisoning." As planned, Neven failed to show up at school.

Vale was confident enough in his prey that he knew Neven would not skip his daily run. Like clockwork, Neven's illness cleared by the time Vale and Red arrived for the male's usual routine. Being the loyal and responsible girlfriend, Perrie would visit Neven after school to look after him—Vale knew it. It was a certainty.

What a pitiful human being, Vale thought as Neven jogged away. He and Red had ten minutes to prepare before Perrie arrived.

"This way." Vale peeled himself from the wall the second Neven was out of sight and darted for the front door.

Red grinned as she caught up with him.

As expected, the door was already unlocked when Vale twisted the knob. He was unsurprised by the living situation inside. The entire dwelling was mundane with its boring cloth furniture and photographs of Neven Lee throughout the house. Vale skipped the sightseeing and headed for the main stairs.

Once on the second floor, he found Neven Lee's bedroom door wide open. The putrid stench of the mortal's soiled basketball clothing violated Vale's senses the second he walked in. Dirty clothes lay on the floor in a pile, neatly tucked into a visible corner of the room. Humans like Neven were filthy and pathetic.

"Time for part two," Vale said as he reluctantly faced a grinning Red. She was clearly delighted by what was to come, her fingers already at the button of her jeans, but the thought of her skin on his again left him disinterested. "Undress."

With eager motions, she unfastened her pants and shoved

them down. Vale removed his own clothing, tossing them beside the bed next to Red's. Not once had he held interest to look at Red's naked flesh as he walked to a dresser covered in band stickers. He turned on Neven's vintage stereo and cranked the music up like Neven Lee would. Even Neven's taste in music unsettled him.

Vale brushed away his distaste for the music and sauntered to the bed. Red was already sprawled naked on the mattress, her back arched, her nipples peaked, wetness pooling between her thighs. Her brown eyes locked on his, the hunger of her want for him obvious. If it were not for the plan and the dying sound of a car engine, he would have walked away.

Now Perrie Madeline was on her way, and she would discover what he wanted her to. The thought of the mortal reminded him of all the things he yearned to do to her—kiss her, taste her mouth and in between her legs, sink into her heat as she shouted his name. Then, like the end to a perfect symphony, his blade slicing clean across her throat so his Bride could rise. Those thoughts had his length hard and ready.

Vale called on a glamour, which shaped his facial features into Neven's. He was used to changing his face when needed, and that was how he knew his plan would work. With one last look at the open door, he leapt onto the bed, colliding with Red's naked flesh, her breasts bouncing. She let out a squeal of pure pleasure as he rolled beneath her and sank into her heat.

As Red moved back and forth on top of him, her filthy nails dug into the skin on his chest, and those fingernails were all he could focus on.

The recognizable sound of Perrie's footsteps echoing outside the room was enough to distract himself. He closed his eyes and imagined it was Perrie Madeline grinding her hips into him instead, or more so, the darker version of herself that would one day find him.

FIVE

The Bride

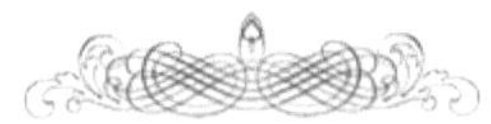

Exhaustion swept through Bride's body, and the electricity at her fingertips barely flickered to life. Vale was right behind her at the next turn, waiting for her to spark up again. They had been at this for weeks now.

"I'm in need of rest," Bride said through gritted teeth, irritated that her energy was running low.

"We can stop for a little while." Vale raked a hand through his blond curls, moving his lower jaw side to side. She knew he wanted to keep going—as did she.

"I'm frustrated too, Vale."

His hand cupped the side of her face, and his thumb rubbed gently against her cheek. "You've done beautifully, my Bride."

His words were the key to lifting her spirits as her shoulders relaxed. Vale was pleased with her work, *their* work. Such elation flowed through her that it felt as though she was floating.

"Where will we go for the night?" Bride asked, fiddling

with the buttons on the front of her dress. Dirt and filth covered the hem of her white gown, proof of their long and strenuous journey.

She brushed a curl from his forehead—even if he wouldn't admit it, he was tired too. A smile, not quite a full one, but close enough, slipped onto his face after her touch. It was a precious gift reserved only ever for her.

"There is an old house a few miles from here that Red is securing for us." His smile dropped, his face becoming unreadable, as he awaited her answer.

A low growl escaped her throat, catching Vale's immediate attention. There was something about Fannie that Bride didn't like, more than the way the immortal was toward her.

"You know she means nothing to me." Vale lifted her chin with a touch of his fingertips. "If I could get rid of her in a second, just for you, I would. But my father wants her here."

With a nod, she clamped her teeth down on her lower lip to keep from speaking words she would rather keep to herself. She had been having more and more thoughts slide in recently, but when she nearly grasped them, they vanished.

Vale held her gaze for a moment longer—his yearning mirroring hers—before he released her face, leaving her missing his warmth. He then silently trekked ahead of her and led the way as she followed behind.

Statue after statue stood frozen, their glass shining beneath the glowing ball of sun in the sky. She smiled at their work, at how complete devastation lingered in their path. Houses destroyed, trees fallen, and streets broken beyond repair. Her smile faltered when a feeling seeped down to her bones—she wasn't fulfilled by the chaos. She needed *more*.

Perhaps sleep would renew the spark within her.

They eventually stopped in front of a Victorian two-story house, surrounded by lush green bushes and a strong iron fence. Bride's feet twitched with a strange warning and for a moment, as she waited at the bottom of the old wooden porch, something within her begged her to run. This would be the perfect opportunity to escape—Vale wasn't paying attention to her. But where would she run to, and why would she want to?

Bride clutched the side of her head and took one step back, then another.

Vale turned to face her and watched her intently. Something like affection sparked in his gaze. "Is something wrong?"

Before she could answer, he scooped her up into his strong arms and carefully towed her through the front door.

The feeling that was inside her vanished, and the sense of safety washed over her instead. Vale was her safety. She rested her head on his shoulder as tiredness took over, hitting her even harder. Bride closed her eyes for a second before Vale set her gently on a soft green couch that her body sank into. She opened her lids and gave him a warm smile.

"Give me a moment," he said and exited the room.

Bride reclined against the back of the couch. The clack of familiar heels sounded as they descended the wooden stairs. Fannie. But Red to Vale. Unfortunately, Bride's moment of peace was now ruined.

Bride hoped if she ignored the immortal that perhaps she would go the other way, but that wouldn't be like Fannie at all.

The immortal bounced into the large living room like a peacock. She appeared clean, her dress pristine, and her red hair wilder than ever. Fannie narrowed her eyes and stepped in front of her.

Bride clenched her jaw. She wanted to tear the immortal's head off with her lightning.

"You're still here, I see. But it won't last. Nothing ever lasts for him."

Baiting her. That was what Fannie was doing *again*. But, Bride stayed.

Fannie sneered, her face turning a bright crimson. "Don't worry, you'll get what's coming to you." She turned on her heels and stormed into another room. The immortal seemed to relish in repeating the same things about Vale to Bride, but when Bride didn't react, that only ignited Fannie's fury.

When they had first walked out of the Glass Vault weeks ago, Fannie had tried to take control, pushing Bride out of the way as much as she could. Bride had stood her ground and Vale had put the immortal in her place once more.

Vale rounded the corner with a shiny metal object, taking a seat in front of Bride on a coffee table cluttered with magazines. With his emerald eyes focused on hers, he picked at his nails with the file.

Bride had noticed this habit for a while, but she wasn't certain what made him do it. Either way, the back-and-forth movements sent a rush of heat straight to her core. As soon as Vale finished, he took out a cloth handkerchief and cleaned the file. Fannie, who had been lingering in the doorway since his arrival, watched him. The way the immortal's eyes danced and the way her chest rose and fell, proved that Fannie was ready to rip his clothing off in the middle of the room just from watching him file his nails. But Bride was too.

"Give me your hand," Vale said softly.

Bride peered up from his file and back into his piercing green eyes. Without a word, she reached toward him and placed her hand in his.

He picked and removed the dirt from under her nails, repeating the same sensual cleaning ritual as before. Once Vale finished, he drew her hand to his mouth and softly blew away the small debris. Bride shivered at the feel of his warm breath on her flesh. A pleased smile crossed Bride's face as she glanced at Fannie, who studied them with revulsion.

"Why don't you ever clean my nails, Master?" Fannie asked while sinking down beside Vale on the table.

He didn't say a word and Bride only smiled wider.

"Come"—Vale released her hand and tucked away his file—"I have something I want to show you."

A new energy rose within her, sweeping the tiredness away. She stood from the couch and followed him down a short hallway, past the flight of stairs, lined with photographs of smiling faces along its beige walls. The people in the photos were dead now, their souls part of the Glass Vault. Bride didn't linger on them long as Fannie clicked her heels. She could tell the immortal was watching her, waiting for Bride to show any sign of weakness.

They passed a large kitchen, and a rotten smell invaded her nostrils. In the center of a table rested a bowl of fruit where tiny flies buzzed around the blackened produce.

Just past the kitchen, Vale pulled open a door that revealed a set of stairs leading down into a dark cellar. Farther down, small candles, already lit, danced in the darkness, their little flames bobbing against the damp breeze of the basement. They could go out any second.

Bride's heart became a steady pound against her sternum.

The descent was slow, and with each step she took, the wood groaned beneath her weight. Her hands slightly trembled, and she didn't know what was happening in that moment—she never felt nervous. Gritting her teeth, she found herself once more and her hands stopped shaking.

Bride pressed closer to Vale, knowing Fannie would attempt to push her down the stairs. She refused to be humiliated by her or anyone.

"And here we are." Vale jumped the last step with an impish grin, making his ethereal face become even more so.

At the bottom of the steps, Bride's gaze settled on a disheveled woman tied up on the cement floor. Her hair was coarse and knotted, her yellow dress caked with mud, and her dark brown skin coated in sweat. The woman lifted her head wearily from the ground, and her brown eyes drifted between the three of them, halting on Bride before growing wide.

The mortal's body shook as she attempted to let out a string of muffled words, despite the cloth around her mouth. Bride felt nothing at the woman's pathetic desperation.

"Pick her up, Red," Vale barked.

Fannie swayed her hips between Vale and Bride, knocking Bride sideways into the wooden rail. Bride's nostrils flared at the slight throb in her back and lightning crackled at her fingertips.

With one hand, Fannie lifted the woman up by her hair, then shoved her down on a metal chair. "Hello, Catherine," she cooed.

Fannie knew her? As Bride squinted her eyes to get a better look, the woman wasn't a stranger—she was one of them.

"We only left you for a moment," Fannie continued, jerking the woman's head back. "I told you we would return."

Bride studied the immortal's features, when something slowly seeped in, becoming familiar… Familiar… A crack of thunder rumbled inside her head, throbbing, spreading. Images flashed before Bride so quickly that she could barely make them out. Lying on a graveled street, in a pool of her own blood, rested a mangled woman wearing a satin yellow dress. Half of her face was mutilated. But the other half? It was the same face as the woman in the chair. Bride inhaled sharply.

"Why is she tied up? Why isn't she out on the streets?" Bride demanded. Something stirred within her, telling her she should not be there, but she ignored the nuisance. Time was being wasted because this immortal wasn't out there gathering more souls.

"We have to send her back," Vale finally said.

Catherine launched herself out of the chair, but Fannie yanked her by the hair and placed a knife at the woman's throat. Fannie slowly led her back to the chair, and Catherine carefully lowered herself down. The knife stayed planted against the immortal's flesh, and a thin line of scarlet ran down Catherine's throat.

"Do you think they're beginning to remember?" Fannie asked Vale.

He cocked his head and stroked his chin, seeming to consider her question.

The question nagged at Bride. *Who is starting to remember? And* what *are they remembering? Is that what keeps knocking at the back of my mind?* She kept her gaze trained on Catherine and her expression neutral as both Vale and Fannie focused on her.

Fannie's eyes slid from Bride's to Vale's like a slithering snake.

"I don't believe so." Vale dropped his hands to his hips and shook his head. "This one wasn't meant for the Glass Vault. Her life was built upon bringing down crime, and in the end, that need to better the world drew her back out." There was an edge to his voice as though he was sickened by the thought. Bride was even more so.

Catherine mumbled hysterically, her muffled wails falling on deaf ears. It was as if she was trying to only tell Bride something, not the others.

"Hand the knife to Bride," Vale instructed Fannie.

Fannie huffed, loud and frustrated. "Why do you keep favoring her, Master? Catherine is *mine.* She's been mine. I should be the one to send her back to the Glass Vault."

"Don't you dare try to undermine me," Vale growled. The hair on Bride's arms and neck stood on end from the deep, enraged tone of his voice, exciting her. Bride was used to Vale's moods with the other immortals. Fannie deserved it— they all did.

Fannie narrowed her eyes at Vale, not even a drop of fear slipped out as she spoke, "I said, she's *mine.*"

"Do I need to send you back with *her?*" Vale appeared calm, but that single sharp note in his last word said it all.

Fannie released Catherine's head with a forceful push. Vale then slipped behind Catherine with one hand on each shoulder.

Fannie sauntered toward Bride with the blade forward as if she wanted to plunge it into her stomach. The immortal curled her lip in disgust at the last second as she flipped the knife and passed it to Bride.

"You are forgetting what she was meant to be used for," Fannie said, staring hard at Vale, "and you are becoming too attached to her. It's starting to feel as if Cupid's arrow has hit you as well." She then stomped up the stairs, slamming the door behind her.

Bride arched a brow at the door before connecting her gaze with Vale's, who was now watching her with a haunted look. Like an emotion was stirring within him, as though he was recognizing something.

Throat bobbing, he turned to Catherine, a new expression on his face taking root, one of pure darkness. His eyes met hers once more, signaling anticipation. "Join me?"

Bride stepped toward him, yet she was uncertain how to go about this. The woman was immortal. If Bride stabbed her, it wouldn't kill her. She would heal. "What do you want me to do?"

Vale's smile grew wicked, every perfect tooth on display. "This one has been a naughty, naughty little thing, trying to stop what we are attempting to achieve. Catherine here will be going back to the Glass Vault with the other souls."

Those were not answers. "She's immortal. Catherine can't go into the Glass Vault, and she will only heal."

His grin slowly fell. "Immortality can be taken away if I choose—if you choose. So will you decide this with me?"

A thrill shot through her. "Of course. And Fannie as well?"

"All in due time, my Bride." This time, his smile became even more vicious. "We have to torture her until she is knocked unconscious, then I can send her soul back before she awakens."

Bride clenched the knife—an emotion washed over her of

how wrong it was, but the other half wanted to slice this immortal in two, then watch the blood pour out of her. Bride had only turned civilians into glass, their souls disappearing as soon as they were turned. This was *different*. Gleefully different.

Her hand tapped the knife silently at her thigh while her heart pounded violently at Vale's pleased expression. She yearned for the gratitude and pleasure he would give her afterward. As easily as her next breath, with her whole darkened heart, she fully gave in to what was right.

Vale held the immortal's head back, her throat ready to be sliced. Tears streamed down Catherine's face as she continued to try and shout at Bride. But her words wouldn't have mattered to Bride, only what Vale and she could do to the immortal together. Lifting the edge of the blade to Catherine's soft flesh, digging in, Bride sliced a crisp line across her throat. Bright red crimson spilled out from the wound—a slight sickness settled in Bride's stomach that should not have been there. But she pushed past the strange emotion and savored the rest with a grin on her face. She then plunged the blade into Catherine's heart.

SIX

Before-Officer Elise Rodriguez

Officer Elise Rodriguez was thorough with her investigation. She'd driven up and down Oak Street two times, deftly aware that she had left no ground uncovered.

She'd gotten out of the car and surveyed the area on foot, inspecting the tree line a multitude of times. There was nothing but trees—some freshly cut down, just like Perrie Madeline had said. Despite her efforts, she couldn't locate the company who'd cut them down in the first place.

Elise had wondered if Perrie fabricated the story, but there was something about the young woman that made her believe she'd been telling the truth. Over the years, Elise had encountered countless, desperate individuals who'd spilled their stories in the same manner as Perrie. Even though it was hard to believe, her gut told her Perrie Madeline was different.

One more time, Elise promised herself at the sound of the toaster. Another early day meant another chance to sweep Oak Street for some peace of mind.

Elise sipped her coffee, lazily tearing at a bagel as she

examined her notes. This case took up more of her kitchen table than her actual desk. Once the reports came in, it was hard to leave them behind at the office, so she'd brought them home. She thought she could piece them all together, find the link that made the puzzle fit for all the missing persons.

If only it were that simple.

The missing civilians all seemed random, except for Maisie Jaser and Neven Lee. She knew from experience that rebellious teenagers often fled their home with a significant other to make a point, especially if the home was chaotic. For Maisie and Neven, it was the perfect answer to the question of their disappearances.

As Elise set down her coffee, she gazed at the cartoon sheep sprawled across the mug, feeling just as tired and hopeless as she had the last few days. It was hard to admit, but she wasn't getting any closer to solving the mystery behind the disappearances. If it wasn't for the phone ringing, she would've drifted off at the table, face planted in her notes.

Elise looked at her phone and didn't recognize the number. "Officer Rodriguez speaking."

"Yes! Officer Rodriguez?" a man's voice frantically asked. "My daughter's missing."

Another missing person? Her shoulders slumped at the thought. The man on the other end was making no sense, his babbling incessant and hard to understand. She rubbed her eyes and took a deep breath. "Slow down, sir. Did you go down to the police station and fill out a missing person's report?"

"I'm headed there right now, but my niece, Maisie Jaser, was reported missing already, and now my daughter, Perrie Madeline, is *gone.* I didn't know what to do, so my sister gave me your number." The man tried again to speak, but his voice trembled with every word. "She said you could help."

Hold on. Now Perrie is missing, too? "Are you sure, sir?"

"Yes, I'm sure!" he cried.

Elise's chest tightened and she rubbed at the spot. Something strange was going on and it went beyond the rapid disappearances. "Go to the police station, fill out a report, and I'll meet you there."

"Okay." Perrie's father's voice faded into the background as Elise tore the phone from her ear.

One more time, she thought again. Already dressed in her police uniform, Elise strapped on her gun and grabbed the rest of her things—notes and files included.

Elise planned to figure out what was going on before anyone else could go missing. She couldn't let it happen again, so she hurried out of her house and hopped in her car, flying down street after street until she reached Oak.

The sun broke through the tops of the trees, casting its light down the street. Elise tapped the brake to slow the car, sighing heavily and feeling defeated once again. All there ever was on Oak Street were trees, and that was all she was seeing now. She thought maybe this time would be different, but she should've known better. Strange stone museums didn't appear overnight.

Then, just as she put her foot on the gas pedal, something appeared in her peripheral vision. She slowed to a stop, her eyes widening in shock by the apparition beyond the tree stumps. A gray stone building now stood there, its large structure casting an eerie shadow across the ground. She'd become an expert on this road alone, and there was no doubt in her mind that this had never been here before.

"This isn't a traveling carnival on wheels," she muttered, studying the old building and its windowless outer walls.

Elise parked the car and rushed out, her heart beating to the pace of her running. She was going to solve this mystery and catch the person responsible. And it was going to happen that day.

She approached a tall wooden door with her gun in hand. A golden plaque was displayed on the door with the words

Quinsey Wolfe's Glass Vault written across in black script, just as Perrie Madeline had said. Elise removed the safety from her gun and held it close—loaded and ready.

To her surprise, she found the door unlocked, which should've alarmed her. Everything about this should've set off warning signals. The door swung gently open without making a single sound. She peered inside and listened for any noise, but was met with silence.

A few feet inside the carpeted hallway, Elise was convinced this area was empty. The door behind her closed with a loud, powerful slam, vibrating the walls. She startled and a streak of sweat slid down her cheek as she aimed her gun at the door. Ignoring the perspiration, she ran back to the exit, and turned the knob—it was locked.

Mother Fucker! she shouted inside her head. But she'd been through tougher obstacles, had been shot at numerous times, had watched her old partner die from one of those bullets.

Blowing out a breath, she pulled herself together and continued onward, down the lantern-lit hallway. The issue of the locked door would have to wait—there were people who needed to be found.

Several hallways later, Elise came to a stop in front of a circular room lined with displays along the wall. Her heart pounded harder as she gazed at what was inside each display— colorful glass-made horrors that made her stomach churn. Some were so violent in nature she couldn't help but gag. As a police officer, she'd dealt with real-life crime on a daily basis, but horror movies gave her the real nightmares.

They always had.

The worst one by far was a display of Jack the Ripper. She knew very little about the cases, but the idea that the sick bastard had never been caught chilled her to the bone. Still, despite the unsettling nature of the museum, Perrie Madeline had been right. Elise fumbled with her phone as she withdrew it from her pocket. The station needed to be notified that the sighting was solid. She scrolled through the cell for the number, ready to hit call, when a violent wind struck the phone from her hand.

"What the hell?" She looked around the room for an open window or door. "Where the—"

A stronger gust slammed into Elise, knocking the words and breath right out of her. She fell to the marble floor, her gun sliding across it and out of her reach. Elise ignored the pain radiating through her body and flipped onto her stomach to crawl to her weapon, but another big burst of wind pulled at her. Screams escaped her as she kicked and clawed at the marble to break free.

Nothing could stop the wind from giving one final pull, throwing her into the display. She instinctively shut her eyes and lifted her hands to protect herself, then waited for the shatter of glass. But it never came.

Elise was off the ground in an instant and bounced onto the wet pavement, finding old buildings on either side of her. The displays had vanished. The museum was gone. Now was the time for panic. Mouth agape, hands shaking, she took a step back and tripped over her own feet. She peered down and gasped when she noticed her shoes were concealed by the skirt of a yellow vintage gown she now wore.

Taking a deep breath, careful of the skirt, Elise pushed forward and bumped into something—*someone.*

"Hello, Catherine," a taunting woman's voice cooed.

"I'm not Catherine," Elise said to the stranger, backing away from the covered woman.

The person in question stood out, dressed in black—cloak, gloves, hat, and shoes. The lamppost nearby, lit by a golden flame, reflected on a lone red curl that escaped from beneath the stranger's top hat.

Who the fuck is this? Elise was too distracted by the odd clothing when the cloaked person charged at her. The stranger was swift, quicker than Elise, and as the lithe figure struck, Elise screamed. A burning pain throbbed at her shoulder.

Elise looked down at her wound, blinking rapidly at the sight of a long red gash torn into the fabric of her dress. Warm blood spilled out from it, sliding against her brown skin, and staining the yellow gown. Adrenaline then hit her and she thought fast, running at the figure and slamming her fist into the stranger's face. The woman stumbled backward, her entire head covered in black cloth beneath the top hat. Without any hesitation, the stranger came back slicing the air with what looked to be a long butcher knife.

She swung her arm up and over, knocking the blade from the woman's hand. Elise punched the stranger in the face again and again until her hand ached. The woman finally collapsed to the ground, out cold.

Elise picked up the knife and ran. Heels clacked hurriedly against the pavement, fabric swishing against fabric as she tore down the cobblestoned street toward a light coming from a building. A *pub*.

Inside were silhouettes of people—people who could help her. The closer she got, the clearer the faces in the window became.

She stopped, her eyes growing wide as they settled on a familiar face. Seated at a table with a young and handsome blond man was Perrie Madeline.

Elise reached out, her fingers nearly brushing against the door handle. Relief filled her at the safety awaiting within the pub—then it was ripped away by two strong hands yanking her back into the shadows. A hand closed hard over her mouth, just as she tried to cry out and scream for help. She brought her arm down to elbow her captor in the ribs, but it was too late. The sting of cold metal burned against the flesh of her throat as hot liquid poured from the wound.

Her words came out gurgled and she struggled for a few more moments, not wanting to give up the fight.

Then the world went black.

Catherine stood outside the brothel trying to remember how she'd gotten there. The stomping of feet down the street distracted her from her thoughts. A woman slipped into view first—Mary Kelly. A young blond gentleman with a lean and strong body ran beside her, one who Catherine would like for herself. "Hey, Mary," she called. "How about you lend your gentlemen to me for the night."

SEVEN

Maisie

The plan was … that there was still no plan. Maisie had been sitting around with Neven for more than an hour with nothing between them besides glass bodies. The concoction of a plan on how to get Perrie back had turned into a gaping failure.

Saving Perrie was still the mission, but neither of them could come up with an idea of where to start. If Maisie's parents were still alive, they would've known what to do.

With them gone, nothing was the same.

No more of her mom's extreme cooking, no more big birthday parties, no movie nights, or her dad's jokes. There was nothing at home to go back to, only what was left behind. But at the end of it all, there would still be Perrie.

And yet, the notepad in Maisie's lap remained blank.

Earlier, she'd searched around the desk drawers at the barbershop, managing to find a pad of yellow sticky notes and a pen. She'd planned to use them for any ideas they could come up with. Not as good as a small spiral pad and pencil, but they would work.

"Do you really need to use the notepad, Mais?" Neven asked, cocking his head. He sat on the floor across from Maisie, while she twirled her pin around her thumb.

"You should know that answer by now." She winked. "Now, are you ready to tell me what happened to you, and how you know August doesn't exist?"

"I never thought this would happen when I went into the museum." Purple bags rested below Neven's eyes, and his lids appeared heavy with exhaustion as though he could crash at any second. He hadn't been open about his experience inside the museum yet, and Maisie had been waiting patiently for the past hour. That had to end now if they wanted to get to Perrie.

"So, are you ready to tell me what happened back in the Glass Vault?" she asked, her tone firm. "If it helps, you can even write it down." She shoved her notepad in his face.

"Are *you*?"

"I never said I wouldn't tell you." She tapped his knee with the end of her pen. "You never asked."

With a groan, he said, "Well, you first. You're not going to like what I have to say."

Maisie inhaled three times since that seemed like the magical number to prepare herself. Her dad had never understood the point of her doing that, but she'd always told him it was because three was her lucky number. Then he would just smile and pat her on the shoulder.

The calm finally took over. "When we were in the Glass Vault, you know, frozen as glass?"

Neven arched a brow.

"We came to life like zombies, right? But not like the breaking out of the coffin and slowly clawing out of the dirt until you break through the surface kind." Pausing, Maisie waited for Neven to say something.

"Do you need to stop every time and wait for me to respond? Just get on with the story in its entirety. You're doing masterfully." He gave her a sarcastic thumbs up and she straightened.

"I'm going to ignore this mood of yours and finish my story."

"You do that." His lips twitched before turning into a smile, one that she couldn't help but mirror on her own face.

Scratching her head with the pen, Maisie gathered her thoughts. "Anyway, when we turned into flesh and began walking out of the museum, and Crazy Maisie started attacking people—"

Neven lifted a hand. "I'm going to stop you right there. You have a name for your alter?"

Why wouldn't I have a name for her? "Yes, don't you?"

He squinted his brown eyes, seeming to mull it over for a moment. "No, because it's still me."

"Well no, it isn't. It's you but some of your emotions are shut off, so it's a new you. But anyway, back to what I was saying before being interrupted. After several days of mass destruction, I was able to escape her claws."

"Can we talk about what happened with you in the Glass Vault?"

Closing her eye, Maisie tried to not let the past tear down the strong walls she'd built for herself. She'd done everything she could to save Perrie back in the Snow White display, and her cousin had still ended up like Maisie.

Neven's warm hand pressed against her cheek, and she didn't open her eye. His opposite hand then trailed up the side of her other cheek. The touch was nice, gentle, and she almost leaned into it. But as soon as she realized what he was doing, it was too late when he reached for her eye patch.

"Don't," she screamed and yanked her face out of his reach, turning away from him. She wasn't sure why she didn't want him to see her missing eye. It wasn't as if he was used to seeing that eye anyway.

"Jesus, Maisie. I just wanted you to look at me with both of your eyes for a minute. I wasn't trying to do anything."

Is that what he thinks I'm afraid of? Maisie adjusted the patch, making sure it was in its proper place before facing him. "That's not it, Neven."

He scooted closer to her, his lips forming a tight line. "Then what is it?"

"My eye is gone."

"What?" His brows furrowed together in confusion.

"I said my eye is gone. Like, it was apparently plucked out by dwarves."

His eyes widened and his jaw tightened, forming an interesting mixture of anger and shock.

"Before you get too mad, when I got sucked into my display, the eyeball was already missing once I got there. I did, however, inherit some memories from Crazy Maisie."

If she had to be honest with herself, those memories were pretty insane. Mutilated dwarves, their eyes, ears, and tongues in a bucket, bloody animal carcasses, and a Huntsman who was in love with chopping off her head or piercing her heart. Once again, she swept those little terrors under the rug.

"What do you mean your eye is gone?" He ignored her last sentence, mouth hanging open as his gaze zoomed in on the patch.

Maisie recalled the time when she, Perrie, and August had reached the barrier to exit the Snow White display. She'd already known she wouldn't be able to make it to the next scene, no matter how hard Perrie had wished for her to escape with her.

When Perrie and August were sucked through, Maisie had darted away from the Huntsman—his hair all flowing in the wind like there was a fan right there blowing at it. It was weird that when she'd looked at him, she had thought of flying hair at that moment, but then his hand came down with a dagger to her chest, and she'd woken in the cottage, the bloody animal fur back in her lap.

The bright side to this apocalyptic situation was the

Huntsman hadn't been trying to hunt Maisie down since they'd exited the Glass Vault. She slid that memory under the rug, too.

"Well, I mean it's gone. Like, there isn't one to display for you inside my eye socket."

He leaned forward and stretched his large hand out again.

She twisted out of his reach. "Stop, Neven!"

"Let me see it, all right? It can't be any worse than me. I have scars all over my body."

"They make you look rugged." Her gaze fell to his visible scars on his arms, hands, face, and neck. In her opinion, they weren't bad at all—slightly raised, pinkish, and spaced a good distance apart. No bolts rested on the sides of his neck, but there were two small circular scars where she supposed they once may or may not have been.

"Did you just call scars all over my body rugged?"

"I did. They look good on you." Maisie lifted her chin in defiance. Flaws were her favorite thing about people. A birthmark here, a scar there… For a moment, she wondered if there were more below his clothing… Her gaze drifting lower, lower still, until she snapped her gaze back up to his face. *Bad, Maisie.*

He cocked his head, his face serious. "Then show me your eye."

Mulling it over for a few seconds, Maisie figured it would only be fair to show him hers since she'd seen his. Slowly, she lifted the blue eye patch and set it in her lap, then continued to stay facing Neven head on.

He studied her for a moment, probably hiding his disgust, but then he smiled. "You look daring."

Unable to stop herself from smiling too, Maisie placed the patch back over her eye socket. Relief washed over her after showing him—it had felt good. As she opened her mouth to tell him the rest of her story, the glass door burst open.

Neven startled, and Maisie leapt up, pressing her hand

against one of the warm glass bodies—a tall man with a comb in his hand. *Had he been planning to use that as a weapon?*

An immortal swathed in shadows took long strides through the door, his gaze fastened to Maisie.

"Ah, you got to them before I did," Dr. Jekyll … or Mr. Hyde said in a raspy voice. She could never tell who was who in this world since both his personalities were a bit on the insane side.

Show time. Maisie skipped up to Dr. and Mr. Evil and screamed to the ceiling. "I sang him a song, a song about dead bloody birds." She giggled and spun round and round.

"What else did you do? What else? What else? *What else?*" He bared his teeth, a deranged smile spreading as he hobbled toward her. Grime caked his crooked teeth, and his hair stood on end as if it had been struck by Perrie's electricity. He wore a disheveled old suit, the sleeve of his blazer ripped at the shoulder, a few of the buttons of his vest missing.

"He got the other ones!" Maisie sang, hysterically jumping up and down, pointing at Neven. She then slapped the pleather of the chair as she watched her friend.

His serious game face was already there, as always, ready to rock and roll. He didn't say a single word, only grunted a poorly-constructed Frankenstein's Monster sound. It seemed good enough for Mr. Two Side, but apparently he'd never seen the movies.

"Tell me more. Tell me more," Mr. Hyde seethed, gripping his hair and yanking out strands. "Jekyll, Hyde, Jekyll, Hyde, Jekyll, *Hyde!*" he shrilled. Turning back around, he took long strides again, this time directly out of the barber shop, still chanting his two names down the broken street.

Maisie bolted to the door and locked it, which she should've done the first time around. She took several deep breaths before pushing away from the door.

"Now," she said to Neven after that rude interruption, "I can finish my story."

"Okay, Maisie. Let's just pretend *that* didn't happen. But go ahead and continue."

So she shrugged, plopped down on the floor, and spilled to him her story of how she'd gotten to the Glass Vault the night she was supposed to start working there. Neven's warm hand slid forward and clasped hers as she continued. She went into detail about how she'd gotten murdered by the Huntsman, her thinking she'd killed him, and how she'd thought she had saved Perrie.

"I have to tell you something, Mais."

"It can't be any worse than my story."

He drew his scarred hand from hers and ran it through his dark hair before looking back at her. "I couldn't do anything. I was chained to that damn wall."

Everything stopped. "What do you mean you couldn't do anything?" When he didn't speak, she urged, "*Neven?*"

"After I came to the Glass Vault, I found August and ended up in the Frankenstein's Monster display. There, I discovered August was Vale. He revealed his plan and plot as he broke me apart. I don't know why he told me all of it, except for the fact I think he knew how much I cared about Perrie and how much it would hurt. Vale put her in a cell with me, completely unclothed. They had … been together, I guess." Bright scarlet seeped into his face and neck. "He killed her in my cell by slitting her throat while I couldn't do *anything*. Then he made her into what she is."

Maisie shut her eye and let his words sink in. She was a firm believer that everything happened for a reason, no matter how lousy. And this was beyond that. Vale had pretended he was August, slept with Perrie, then killed her. To anyone, it would be a tough pill to swallow, but she and Perrie could work with it. Her cousin was still alive and that was what mattered, even though Maisie didn't know if Perrie would be able to get through all of this. But Maisie would be there to help her, always.

Opening her eye, feeling a new-found sense of hope from that messy darkness, she rose to her feet. "The only thing left to do is find Perrie and save her. Using her lightning power with my singing skills, and your strength, we will get Vale back in his vault somehow."

Neven blinked several times, his lips pursed. "We don't even know where to start. I haven't seen Perrie since before we left. I mean, do you even know where she is?"

"No. Do you have a better idea?" she challenged.

He rolled his eyes. "No."

She offered him a hand to help him up. Neven's lips twitched before he gave her a half smile and clasped his hand with hers. It was mostly him pushing his tall body off the floor than her doing the work.

Spotting the small over-the-shoulder purse she'd found earlier, Maisie picked it up and emptied its contents on a chair, in case the owner ever came back to claim them. Most likely that wouldn't be happening, but she took the top sticky note and scrawled a short note, apologizing that she'd needed to borrow his or her purse. Then she pasted the yellow sheet directly next to a small wallet.

Neven rolled his eyes again, which must've been his main habit of the day—even more than usual. She took two candy bars from a desk drawer and tossed one to Neven. He easily caught it with one hand, and she gave a nod of approval, quite impressed.

"You know we don't have to eat, right?" Neven asked as he unwrapped the chocolate bar.

Maisie had figured out the first day that she never got hungry, yet she still delighted in eating what she could find. Besides, her taste buds were still there—she wouldn't want to deny them their bliss. "We need to have some pleasure in immortal life—chocolate is the answer."

She unwrapped her bar and stuffed it into her mouth as she led Neven out of the barbershop. For now, she swept what had happened between Vale and Perrie under the rug. Placing a hand to Neven's strong chest, she looked both ways to make sure the two-sided maestro was gone. He appeared to be.

Neven's brow stayed lifted while he studied her hand.

"What?" she asked, slipping it back by her side.

"Nothing, Mais." He shook his head and smiled. "Nothing at all."

They'd only made it a few feet away from the glass door when a body darted around the corner of the building and slammed hard into Maisie. Her candy bar went flying, and she crashed to the ground, her head striking concrete.

For an instant, Maisie thought she was dead with blood pouring out of her throbbing skull—a heaviness strapped her down to the cement.

The weight then lifted as a loud smack echoed from somewhere. Neven knelt beside her, holding her head up.

"Are you all right? Please tell me you are," he pleaded.

Maisie guessed he'd forgotten they couldn't die. "Immortal, remember? Where's my candy bar?"

A deep chuckle escaped his throat as she sat up and located her delicious treat. She brushed the dirt off it and looked up at Neven, who had vanished from her side. A guy with white hair was now in Neven's grip, backed up against the wall, lifted so his toes were dangling off the ground.

"What are you trying to do to her?" Neven demanded, then continued with a line of similar questions. Maisie stood by watching while she finished her chocolate.

"I'm not like them," the guy cried, his pale skin flushing a bright pink. He was an immortal, but he was right, he wasn't lost in la la land.

Maisie folded her arms and leaned against the wall beside them. "Neven, quit acting like a beast and set the poor guy down."

Neven lowered him, but didn't release his grip on the guy's shirt.

Staring at the immortal for a moment, Maisie blinked in recognition, her mouth opening in awe. She lifted her index finger in the air, ticking it back and forth. "I know you! Ben Johnston!"

He backed up all the way into the wall for safety as though she was going to sing him to glass right there, even though he was an immortal.

"You know, I had my own plan prepared to search for you before I went missing myself." She grinned.

No one said anything, both guys just stood staring at her. With a shrug to herself, she asked Ben, "How and when did you come back to yourself?"

Ben's fright seemed to wear off a bit, but based on his rigid shoulders, she figured he would bolt soon. "I don't know how. It was only a few minutes ago—before I took off running. I had been feeling more and more myself as the days went by until the memories hit me all at once."

I wonder why that is? Why we aren't getting all our memories back at the same time or not at all. Nothing was easy to piece together. If Perrie were here, Maisie was sure they could draw some conclusion together like they always had—whether it was games or real-life situations.

"Do you want to come with us? We're leaving to save Perrie." Three would be much stronger than two since going up against Vale would be a difficult task.

Ben furrowed his brow. "I have no idea who Perrie is—I'm sorry."

"She's the Bride of Frankenstein. Well, really it would be the Bride of Vale." Not that they were married, so Maisie didn't know why she was referred to as the Bride. Vale *was* like Victor Frankenstein by making the monsters, though.

A look of pure horror crossed Ben's face. "Absolutely not. No way." She probably shouldn't have mentioned the Vale part...

Maisie reached out to stop Ben, to reassure him they had a

plan and that everything would be fine. "But—"

"If I were the two of you," Ben cut her off. "I would steer clear of any path that might take you to Vale. Your friend, this Perrie, she's his now." He turned to leave but stopped just short. "Good luck, though. Also, if you see the redhead named Fannie, stay away from her." Throat bobbing, he scurried off without a backward glance. His boots thumped against the pavement, growing fainter, until only quiet filled the air.

Perrie had told her Ben's story, of what had happened to him in his display, and it wasn't the prettiest of tales. Maisie hoped Ben didn't run into anyone who could hurt him again. However, that was not in the stars for her and Neven.

Neven worried at his lower lip.

She wrapped an arm around his waist and drew him close. "Let's find Perrie."

EIGHT

Before-Ben Johnston

Ben unzipped the fluorescent-orange fanny pack at his side, and drew out his handy pink bottle of sunscreen. The day was an excellent day to take photographs. He'd been trampling through the wooded area of Oak Street for the last hour, snapping photo after photo of the lush green foliage. The day had been mostly cloudy, but now that the sun was coming out, he needed to re-apply.

He fired open the spray and let the cool beads hit against his exposed arms and legs—it was refreshing, to say the least. Then he fished out a stick of sunscreen from his pack and spread it generously across his face. Sometimes the sunscreen felt more like an addiction than a necessity, but with having such pale skin due to his albinism, he needed to keep the rays out.

Ben placed the items back in his fanny pack and zipped it up with one quick pull. He raked a hand through his white hair, shaking it out before lifting his camera up to his face. A twisted old tree with gnarled limbs and a crooked trunk, not ten feet away, practically shouted his name.

"Hello."

Startled by a female voice and the snap of the camera, Ben stumbled back and caught himself against the base of another tree. Thankfully, Oak Street was lined with them.

Ben felt the light touch of a hand on his arm and glanced up, meeting two brown irises.

"Oh, I'm sorry." A young woman with bright red hair smiled. "Are you okay? I didn't mean to frighten you."

His heart thumped wildly. "I'm fine." He pushed himself up and checked the lens of his camera for any scratches. Truthfully, he wanted to avoid her eyes, which were focused on him. He wasn't good at talking to women.

"So, what are you taking pictures of?" Her voice was soft with an English accent.

Ben finally looked up, positive the blush on his face was as red as a ripe tomato. He scanned her up and down. The swells of her perfect breasts didn't escape him, as her chest was the first thing he couldn't tear his eyes away from. He swallowed his nervousness and hurried to meet her face before she thought he was a pervert. But he couldn't stop the question from slipping into his head of what her breasts would feel like in his hands.

"Um, just some trees," he stuttered. Finally calming himself, he then noticed her unusual outfit. "What are you wearing?"

Her blue dress was completely out of place in the middle of Oak Street. It was old-fashioned, adorned with vintage buttons, a stiff bodice, and a full skirt that flared at her hips. Her hands, which she clasped below her chest, were covered with olive gloves. He found the whole scenario to be more than weird.

"Oh, this?" She chuckled and brushed her gloved hands over the skirt of her dress. "It's part of my work but it's been slow, so I decided to take a break and go for a walk. Did you think I would actually be wandering around town wearing this?" A smile lingered on her face.

Ben smiled in return and ran a hand along his jaw. "That must have been a long walk then."

"Not at all. I work at the end of the street."

He wrinkled his nose. "There isn't anything on this street besides trees." Maybe she'd meant she was practicing for a play somewhere close by. Theater kids would do that all the time at the park on the other side of town.

Still smiling, the woman twirled a wild curl with one of her gloved fingers. "You didn't know? There's a museum at the end of this street."

A museum? There wasn't any museum out here. She either had to be mistaken or she was screwing with him.

Sensing the question hanging between them, the young woman giggled playfully. "You don't believe me."

"I didn't say that." Ben tugged at the collar of his shirt nervously.

One of her auburn eyebrows rose. "Have you been to the end of the street today?"

He shook his head. "No, but I was at the end of the street last week and there wasn't anything there."

"Why don't you follow me, then?" The redhead turned on her heels and swayed her hips as she sauntered away.

Ben didn't want to stop talking to the pretty woman. Without hesitation, he jogged after her. "What's your name?"

The edge of her lips quirked up, and she wrapped her hand around his bicep. "I'm Fannie."

"Fannie," he said softly. He liked the taste of her name on his tongue—he liked the touch of her hand on his bare arm even more.

"And yours?"

"My what?" he asked, startled.

"Your name, silly." She gently swatted at his arm, causing heat to creep into his cheeks once again.

"Ben. My name is Ben Johnston."

They trekked slowly through the trees, a mysterious redhead on his arm—he couldn't complain. As they walked, he snuck quick side-glances at her, noticing the light sprinkle of freckles running across her nose to her chest. He hadn't seen them from afar.

Up close, she was more than pretty—she was *beautiful*.

In his twenty-three years, Ben only had a handful of short-term girlfriends. It had been more than two years since his last, and he was ashamed of himself. It was hard to have a meaningful conversation with another person when one was a hermit. Fannie seemed nice though, unaffected by his condition, and genuinely sweet. He wouldn't mind hanging out with her sometime.

"And here it is," Fannie said.

Ben's pale blue gaze flicked from Fannie to the end of the street, and he gasped, his eyes bulging. A building much older than anything built in town stood tall before them. It was magnificent. There was an angle in there somewhere just waiting to be captured—he could feel it buzzing in his fingertips like anxious bees.

"You weren't kidding, were you?" He turned his head from Fannie to the large stone structure, then back at her. "This … this wasn't here before."

She looked at him as if he was crazy. "It's been here a while. You must not have been paying attention."

He wiggled out of her grasp. "Look, uh, Fannie. I come out here every week. Believe me, I would've noticed this place. How could anyone not notice it?"

"The trees were cut the other day." She pointed at the tree stumps surrounding the building.

Ben narrowed his eyes at the trees like they were hiding all kinds of secrets. "Something isn't right here, Fannie. I think I better go and talk to someone." Who was he going to ask? His non-existent friends and family? He could ask one of his neighbors, though.

"Wait." Fannie grabbed his arm again, tighter than before—a little possessive even. "Come with me inside, and I can show you around. It's only me today."

Ben studied the curved arch of the doorway, skeptical of the mystery as though it still wasn't real. He couldn't believe his eyes. His gut told him to go back the way he'd come, back to the safety of the forest where he could continue taking pictures. But that pleading expression on Fannie's face pulled at him more.

"Okay, but only for a bit." He could talk to his neighbor once he got back home.

"Perfect." She tapped the tip of his nose with her index finger.

Once they crossed the archway, Fannie reached for the golden knob and opened the door. Ben closed it behind him and followed her down several hallways, paying more attention to the sway of her hips—how they dipped from side to side—than any of the surroundings. A heat spread through him, shooting straight to his length. Ben adjusted his pants, but he could still feel himself straining. He started counting backward before he embarrassed himself. If she turned around and peered down at him, he would bolt.

Just as he relaxed himself, Fannie came to a complete stop at the end of the hallway.

"Where are we?" he asked, moving past her into a circular room.

"The belly of the beast."

He took a hard swallow—the room they were in was oddly arranged with various glass statues. There were no windows and no doors in the new territory he was about to enter. The gruesome and unique aspects of the glass statues had Ben reaching for his camera to capture the moment, but Fannie entwined her fingers with his and pulled him to the middle of the room.

His gaze fixed on a display and he wandered away from Fannie, taken by a glass scene of Peter Pan. This was one of his favorite stories, and to see it so twisted and different made his fingertips twitch with the need to snap a picture. Peter hovered in the air above Wendy, a knife hidden behind his back. Wendy's hand was in his other, following wherever the Lost Boy might lead. Her expression was taken, wondrous even, because a boy could fly.

As Ben raised his camera, he somehow knew Wendy wouldn't be able to escape the danger.

"This way, Ben," Fannie drawled. He turned around and walked to where she was standing, now in front of a Jack the Ripper display. "This one is my favorite."

"I can't believe they never solved that case." Then again, the technology wasn't as sophisticated during that time. Ben took another photo, wishing he'd brought his digital camera instead of his vintage film one.

"*She* was incredibly smart."

He puckered his lips. "It wasn't a woman." It wasn't that he believed a woman couldn't commit the crimes, but rather what the evidence had said. The letters were signed by Jack.

Fannie smiled, a bit too wide, and something about it didn't feel right, snapping him out from the distraction of this place and her. Ben always found himself caught up in taking pictures versus what he should be doing. He needed to leave.

"I gotta go." He stepped to the side, placing him in front of a display that held a large bridge, naked trolls underneath, and a broken goat on top. *Three Billy Goats Gruff.*

"Sure." Fannie cooed, her grin growing wider.

Before he could respond, a violent wind knocked Ben to the floor. His face smacked into the marble, sharp pain radiating through his teeth. Warm blood filled his mouth as he tried to push himself up. The invisible force picked up again, pulling him and his camera toward the display.

High-pitched laughter echoed in the room that could've

only come from Fannie.

Ben closed his eyes. The feeling of falling was harshly interrupted by the impact of his body against solid ground. He opened his eyes, blinded by the bright rays of an orange sun hanging overhead. Was he back in the forest? He had to be dreaming.

Fannie was nowhere in sight.

Slowly, he pushed himself up to all fours, still dizzy from whatever had happened. He was right about one thing—he was beside a forest with the beginning of a path that led to a hulking bridge. Ben brought himself to his feet, eyes on the bridge as he reached absently for the fanny pack at his waist.

Only, it was *gone*.

In its place was a sword. His whole body trembled as he spun in a circle, trying to spot anything familiar. Nothing.

Panicked, he shot forward and sprinted for the bridge, hopeful he would just wake up if he kept running. Halfway across the stone structure, he tripped over a small rock, losing his footing again. For the third time that day, he was knocked to the ground. He'd never fallen so much in his life.

This is madness, he thought. He started to push himself up and came to an abrupt stop when a naked woman with olive skin and thick black hair lifted herself from over the side of the bridge. His jaw fell open as she walked toward him with rosy peaked nipples and perfect dark curls between her thighs.

"You are mine," the enchanting woman growled. She was extraordinary, radiant, and sparkling like sunshine. He couldn't rip his gaze away from her, even if he wanted to.

Ben yearned to kiss down her throat, feel her nipples in between his teeth, press his digits into the heat between her legs. He wished he had his camera to keep a piece of her. The actual sunshine from the sky blinded him for a split second, and once it cleared, he was no longer face to face with a gorgeous woman. Instead, he met the eyes of a malformed beast with saggy skin and rotten teeth who stood as tall as a giant. What was in front of him, he'd only seen in books or movies. There was no way it was real—but then again, the sword on his hip was tangible.

Troll.

Heart pounding out of his chest with fright, he spider-crawled backward to avoid the beast. Ben stopped as something washed over him, as if a spell was drawing him to the creature, its allure. He closed his eyes tightly to push the pull toward the troll away as he stood to take off running. The scent of decay invaded his nose and his lids flew open. He shouted as the beast's monstrous hand swiped at him, plucking him up from the ground. Ben's ribs bit into his lungs, cutting off the oxygen that he was desperate to drink in. He wanted to rub at his throat for air, but his arms were trapped in the troll's deadly grip.

As the sun scorched his pale flesh, all he felt was the burning and lack of air supply, until there was nothing left for him except blackness.

Billy rubbed at his head, feeling a little dazed about where he had just been. He stared at the foliage around him and out toward the bridge farther ahead. It was about time he took an adventure, so he began his journey to discover what lay on the other side of the bridge.

NINE

The Bride

Bride helped Vale carry the remains of Catherine's body up the stairs. Fannie was nowhere in sight. The dejected deviant was most likely skulking about through the city, searching for any remaining mortals. Vale's decision to let Bride lead the torture was enough to spark Fannie's anger. Despite the notion of torture, Bride was more pleased by the immortal's dramatics than anything.

As they stepped out onto the backyard patio, Vale tossed the limp body onto the pyre. The heap was made from old tomes and the stack of chopped firewood beside the garden shed.

Vale picked up a can of gasoline, a token he'd found earlier in the garage, and sloshed it over Catherine's body. The pleasure of torturing another soul had brought Bride a sense of foreboding. She pushed it away and focused on the scarlet splattered on her own arms, wondering what it would taste like. Victory? The strike of a match drew her away from her thoughts, and she watched as Vale tossed it toward the bloodied corpse.

Fire ignited under the dark sky, crackling and burning while each flame licked away Catherine's flesh, peeling it away from the bone. Bride couldn't conceal the sparks at her fingertips as giddiness stirred within her at the sight. If Vale were able to use his stronger abilities, she could only imagine how powerful the fire would have been. Outside the Glass Vault he was limited, but inside he could do anything.

He longed for power. Sometimes, Bride believed she craved it even more.

Together, they mourned how great Catherine could have been. Even with her betrayal, she was still one of them. The flames continued to eat away at the immortal until she was nothing but ash. Vale's eyes hadn't once left the blazing orange, but as the last flicker snuffed out, he turned toward Bride.

"You were miraculous in there," he murmured, pressing his forehead to hers, his fingers trailing the length of her spine.

"I felt miraculous, Vale." She was the only one allowed to call him by his true name, even Fannie had to refer to him as Master.

"Because you are. You are remarkable. You can get cleaned up if you wish. There is a shower on the second floor." He lifted his forehead from hers, his expression now unreadable.

What Bride wished in that moment was to be with Vale right here in the open, surrounded by Catherine's ash, but her skin ached to be washed, for her to remove the dirt first.

With a nod, she went back inside the house and up the stairs. A throbbing came at her chest, similar to the pounding in her head, but she ignored it. Bride needed a distraction, and she found it as soon as she stepped into the bathroom. On the countertop, a towel and rag were already set aside for her. Bride stared at her reflection in the rectangular mirror hanging above the sink, and she didn't recognize her face beneath the blood and grime.

Long, brown hair, wild and untamed, hung below her shoulder blades. A thin streak of white hair rested on each side of her temples, weaving themselves into the tangles. Deep brown eyes rimmed with black circles from lack of sleep peered back at her from the glass. They focused on a part of her throat hidden in shadow. Just a few inches above her collarbone sat her pale scar.

It seemed to smile at her, as though it knew something she didn't.

For a moment, Bride didn't know who she was or *what* she was. The ache in her chest pulsed faster, sharper. She gripped the fabric above her heart and took a deep breath, knowing who she was, what she was. She was the Bride. Vale's Bride. She was his chosen leader, his Queen of the Glass Vault and all living creatures inside of it.

Shedding her blood-smeared gown, she took a step into the shower.

Cool beads of water pelted against her flesh as it washed away the grime, red and brown mixing with the clear water. Bride gathered her electricity and ignited it to heat her skin. As her current crackled, the liquid now felt warm when it hit her skin. The dull pounding in the back of her head shot forward, sending a path of shocks through her body, and she couldn't fight it anymore.

Bride's knees buckled and she caught herself on the floor of the tub just before slamming her head against the wall. A flash of pain still twisted inside her skull, crashing into memories she had never once seen.

A shadow... It morphed into a young woman with obsidian hair and a bright blue eye. This was no stranger—she was the same immortal wearing an eye patch that Bride had seen at the museum. She squeezed her head between her hands. The pain … it wouldn't go away, and the more it pounded, the clearer the vision became.

Nev came over to watch movies while Perrie's dad was at work. Her dad hadn't looked himself this morning, and she knew why. It was the anniversary of when her mom had left them. Years might've passed, but to her dad, it was like yesterday. She preferred not to think about it.

They were waiting for Maisie to show them her surprise. Her cousin had told them a week ago that she'd come up with an idea but wouldn't let either one of them know what it was.

Maisie had said she planned on starting it in a month when summer break began after their sophomore year, but she apparently couldn't wait a second longer.

Nev sat in the chair, already enchanted by an old werewolf movie Perrie had turned on for him. He hadn't seen many of the old classic horror films, so Maisie had made it a purpose for him to start a few weeks ago.

"What do you think she's going to surprise us with?" Perrie asked, fiddling around with a Rubik's Cube that she could never fucking solve.

Nev cocked his head and smiled as he seemed to mull it over. "I'm thinking it has something to do with what she's been into recently, which has been pirates."

That was true. Maisie had been carrying around a lot of different books lately. Perrie believed two of them may have had a pirate ship on them. "So, your guess is a pirate accent?" She laughed.

Rolling his eyes, Nev looked back at the TV. "If she got this worked up over a pirate accent, I'm going to be thoroughly unimpressed."

A knock came at the front door, and Nev bit his lip anxiously toward the sound. Perrie frowned, unsure what he was nervous about. It was only Maisie, not a werewolf creeping out from the TV screen.

Perrie checked the peephole and released a birdy whistle when she confirmed it was her cousin. Maisie stayed turned to the side as she whistled in return.

As Perrie swung open the door, Maisie jumped through the space and waved her hands in the air. "Surprise!"

Nev leapt around the chair and ran to Maisie, cradling her face in his hands. "What the hell happened to your eye?"

Maisie's smile grew wider, and she patted his hand away. "You like it?"

Okay, so Nev was right. *"Pirates, remember?" Perrie said, glancing toward him as he studied Maisie.*

"Damn it, Mais." A scowl crossed his face for a brief moment before he smirked, most likely impressed with himself for knowing her surprise had something to do with pirates.

Perrie took a closer look at the blue and red eye patch, appearing to be well crafted. The patch part itself was the body of a parrot. A head poked out on one end, tail feathers on the other, and tiny feet at the bottom.

"I'm surprised you didn't add a pirate hat with a skull on top of it." Perrie laughed.

Maisie tapped the side of her head with her pinky finger. "I'll add that thought for another day to my growing list."

"What list?" Nev piped in, his interest piqued.

Clapping her hands together, Maisie brought them in front of her mouth. "I'm starting my own business. Time to do away with boring black eye patches. Those with one eye deserve to express that you don't have to hide the eye, you can embrace it."

"Technically, the eye would still be hidden behind a patch," Perrie pointed out.

Maisie waved her index finger around like a pirate's sword. "That's true, but the barrier protecting the eye can be vibrant. To show my support, I will wear one from now on."

It was a Maisie sort-of-idea, but Perrie liked it. "Go ahead."

Nev shook his head and sank back into the chair, seeming to not quite get what the hell was going on.

With a laugh, Maisie rumpled Nev's hair to bug him, then

The image disappeared. It all vanished. There was something there—Bride knew it. She tried to bring the pieces back, but she couldn't. It was gone and she was here in the shower, the water once again cold. Bride pressed her hands to the sides of her head and squeezed, urging the memory to resurface, but it didn't. Instead, she was left with a dull throbbing in each temple. Grounding her teeth, she slapped the bottom of the tub as hard as she could, the small puddle of water splashing against the walls.

Beads from the shower head continued to pour down on her, and she slowly felt herself once more, no longer caring about what had been there. Bride turned off the water and wrapped herself in a towel while staring at the fog-covered mirror. She leaned forward, lifting a finger to the glass and drew a picture of a flower.

"Strange," Bride said to herself, wondering what would make her do something so pathetic.

Shaking her head, she finished drying off and bent down to pick up the dress from the tile floor. The ensemble was back to its impeccable condition—pure ivory, not a speck of dirt or blood. Stepping into the silky material, Bride buttoned it back up.

As she opened the door, Vale leaned against the wall, file in hand. His hair was damp and curled slightly against his forehead—he must have showered as well.

"Took you long enough," he said almost playfully, running the file across his perfectly-shaped fingernails.

Shame slithered forth within her as she thought about the weakness she had just experienced in the bathroom. She was too ashamed to confess the words aloud, even though Bride knew Vale would help her. He always answered any questions she would ask.

"I wanted to make sure I scrubbed my nails thoroughly and made them extra clean," Bride lied, holding out her hands and splaying her fingers for inspection.

Vale ran the tip of his tongue across his lower lip, his smile turning into something like a dare.

His luscious, full lips drew her gaze. Everything was forgotten, the world *forgotten*, except for him. With a grin, she whirled away from him and slowly walked toward the bedroom, knowing he was following behind. She *wanted* him to follow her.

The room appeared clean, finely decorated with a large bed, a white-washed vanity, and an antique desk with a closed laptop resting on its surface.

Quiet filled the room, and it was all theirs for the night.

"You know the effect you have on me, don't you?" Vale pulled her to him, turning her in his arms. He placed his forehead into the crook of her neck for a moment, breathing her in, before reuniting his eyes with hers.

She did. These were the times when Vale was almost vulnerable. These were the times she went mad with lust. Bride's hands traveled up his chest, stopping at the place where his heart sat, but nothing beat against his rib cage.

Vale lifted his hand and gently trailed his fingers along the scar on her neck. "You never asked me how you got this," he said softly.

"Because I don't care." However Bride became what she was, she truly didn't care—she relished in what she was, loved doing the things she did. She felt powerful.

"I will always answer anything you ask. *Anything*."

"How about you tell me tomorrow, then. There are more important matters at hand." Bride licked her lips, inching closer to him. To her delight, his breath quickened.

That was all it took.

Vale's mouth crashed to hers, his body pressing into every part of her. The kiss was so rough that Bride tasted metallic on her tongue. They plunged back into the desk and her thighs pushed into the edge of the surface. She kissed him with the same level of intensity, but her body ached for more.

Vale flipped her around, and Bride steadied her hands against the desk. His fingers skimmed down the sides of her rib cage and to her hips. Everything within her ignited at his caress, the rush it sent through her. Releasing a growl, his digits dug into her flesh, tugging her closer.

Bride's heart sped with yearning as he pressed into her from behind. His touch captivated and rendered her nerves senseless.

Vale's warm breath fluttered against her ear as he purred, "Should you hike up your dress, or shall I?"

He removed his hand from her waist and ran it along the inside of her thigh while the other hovered just below her breast. She let out a moan that she didn't want to hold back when he cupped her breast and did wicked things with her nipple, even with the cloth barrier between them.

"You do it," Bride pleaded.

Vale released a low groan. The zipper of his pants slid down, the only other sound besides their ragged breaths, then he yanked up the skirt of her dress. He trailed rough kisses down her neck and nibbled the skin just below her ear.

With one quick stroke, Vale buried himself inside her, and she inhaled sharply at his delicious movements. Again and again, he thrust—each time she moaned louder, needing even more of him. He seemed to know exactly what she wanted as he increased his pace.

When his fingers came to her center, circling in an enticing pattern, she shouted his name for more. And he answered with *more.*

Bride closed her eyes as her electricity lit up the entire room, roaring with bliss. She never wanted him to cease.

The smell of clean cotton sheets disturbed Bride from sleep.

Her eyes fought against exhaustion as she turned onto her side, pulling the covers back up to her shoulder. The muscles in her legs ached, but it was an exquisite feeling to have, knowing that Vale was still beside her. He had dozed off to a well-deserved rest after he had taken her multiple times, but to her disappointment, he was on the edge of the bed, out of reach.

Always when they slept, he drifted farther away and didn't touch her, as if he was afraid of letting himself feel too much. Bride reached out to him, and he rolled onto his back at the last second, straight into her extended hand.

It happened so fast she couldn't stop the little spark that escaped her finger.

Vale jerked against the light jolt, and Bride yanked her hand back, horror on her face. She waited for his eyes to flick open, worried she may have hurt him, but it didn't happen. He was still sound asleep—not a hair on him had been moved out of place to cause a disturbance in his slumber.

"Vale?" He didn't answer, so she touched his chest again and felt it against her palm. *Thump … thump … thump.*

She withdrew her hand and hurriedly placed her ear to his chest. It pumped, though weak and labored, begging to be heard. Its voice was tinier than most, but his heart was crying out. Possibly for her.

Vale's heart was *alive*.

Frantically, Bride tried to shake him awake. Vale rolled toward her with hooded eyes.

She sighed in relief as he studied her.

"Perrie," he murmured. A small boyish smile appeared when he said the word—the type of smile Vale never wore.

Bride didn't recognize what he had said. Before she could speak, Vale reached for her waist and drew her closer. He rested his forehead on hers, one hand lightly cupping her cheek, then he softly brushed a kiss against her lips. Something slammed inside her, trying to break free—it pressed against the back of her skull.

Ever since Bride had first awoken in the Glass Vault, Vale had never kissed her in this manner. Their kisses were more passionate, never this subtle, this tender. His caresses tingled against her lips, sweet and gentle like the soft brush of a feather. His hand drifted to the small of her back, lightly stroking the area—then he pulled her even closer.

Vale trailed delicate kisses along her jaw, down her neck to her collarbone and right back to her mouth while gracefully entangling his fingers through her hair.

Vale kissed her gently one more time before Bride rolled away from him, a strange emotion pouring over her. He settled behind her, encircling her mid-section and resting his forehead between her shoulder blades. His heart barely thrummed against her back. But that kiss felt *wrong*—something was wrong with *him*.

This wasn't *her* Vale.

Before she could sit up to shake him back awake, the pounding in her head returned with a ferocity unlike before. It was the same as in the shower, only this time she could *feel* the memories falling back into place, like tiny pieces to a puzzle. Names, faces—they all came flooding out from the depths of her mind. A tidal wave that consumed her.

Warm blood poured down Perrie's throat, Neven chained to a wall, Vale dragging her by her hair as she thrashed. Then she was lying naked in a bed with a flushed August—there were crazed blackbirds flying before that—then the Huntsman was going after Maisie. She remembered it all, right up to the moment she entered Quinsey Wolfe's Glass Vault.

Everything was on rewind, and the sting of hot tears filled her eyes.

She couldn't stop the memories from coming—part of her tried, but she fought back. Perrie had forgotten about everyone—including herself. She'd lost everything inside the

Glass Vault and then, because of her, she lost everything outside of it, too. Her dad, Uncle Jaron, and Aunt Krista—they were all dead.

The pounding in her head lightened to a dull throb, then it was gone, leaving behind a terrible panic. Fear rose inside her, clawing its way into her chest as she realized where she was—and *who* she was with. His arm was looped around her waist, an anchor that had her trapped in the middle of the ocean away from any sort of land or freedom.

I need to get the fuck out of here. Now! Her heartbeat kicked up.

Tears streamed down Perrie's face, but she needed to keep quiet. After she got out of here, she could scream all she wanted. Slowly, she lifted Vale's warm hand away from her stomach. She prayed to any god listening to let Vale not wake up. Just this once, she desperately hoped someone would hear her prayers. *I have to get out of this house—I have to escape.* She repeated it over and over again in her mind until Vale's arm was safely removed.

With a steady hand, Perrie lowered Vale's arm to the bed beside his hip. He rolled to his back with a low groan and she froze, waiting. His eyes remain sealed, undisturbed. Carefully, she shifted her feet to the floor and pushed up from the mattress, glancing back only once to check on him. Her chest tightened. He looked like August Hartley, but he wasn't. The sleep-tousled blond curls and peaceful expression couldn't conceal the monster underneath the boyishness anymore.

Perrie tip-toed across the carpet toward the door, grateful the floor wasn't wood that could squeak. She left her boots behind and wouldn't risk her safety for a pair of shoes. No matter what, barefoot or broken, she would be running for her life. And if what she knew about Vale was true, then she would most likely never stop.

As Perrie descended the stairs one slow step at a time, Fannie rounded the corner from the living room. Perrie folded her face into a blank expression when everything inside her was shivering to the bone, her heart screaming.

Fannie sneered as she passed and clicked her heels down the kitchen tile toward the basement. Perrie breathed through her nose, a little too rapidly and loud for her own comfort. When the immortal closed the basement door behind her, Perrie padded toward the front exit and turned the knob.

The door swung open and she closed it behind her with a soft click. Relief thrummed in her veins, but it didn't last long—she wasn't far away enough yet.

The early morning welcomed her with a warm breeze. Stumbling down the steps of the porch, Perrie inhaled as much fresh air as possible. Her body tingled, and adrenaline vibrated in her toes, urging her feet to move faster. Perrie might be free, but she wasn't safe yet, so she ran to her goal number one—the sidewalk. Then she reached goal number two when she passed the second house. Then Perrie struck fucking gold when she hit the third, and she continued to root for her achievements as her legs pumped as hard as they could. The only thing she held a firm grip on was her scream.

Wind rattled in her ears—the sound of her feet slapping against concrete flushed out the damn insanity, and everything in the world she passed became a blur.

Even when she'd distanced herself, she kept running away from the house, away from Fannie, away from Vale, away from it all. She didn't once look behind her, afraid if she did, Vale would be there to catch and drag her back by her hair to his world of hell.

TEN

Before-Neven Lee

Neven started his car and left Perrie's house in a rush. He hauled ass to Oak Street, pissed off at Perrie. Why couldn't he just let the girl go? She was obviously out of her damn mind. She'd been in a delusional state over something that never happened.

He took several long minutes to think about how she was with August, and he slapped his hand against the leather steering wheel. It was different. She looked at August with a completely different intensity than she'd ever looked at him. She may not be aware of it, but he was.

In a way, the day's events had helped him understand after all that had happened between them, they could just be friends. Now, if only she would talk to him. Just the other day he'd thought they were the real deal, but everything had changed. He would prove he'd never cheated on her, though. That situation was a fucking mess that boiled the blood beneath his skin every time he thought about it.

Neven turned down Oak Street to confirm to himself that,

yes, there was a museum, and David and the other guys were full of shit.

He sped down the street and came to an abrupt stop when he spotted August's silver car. "What the hell?"

August's blond head moved closer toward the stone building. The squeal of Neven's tires caught August's attention—he stopped in his tracks, turning his head back to Neven with an expressionless face.

A run-in with August these days was a bucket full of fucking fun, and this was one encounter Neven didn't want to deal with. August used to be cool, but ever since he'd thought Neven cheated on Perrie, that had changed. Then again, if the situation was reversed, and he'd heard August cheated on Perrie, he'd be damn angry, too.

Hopping out of his car, Neven slammed the door shut and jogged up to August. "What are you doing here?"

August lifted a blond brow. "I could ask you the same thing, Lee."

Neven and August stared at each other for several seconds, neither saying a word. "Okay, this is dumb as shit," Neven said to cut the tension. "We know we're both here for the same reason."

A crease appeared on August's forehead. "We do?"

Standing out here with August was getting Neven nowhere. "Yes, we do." He shifted closer to August, hovering over him.

August's lips twitched and pulled into a smirk. "Lee, you have no idea."

"Moving on." Neven shook his head, stepped back, and pointed straight at the wooden door. "You see this building? Where the hell did it come from? And why did it appear out of nowhere?"

August cocked his head as if thinking *really* hard about the building. "You think I know these answers?"

Neven let out a long, exasperated sigh. "No. I don't think

you know the answers, but I thought you might've drawn a better conclusion than I could've. The guys I asked at school haven't seen this place."

"We can go inside and take a look." August shrugged and strolled toward the door.

"I already came here this morning. The door was locked, so I can guarantee you right now it's still going to be," Neven said, following closely behind.

Once they stood in front of the door, August brought his fist to the wood—a loud bang that screamed to whoever was inside.

"What are you doing?" Neven yanked August's hand back.

"I'm seeing if anyone is here. Isn't that obvious?" If Neven could've punched August, he would've, but it would only piss Perrie and Maisie off.

They waited around for about a minute, and no one answered. August twisted the knob, and the door opened without making a single sound.

"I guess it isn't locked," August said with a cocky smile. Neven rolled his eyes, vowing to himself that he *would* punch the jackass later.

"I guess it's unlocked now, but it wasn't this morning," Neven mumbled.

"Do you want to go in, or do you want to go back to your car?"

Ignoring August's sarcasm, Neven brushed past him with two long strides. "I'm going in."

"Your choice." August closed the door, his words trailing behind Neven.

Coming to an abrupt stop, Neven turned around to face August. "Enough already, okay? I get it. You think I cheated on Perrie, and I didn't." Neven marched toward August and poked his index finger to the idiot's chest. "Even if she doesn't completely know it, I see how she looks at you. She never looked at me like that, so I'm done trying to be with her, but

I'm going to get my friend back."

August stared him down with that stupid blank expression again. "I understand."

Neven shook his head and continued down the carpeted hallway filled with lanterns. "Now that we have that settled, we can maybe get some sort of answer around here about why this place came out of nowhere."

"Good idea," August called from behind.

The lanterns' shadows swayed along the walls as Neven walked to the end of the hall, then turned down another. A single line of chandeliers hung from the ceiling in the new hallway. He ignored the rest of the decor and proceeded down the corridor when, eventually, he needed to take a turn to another long hallway.

"Feeling lost yet?" August asked.

Neven glanced over his shoulder at August and shot him a glare. "How can I feel lost if the hallways are leading me in what direction to go?"

August let out a dark laugh, and Neven chose to ignore that too. The end of the hallway neared, and he entered a room filled with displays of some sort. He moved at a quicker pace until he stood in the center of the room, able to view the details more clearly.

"What is all this shit?" Neven asked more to himself than to August. Everywhere he looked, there were statues made of glass. He strode to a display with a crooked sign that read: *Beware the Black Plague*. Inside rested two glass statues. One of the man's arms was missing, while a blackness spread from fingertip to elbow on the other.

"This is strange," Neven said as he faced August, but he was no longer there. "August?" Neven stepped away and scanned the different scenes, as if August would creep out of one of the displays.

"August? This isn't funny, man." Neven observed the new scene before him for a moment, wondering what the hell to do.

Before him stood a glass statue of a man wearing a white dress shirt and black slacks, positioned with his back to Neven—an empty medical table at his side. He turned away from the scene to search for August, when something tugged his shirt.

"Cut it out, August. That was stupid of…" His words trailed off as his gaze connected with no one except for the statue. He gnawed on the inside of his cheek, knowing it was time to bolt. Whirling around, he lunged forward but was thrown back with one forceful pull from an invisible wind. He flew through the air, landing hard on his back against the rough floor inside the display.

Groaning, Neven stared at the ceiling for a second as pain radiated through the length of his spine. He brought himself to a sitting position and studied the display, his chest heaving. No, not a display, a cage. Heart pounding, he rose to his feet and ran toward the metal bars. He shook the door, making it bang throughout the entire room.

The sound of squeaky wheels rolling down the hall echoed against the walls. Neven paused, his hands still gripping the bars. August strolled toward him, pushing a silver tray on wheels. He now wore black slacks and a white shirt with ruffles down the center.

"When did you have time to change?" That was the best thing Neven could think to say because he had no idea what the fuck was going on as confusion swirled within him.

August's upper lip curled. "I am going to avoid that question, but I will answer one from earlier. I know you did not cheat on Perrie because that was all me."

Neven stilled. He felt like all the reasons for the strange things happening were about to be revealed, and shit was about to hit the fan.

"First, I'm going to explain it all to you." August glided his hand over a set of tools on the tray before lifting a pair of medical scissors. "Then, we are going to have a little fun."

ELEVEN

Maisie

The past couple of days had gotten Maisie and Neven nowhere. If only Maisie had some sort of psychic ability to locate Perrie, but she didn't even know if they were heading in the right direction.

She and Neven had stayed to the trees, away from the main streets. From the look of things, it seemed as though all the immortals had already left to set sail on their own adventure to their continuation of ruination.

The first night after she and Neven had left the barbershop, they'd made themselves a little camp in the forest nearby. *By camp, I mean one of us would fall asleep in the grass while the other kept watch for anything strange.* While Neven had been dozing off, Maisie left their hideout and decided to poke around near the edge of the forest, in hopes she would find *something.*

The sound of loose rocks scraping gravel had come from straight ahead, and Maisie prepared herself to go in for the attack and save her cousin from Vale. Maisie's shoulders had slumped as soon as she caught sight of the scraggly mermaid. Her dark skin, cerulean hair and matching tail, all seemed to glow beneath the silvery moon. The creature had slowly dragged her body across the gravel, her tail half ripped from her abdomen. Something oozed from the wound, leaving a liquid trail in its wake. Maisie hadn't been sure whether to be impressed for how many weeks the mermaid had towed herself across the land, or worried she might spot their camp. She leaned more toward being impressed.

After the mermaid crawled on by, Maisie had made it a point to stay by the fire.

Day two had been anything but action-packed. No immortals were anywhere to be found, only an endless supply of their finished business—glass statues. The town was so deserted, even more broken than the last, that she'd expected to see a troop of tumbleweeds pass her, but that most likely came from another movie.

Now, at the end of the day, Maisie couldn't focus on anything else except for how much she missed Perrie, her family, and the eye patches crafted by her own hand.

"Neven?" she asked, leaning against a tall tree, its pinecones scattered around her.

"Yeah?"

"Do you miss Perrie?" A look of confusion spread across his face, so she needed to break it down further—as if it wasn't obvious enough, though. "I mean, do you *miss* her, like are you still in love with her?"

Neven frowned for an entire sixty seconds. Maisie knew because she counted.

Finally, he shook his head. "No. I think it's more like I miss her friendship. Besides David, I was always around the two of you, and then I wasn't. I did love her, and a part of me always will, but I was wrong about a lot of things."

Maisie let his words sink in. She wasn't sure if she believed him. Just a couple days before he'd vanished, Neven was all about getting Perrie back. He hadn't lurked around corners or anything to talk to her, but he'd still tried every now and then.

"What?" He shot her a hard stare. "You don't believe me, do you?"

Maisie bit her thumbnail and didn't say anything.

"Believe what you want."

"I don't know, Neven. You seemed pretty persistent about getting her back before you disappeared."

He sighed. "I know, but after I left her house that day, something hit me, and I knew she looked at August differently than she ever did at me."

"Okay, but just because you thought she felt something more toward August, it doesn't counter your feelings or make them vanish."

"Look, I can't explain it, but I cared more about our friendship than anything else and that's why it was so important to get her back. Yes, I told Perrie I loved her when I left her house, because I do. It's just not in *that* way anymore. Does that make sense?"

It did. His words did make sense, but she still wasn't sure.

As Neven stared out at the fallen and cracked telephone poles near the street, something in his eyes grew distant, and an old feeling stirred within her as she watched him.

"Speak, don't forever hold your peace," Maisie said.

He whipped his head to hers. "Seriously?"

"What's wrong now?" Maisie scooched closer so her arm was pressed to his. He needed someone in that moment, and she wanted to be there for him.

"I thought maybe I could help be a hero after what happened to my mom, but the past few days proves I'm just a monster who can do nothing."

"You're not a monster." Maisie patted his back. "You're going to be a hero with me. Frankenstein's Monster was never the villain of the story."

Neven slung his arm around her shoulders and held her close. "Easy to say, Snow White was the ultimate innocent."

"Ah, my dear friend, but I've actually turned people to glass, while you were fine and dandy after exiting Vale's funhouse." Neven was luckier than all of them, and she was glad for it.

"Under all that upbeat attitude you always have, you're *still* positive and I sort of admire it, even though it's a very oddball reaction to this new existence."

"Why, thank you. I couldn't have said it more perfectly myself."

He didn't look as miserable for the time being, and Maisie didn't want to rehash and think about his feelings for Perrie. So while the sun set, Maisie stayed pressed against Neven, his comforting minty scent enveloping her, as they studied the cracked streets, the stalled cars, and the smoke curling into the air farther away where buildings had been burned to the ground.

Once Vale was gone, Maisie, Neven, and Perrie would help to return this world to its former glory. That was a promise.

As the sun's rays crept out for morning to bring about the day, Maisie's eye flicked open. A feeling of adrenaline pulsed within her. She was fresh and pumped to continue their mission in the next town.

Maisie propped herself up against the tree trunk and shook her legs out to get them ready to roam about. Neven yawned as he stood and stretched his scarred arms toward the sky. The insides of her stomach performed a little dance as she studied the sliver of skin where his shirt was lifted. A trail of dark hair rested below his belly button, leading to… She hurried and looked away. That old feeling had been there, a link to the past, and a part of her kind of *liked* it.

"Ready to go?" Maisie pushed herself up from the cool grass and brushed off the dried leaves and specks of dirt clinging to the skirt of her dress. Neven plucked a tiny leaf stuck to her back, and his touch sent a thrill through Maisie. She maneuvered away from him as she pretended to adjust her patch.

He chuckled. "More walking, right?"

She peered up at his face, and the light hit his jaw just right. He had an intriguing jaw. Maisie shook her head, needing to not think about his features. Any of them. Regardless of how pleasant they may be to look at.

"So, no walking today? We're just going to stand here?" He pointed to the ground.

"No." Somehow, Maisie tripped over that one-syllable word. "I mean, yes, we're going to walk." She pivoted on her heel and headed to the street, becoming her own compass since she lacked one.

Neven jogged up beside her. "You're acting weird, Mais."

She laughed, feeling back to normal, *focused*.

"Well, weirder than usual." He cracked a half smile.

"I adapt to my environment."

Debris and broken branches littered the road and leaves crunched beneath their feet. They hadn't talked to another living soul since Ben. Maisie wondered how far he'd gotten after leaving them in the dust. She hoped he'd made it to somewhere safe. What about Josselyn? Had she managed to snap out of it, or was she still out there creating headless glass statues? Maisie may not have been able to save her parents or Uncle James, but she was determined to save Perrie. Unknowingly, Maisie shook her fist in the air.

"You all right?" Neven asked, latching onto her arm. His hand was warm, comforting.

"Yeah, I'm fine. I'm just thinking."

"About what?"

"Ben. Josselyn." She paused, taking in a breath. "My family."

He nodded, understanding. Since the world turned to glass, Maisie doubted he'd stopped thinking about his mom once.

"Mais, listen—" Neven didn't finish his thought. A loud rustling in the trees stirred, directly above them.

They halted and exchanged a glance. Maisie thought for a second that it could be animal life, maybe squirrels or a raccoon, but a decaying odor permeated the air, and she knew she was wrong. Something twisted in the branches, shuffling through the leaves. Maisie squinted her eye to get a better view.

Without hesitation, the thing dove from the tree, and Maisie pulled Neven out of the way just in time.

"What the hell is that?" Neven's words echoed above her head.

They slowly backed away as the questionable thing rose from the ground. Human eyes stared back at them, unblinking, from a mask of rotted flesh. The greenish skin, which was far too large and sagging in places, revealed a hidden wooden body beneath its surface. The putrid smell of decay became stronger, drifting straight from the creation. If it weren't for the long wooden nose and too-big wooden hands protruding from the flesh, she wouldn't have known who it was.

"It looks like Pinocchio in a skin suit," Maisie whispered.

"We need to run," Neven hissed in her ear.

"We can't run. He knows we aren't part of the club anymore." Besides, if they escaped his presence now, then flesh-wearing Pinocchio might locate Vale before they had the chance to find Perrie. Then the whole saving Perrie mission would be finished before it had even begun. "Stay here—I've got a plan."

"Oh fuck, not another one."

Pinocchio hadn't moved a single wooden muscle—his

dark eyes remained unblinking, possibly waiting for them to make the first move. Maisie put on her best soothing face and inched closer to Pinocchio. He held his stance, chest puffed out, proudly wearing the dead skin.

Preparing her ammunition, Maisie cleared her throat before softly whistling a little melody. Pinocchio's head tilted to the side, creaking with each twist of his neck. It was working—Maisie had his attention.

A tune escaped her lips, one she sang just for him, "Pinocchio wants to be a live boy. He created his own clothes out of skin. It's time to fall fast asleep and—"

"What are you *doing*?" Neven demanded, hauling her to him, her back pressing against his firm chest.

"See, it's working. I'm hypnotizing him with my powers!" She pointed frantically at the wooden boy.

Maisie's gaze latched onto Pinocchio's and she opened her mouth to sing again, when he lunged at her. With each step, a groan sounded as he bent his knees. They whirled out of the way right before his hands connected with her throat. She should've known her ability wouldn't work on an immortal.

Pinocchio spun around to attack again, but Neven charged forward first, slamming the immortal into a tree trunk. The wooden boy clawed violently at Neven's chest, shredding his shirt and skin until blood bloomed to the surface.

Heart pounding, Maisie had to help Neven. Searching around the forest, she spotted a fallen tree branch on top of a bush that she could use as a weapon. She barreled for it, hoping Neven could hold the immortal off. Neven's power was strength, after all.

Pinocchio viciously gnashed sharp teeth at Neven's forearm as Maisie snatched the branch. She rushed back, swinging for the savage immortal's head until she finally thwacked the heavy wood. He howled an ugly sound, distracted enough by the blow to lose his grip on her friend. Neven took the opening and grabbed for Pinocchio, pinning the immortal's arms and legs to the ground.

The wooden creation hissed as Maisie lifted the branch over his head once more. Without hesitation, she brought it down hard, over and over again. He bucked and thrashed, shaking Neven's body with the movements. No matter how many times Maisie struck Pinocchio, he didn't surrender, wouldn't give up his battle.

"I don't know what else to do!" Maisie yelled. "Nothing's happening to his head."

"Screw this." Neven took Pinocchio's head and twisted it side to side. The immortal's sharp, wooden teeth snapped at Neven's hands, and she wondered if Neven's finger would grow back if Pinocchio bit it off.

Neven gave the head one more good twist, then it cracked off. Pinocchio's body turned limp and something like sap oozed from his neck. Neven's shoulders relaxed and he appeared pleased with himself as he tossed the wooden boy's head to the side like a piece of dirty clothing.

"Well done." Maisie grinned.

"Thanks, I—holy shit!"

Pinocchio's body sprang to life where Neven was kneeling. Maisie hurled herself toward Pinocchio's arms while Neven went for the legs. It had been too soon to celebrate. Using his inhuman strength, Neven ripped both legs away with a snap, then finished by cranking off the arms.

Neven hadn't even broken a sweat. Maisie, however, was drenched, and beads of sweat trickled down her flesh.

"Now what?" Neven asked.

"Do you think he can magically put himself back together?"

It was entirely possible. In her display, Maisie had killed the Huntsman once, and he'd poofed right back to life. From her experience, dead things didn't always stay dead.

"I don't know," Neven started. "Maybe we should bury him? Well, his pieces I guess."

A finger twitched on Pinocchio's severed arm. "Maybe bury them separately," she said.

"Good idea."

Neven found a patch of dirt and clawed at it with his hands. He dropped one twitchy leg in and hurried to cover it.

He made quick work of the remaining limbs while Maisie hunted down the head. Pinocchio's eyes were glazed over, glassy like the statues left behind. She pressed her fingers into the cool dirt and tried to make a grave for his head, even though she couldn't tear the ground up like Neven.

Giving her a lopsided smile, Neven patted her shoulder and gently took the head from her hands. "I got this."

Pinocchio snapped his teeth at Neven, but he buried the head casually, as if it was totally normal to dig a hole for an almost-dead marionette.

"So, singing to Pinocchio, *really*?" He laughed deeply when he stood.

Placing her hands on her hips, Maisie jerked her chin toward the fresh plot. "It's not like I knew for sure it wouldn't work on him, but I kind of forgot he wasn't human."

"The dead skin, wooden head and hands didn't give it away?" Neven held his hands in the air, and she gave each one a high five. He laughed again, the beautiful sound singing in her ears, as they headed toward the street.

"How's your chest?" she asked, lifting his torn shirt to inspect the wounds, but they were already healed. Only blood and taut muscles on his strong chest were there.

"I'm all right," he said, voice low as they stared at one another.

Swallowing, she dropped his shirt and peered down at her hands. "Can we find somewhere to scrub this syrup off *unless* you want to go search for some pancakes?"

"That's fucking gross, Mais."

Maisie laughed. "Come on, I'm pretty sure there are some houses a couple blocks away." She took one confident step forward before Neven stopped her.

"Look, I know you want to get Perrie back, and I do too, but we need to be more careful. That was close, too close," he said, his voice firm. But his expression held something softer, concern.

Even though the expression on his face made her heart sing, telling her to take a step toward him, she had to take a step back. "Aw, are you worried something's going to happen to me?"

"I'm serious!" His shoulders slumped. "I'd miss you, Mais."

"You've been fine without me for months and months, you'd be okay. If something happens to me on the way and it helps save Perrie, that's fine—she's all that's left of my family. There's no one else."

Neven tugged at his hair with a dirt-covered hand. "I didn't try to talk to you because you were harder to get through to than Perrie, and that's saying a lot."

His big brown eyes found hers, and she could tell he wanted to say something else. But then he just shook his head and scowled. He didn't have anyone left either, so she understood where he was coming from, but she needed to try. Perrie had come after her without a second's hesitation when Maisie had gone missing.

"Let's get going." She patted his back a couple of times with a reassuring smile.

He ran a hand down his face, then surprisingly, he laughed. "That's it? You give me a pat on the back and everything's fine now?"

"Yes. Now let's get going before Pinocchio becomes *Day of the Dead*."

"That's the best idea you've had so far."

TWELVE

Maisie

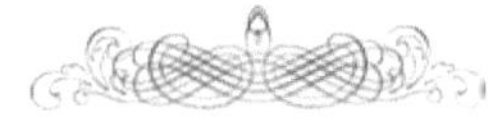

Maisie and Nev headed down a street where several crashed cars rested. A truck was smashed into a tree with a family of four inside—all glass. Another had taken a nose dive into a grassy ditch. Two smaller vehicles were rammed into one another, pieces of their cars scattering the ground. Maisie blew out a breath and pushed forward.

A few roads down, past a shattered gas station, rows of houses lined unbroken pavement. Thankfully, it hadn't been a long walk from Pinocchio's graves to sunshine in suburbia. Every house was the same exact make and model with a couple alterations in windows and mailboxes.

Maisie threw her hand out to the side, stopping Neven. She looked both ways before they crossed the street, making sure she didn't see any sign of another immortal. When the coast was clear, she grabbed Neven's hand and booked it across the street with him in tow.

"You know, Mais, you don't have to be my protector. I did just defeat that thing back there." Neven drew her to his side as they came to a halt.

"Sure, Neven." She patted his back.

Maisie believed he could take care of himself, but he wasn't the best at observing situations. Maybe she wasn't either because neither one of them had spotted Pinocchio up in the tree. She wouldn't say it was her fault though—his woodenness had blended in with the tree, while the hunk of skin he'd worn was a shade of green that fused with the leaves. A little chameleon, he was.

"Take your pick," Neven said, scanning the mostly beige houses.

"The middle one."

"Why the middle?" He cocked his head, clearly skeptical of her choice.

There was always a method to her madness. "Besides for it looking rather cozy in the center? Strategically, it's the safest point between the beginning and the end."

"How?"

"If anyone is looking for us"—Maisie gestured at both ends of the street—"they'll check the first couple houses. They won't keep looking if the first two are empty—they'll just move on." Plus, she would feel more protected by the barriers of the other homes.

Neven palmed his face in both hands and groaned. Sarcasm laced his next words. "And what if they choose the middle house first?"

Maisie chewed on her thumbnail for several seconds, pondering what he'd said. "But what if they don't?"

"You can't answer a question with *another* question!" he hissed, his voice cracking.

She couldn't help but giggle. "Trust me, Neven. The middle house is the safest place to be. Come on"—Maisie strode toward the house in the center—"and join the fun side."

He gave her a side stare and attempted to conceal a grin.

Overgrown grass and lawn gnomes surrounded the house.

Not one or two small little smiling men, but about fifty. This house was right up her alley, other than the statues slightly resembling the dead dwarves back in the Snow White display. But since there were more than seven, relief washed over her.

"Are you sure you don't want to pick another house?" Neven asked, lifting the closest gnome from its place beside a bright pink flower. The figure held a watering can and his grin took up half his face.

"No. It's perfect," Maisie said, placing a hand on her hip. "You know they aren't real."

He arched a brow and set the gnome back on the ground. "I know, but it's still fucked."

Maisie brushed past him and reached for the knob, finding it locked. Neven shrugged, rising on his tiptoes to look through the half-window above the door.

"Looks like there's a backdoor," he said.

They walked around the house to the back, not completely away from the gnomes since more littered the backyard. The backdoor didn't do them much good with it also being locked and all. Neven discovered another entrance by punching through a window.

"I'm not paying for that." She grinned.

Neven rolled his eyes. "Whatever, just get over here so I can help you inside." He cleared away the rest of the glass with his shirt and lifted her up. His fingers trailed down her sides as she crawled through, and a warmth spread through her. She ignored the feeling and unlocked the door for his larger frame.

Maisie set her borrowed bag down and decided to search the house while Neven patched up the window. It was a quick process—three bedrooms and one bathroom. The living room and the kitchen were connected, both appearing clear—no villainous immortals and no glass statues. Photographs lined the hallway and several more stood on a shelf beside the TV. It looked to be a single mom and her two high school kids. Maisie wondered if they were caught on the street in one of the cars she'd passed, or had they been able to escape?

She rooted for the latter.

"All done with the window," Neven said as he joined her in the kitchen.

"Shower time. You go first."

"Oh no, ladies first." Neven tried to prod her to the door in the hallway.

Maisie wiggled out of his arms. "I don't think so. You're covered in more of Pinocchio's sap than me, Neven. And I need time to brainstorm."

"You do that."

"You seem to enjoy saying that," Maisie called to his back.

A few seconds later, the sound of the shower turned on and a string of loud curses followed. She softly laughed to herself—it seemed Neven had forgotten the water wasn't going to be hot.

Maisie took a seat at the perfectly-round kitchen table, her fingers silently tapping the wood as she thought of a strategy. Finally, she wrote down, *Make sure to have a weapon.* That was all she had... She needed a distraction. The fridge took up a corner right next to her, practically begging her to look inside. She drew the door open. And … she should've kept the forsaken thing closed.

A rancid odor invaded her nostrils and she gagged. Not that any of the food would've still been good without power, but she would've probably still eaten the cheese slices if they didn't have mold growing on them.

The pantry, however, had her bouncing in place. It held a box of crackers, a can of spray cheese, and a few packs of breakfast bars. Maisie snatched the crackers and cheese can before resuming her brainstorming.

By the time the shower turned off, Maisie had managed to jot down a few more ideas.

"Be prepared. The water is freezing." Neven padded into the kitchen, shivering.

Maisie took a blanket from the back of the couch in the living room. Opening it, she laid the fleece across his shoulders as he watched her with a curious expression.

"What?" Maisie asked as she tucked the ends together for him to hold.

"Nothing."

Not really an answer. But then Maisie remembered her notes. She grabbed her notepad and handed it to him. "Here."

As he scanned over the notes, a large bead of water slid down his cheek. She reached to wipe it away with her fingertips, and he threw his head back as if she'd struck him.

Maisie frowned, confused. "What?"

"Nothing," he muttered while avoiding her eye.

"You had water on your cheek."

At that, he looked at her, his lips set in a tight line. "Thanks. It was just unexpected."

Is he thinking about what happened with Vale? Maybe he had a problem with being touched after what he'd gone through with that monster. Even though she'd already touched him several times... "You know you can talk about it."

"What?" A puzzled expression formed on his face.

"I get it. Your situation with Vale caused you to not want to be touched." Maisie wanted to reach out and put her hand on his arm, pull him close, but the reaction might cause him to fold into himself.

He slapped his forehead and slid his palm slowly down his face, shaking his head. "You don't even know the half of it. But no, I'm fine about Vale. I mean, as fine as one can be after having your body torn apart, but I don't have any of those effects from it." He handed the notes back to her before she could give him a response. "What I'm more concerned about is that the maniac who did these things to me has Perrie. We're going after him and all we've got to defend ourselves is a little notepad with a bunch of useless ideas. You have no hows." Neven caught himself at the last second, seeming to realize what he'd said.

"Well, how about you write the hows while I take my shower then," Maisie mumbled, tapping the notepad three times in his face before tossing it back on the table. She stomped away without looking back.

"Maisie, wait!" he stammered. "That's not what I meant— I'm sorry!"

Bring weapons! Find Perrie! Put Vale in a display in the Glass Vault! Destroy the Glass Vault! Those ideas are good! Maisie slammed the door shut and practically ripped off her dress. She threw it at the floor, along with her eye patch. Anger rolled through her in waves and she didn't realize how mad she was until she stepped into the shower. All because of Neven. She never got mad—occasionally frustrated, but never angry. Taking a deep breath, she focused on something else— eating the cheese on those crackers once she finished showering.

Her hand drew the curtain closed, and she turned on the shower. When the freezing blast of water pelted her skin, Maisie released a high-pitched shriek. She'd forgotten to prepare herself for the blasted cold.

"Maisie? Are you all right?" Neven shouted, his voice shaky as he barreled through the door.

She startled before clenching the curtain and wrapping it around herself. "I'm fine. I just forgot the water was going to be so cold," Maisie said, trembling while peeping her head out at him.

Relief filled his eyes as he stared at her, his hand clutching his chest as he worked to slow his breathing. "Next time, can you not scream like that?"

"I would have prepared myself if you hadn't made me mad earlier," she pointed out.

Neven pinched the bridge of his nose. "Look, I didn't mean what I said. Your notes are more than what I have."

Maisie's teeth chattered as the cold drops met her flesh.

"Are we going to stand here and chat all day? I need to finish."

Neven's cheeks reddened when his gaze focused back on hers. It must've hit him that she was showering while they were having a chat. A grin spread across her face. She didn't know why he felt embarrassed—he was only seeing her head, and the curtain concealed her entire body. Really, he'd seen more of her earlier in the dress with her arms exposed.

"You're forgiven!" Maisie yelled as he hightailed it out of the bathroom. She leaned back against the wall of the shower, finding his reaction rather cute. Then she remembered he was in this very shower just before her... Images of him naked while washing floated in her head, and now *her* cheeks were heating.

Cheese. Crackers. Cheese. Crackers. She repeated the words like a mantra in her head as she finished showering.

Once Maisie slipped her magically pristine dress back on, she headed into the living room, clean but shivering. Neven pounced on her with the blanket she'd used on him earlier.

"Why thank you, Neven." Maisie snuggled down into the soft fleece.

"No problem, I knew you'd be cold since I'd been." He smiled, resting his hand on her shoulder.

Maisie's eye locked on it, remembering her earlier shower thoughts. As if reading her mind, he drew his hand away. She tugged the blanket around her until she was as snug as a burrito, which reminded her of food, which reminded her of cheese in a can. Darting for the table like her life depended on it, she halted when she reached the now-open can.

Throwing the blanket to the tile floor, Maisie lifted the can and cranked the tip to the side. A remnant piece of yellow cheese rose to the top before falling to the table. Her heart plummeted.

Maisie slammed the empty can down on the table, releasing a metal clank throughout the room. She shut her eye, her chest heaving as she took deep breaths.

That's twice in one day and less than an hour apart? Frustration coursed through her veins, and her fingers vibrated from how mad she was. Neven hadn't spoken a word, but she knew he stood a few feet away, silently watching. She opened her eye and turned to face the culprit. He didn't so much as blink.

"My cheese!" she finally shouted, marching up to him with her fist shaking in the air. "If I could sing you to glass right now, I would!"

His eyes widened. "How the hell was I supposed to know you wanted that cheese? It was just sitting there!"

"*Maybe* because it wasn't there when we came in? *Maybe* because it was sitting next to my notepad? *Maybe* because it was right in front of the chair I was sitting in!"

Suddenly, her feet were off the floor and she squeaked, finding herself in Neven's strong arms. He carried her to the couch and plopped down onto the cushions. His gaze held hers, and she could feel the beat of his heart against her. He then gently set her beside him.

"What was that for?" She laughed.

"You were getting a little too intense—*over fucking cheese.*"

"Well, it was *mine*, and I would have happily shared half the can with you if you'd have waited." She rumpled his almost dry hair, messing it up like she used to do, feeling back to herself.

"Next time I find food, I'll ask first. Do you want me to get you the box of crackers?" He rose from the couch, and she pulled him back down beside her.

"A cracker without a partner isn't fun."

He rolled his eyes *hard.* "I'll stack it with two crackers, then."

"Fine," she drawled. "If you insist."

Neven left her on the couch, her gaze sliding down his flexing muscles to his backside. She swallowed and looked away.

He returned from the kitchen with both the blanket and crackers in hand. With a smile, and a rush of something else pulsing inside of her, she dug into the box. As she bit into a cracker, she was still reminded of what amazement the crackers could've become if only she'd had that cheese. But the warmth of Neven beside her made it all better.

THIRTEEN

Maisie

"What do you think Vale's doing with all the collected souls?" Maisie asked.

Neven handed her the last two crackers. He'd been generous enough to let her have more than half the box since he *did* eat all the cheese.

He considered her question a second longer, staring deeply into the darkness of the empty cracker box. Maisie waited patiently so as not to disturb his train of thought.

"I don't know." He shook his head. "I mean, I may possibly have a clue."

She perked up and pulled the blanket tighter against her body. "You do? Why didn't you say something before?"

"I didn't think it was important?"

"It's definitely important now, Neven!" Maisie practically jumped into his lap, which caused him to fall back on the armrest, dropping the empty box.

"Aug—I mean Vale—mentioned something about power. He said the Glass Vault was the source of it all."

"It's a start."

"Now if only—" Neven didn't get to finish his sentence as the vibration of a violent tremor shook the couch.

No, not the couch, the entire house!

The walls, the windows, everything quaked. Neven grabbed her arm at the same time she leapt to the floor like a flying squirrel, arms opened and all. He dove next to her as the wood beneath them rattled, her teeth clacking together from the movement.

"What are you doing?" he whisper-shouted.

She put one finger to her lips and another to his, giving him the quiet signal. His lips were soft against her digit, but she didn't have time to think about that as she pulled it away. The briefest of pauses occurred between each tremor, which made Maisie wonder if it was footsteps and not an earthquake. Maisie pointed toward the window at the front of the room, ignoring Neven's dirty look, and army crawled to it.

Neven sighed and joined her, peering over the top of her head as she peeled the curtain back a fraction of an inch. Her eye widened when it fell on a massive troll stomping along the wide street, creating craters in her wake. This troll was just as filthy as the last one Maisie had seen days ago. The immortal's flesh sagged, her large breasts flapping against her belly, and matted hair clung to her back. Maisie scooted away from the window and leaned against the wall. Neven followed suit, his arm shaking as he wrapped it around her shoulders.

"What was the point of that?" Neven hissed in a low voice.

"I had to see what it was."

"What would you have done if the troll was coming in here?"

"We would've run out the backdoor." She shrugged—it was that simple.

Neven rolled his eyes and drew her closer.

As if on cue, a loud crash tore through the air at the end of the street. The ground rumbled once more, lasting for only a few seconds before everything turned silent. Neven's chest heaved, his breaths coming out rapidly through his nostrils. Maisie wrapped her arm around his waist and held his free hand to quiet his nerves. The crashing hadn't been too close, so her nerves weren't as loud.

The antsy part of her wanted to run outside and see what had happened. She attempted to calm that part of herself by stroking Neven's hand with her thumb, drawing soothing circles to help his fright at the same time.

After about fifteen minutes, Neven's breaths came out even and she couldn't control herself any longer. Maisie unfolded herself from him and jumped to her feet before racing for the front door. She drew it open and hopped down the steps past the gnomes.

"Oh, come on, Maisie!" Neven called.

At the end of the driveway, past the curb and mailbox, she peered out at the end of the street. Dust billowed upward from a pile of rubble. The troll seemed to be long gone.

"What?" Neven rasped when he caught up with her. Then he spotted the destruction, his lips parted before giving her a hard look. "Don't even say it."

Maisie couldn't help it—her lips curved into a wide grin. "So, we should've chosen a house at the end of the street, right? Not one in the middle?" She laughed, gesturing to the crushed one-story home at the end of the road. To see a house in shambles like that was still a devastating sight, but no worse than anything she'd seen thus far. Thankfully, no one was likely there to get crushed, but turning to glass wasn't a much better option.

Neven tried to hide his smile. "I was talking about us staying at the *other* house at the *other* end of the street."

"Sure, Neven."

The sun was quickly fading, the sky turning hues of red and orange. The moon, the stars, and the night would be peeking out soon, so they headed back inside in case troll number two decided to venture back.

"We should probably hit the sack." Neven yawned.

"You can take one of the beds." She nodded in the direction of the bedrooms.

"Where are you going to sleep?"

Maisie held out her arms, then fell gracefully onto the cushions of the couch and closed her eye. "Right here."

"Why not a bed?"

"I would, but I don't know the people who slept in it, or how clean the sheets are. It's too weird." Plus, some people slept naked in their sheets, and who knew what sort of bodily fluids leaked from them there. Just because she was immortal didn't mean she stopped thinking about things like that.

"But you're going to let *me* take a bed?" he countered.

"Yes." She opened her eye, her expression sheepish.

"Gee, thanks," he said, folding his arms and inching closer to her. "Move over and make room."

"What?" Her heart slammed against her sternum, but not from fright as he stood above her, waiting for her to make room—something else.

"Look, we stay together." Neven pulled at the edges of his hair. "If that thing comes back and we have to bolt, I want us to be ready to go."

"All right." That made sense, yet it didn't stop her heart from singing to her.

Neven took the other side of the couch and lay down, his body too long to fit on it comfortably. As he adjusted his head, her heart sang louder, thumping and thumping. And when his arms opened up for her, the blasted organ screamed.

"*What?*" she asked, her voice high-pitched.

"Seriously, Mais?" Neven sat up and drew her down with him. "You're not going to sleep with my feet in your face, and I'm definitely not sleeping with yours in mine."

After nervous laughter and awkward shifting, they settled into a comfortable enough position. Neven wrapped his arm around her waist, and her back pressed against his firm chest. She could feel every single one of his deep breaths, every single one of his heartbeats.

It was actually kind of perfect. *Perfect? No, I can't be liking the snuggling session with Perrie's ex!*

Maisie was about to break out of his arms and go for a bed, regardless of a stranger's potential semen, blood, or sweat. But then Neven held her tighter, and she didn't know what to do. He was warm and comfortable, and she fit perfectly in the pocket of his arm and chest.

Stop it! Maisie needed her notebook to distract herself, but it was across the room, and by the sounds of his laborious breaths, he'd already fallen asleep.

But the tiredness she'd been feeling had already left as her mind raced about all the wrong things concerning Neven. He was Perrie's. He'd always been Perrie's, ever since the day they'd met.

They would rescue Perrie, and her cousin and Neven could live happily ever after. That was the way it was supposed to be. That was the way it always should've been.

A memory sprang forward from the rug she'd shoved it under. Despite her best attempts at sweeping it away, it found its way back out in her dreams when she'd finally fallen asleep.

"Perrie, are you sure you're going to be okay?" Maisie asked.

"I don't know. I may die tonight, and you'd have to figure out a way to revive my corpse." Perrie tried to smile, her skin pale, while she clutched her stomach, still on the verge of throwing up.

"Eh, you'll live." Neven shrugged but still looked concerned as he waved her a goodbye.

After Maisie closed the door, she turned to face Neven. It was always the three of them, Neven and Perrie, or Maisie and Perrie. But she would give it a little variety this time and make it Maisie and Neven. "You coming to watch the movie?"

"I can walk home." He glanced out toward the door.

"You want to leave?" Maisie asked, confused.

"No. No. Only if you don't want me to come." He smiled, a flush creeping up his neck.

"Nah, I don't want you to leave. You're going to be my movie partner in crime." Too bad Perrie was going to miss out on such a Phantom-tastic day.

Maisie ran into her room as soon as they made it over the threshold and grabbed two masks—one was hers and the other Perrie's. She tossed a mask to Neven when she padded back into the living room. He rolled it over in his hands, giving it a peculiar look over.

"Put it on," Maisie said, but he continued to stare at it. "Here. Let me help you." She took the mask from Neven's hands, and he hunched down a little so she could easily bring the elastic cord over his face. Her fingers brushed his skin, and she found it to be one of the softest she'd ever felt. "Perfect. You look exactly like the Phantom."

His eye on the masked side shifted from side to side. He didn't speak a word, just continuously blinked at her, seeming unimpressed.

"Let me put mine on." Maisie tugged the elastic cord over her head, slid the white mask onto her face, and smiled. "There."

Neven grinned and shook his head.

Now that they were in character, it was the perfect time for her to start the movie.

During the film, Neven's arm brushed hers, but she didn't think too much of it besides it feeling nice. Their bodies were pressed close together, but Maisie always relaxed like this with Perrie too.

Throughout the remainder of the movie, Neven fidgeted and tapped his knee constantly, making it jerk. Maisie wanted to ask him if he was trying to perform the knee-check-thing a doctor did, but she let him continue his leg dance.

As soon as the Phantom drew to a close, she glanced at Neven to see what he thought about it. Only, he already faced her, watching her nervously. He then leaned forward and pressed his lips to hers, soft and warm. She'd never felt anything like it before. A crinkling came from their masks when their noses rubbed together. He was like the perfect Phantom.

As she realized what was happening, she froze, then pulled back and released a small scream.

Leaping from the couch, she booked it to her room, shut the door, and locked it behind her. Hands shaking, she backed away, like Neven might possibly break it down.

The mask was stiff against her face and it reminded her of the kiss, so she took it off, burying it underneath her bed.

Did I want him to kiss me? *Maisie wasn't sure, but if he did it again, she would want him to. She would want to feel those soft lips on hers one more time. Her heart quickened at the thought, the anticipation. This time she wouldn't run off screaming like a sacrificial animal.*

After Maisie calmed the singing birds in her stomach, she casually unlocked and opened the door, walking out of the room as if nothing happened. Neven still sat on the couch, his spine stiff, but the mask was no longer on his face.

"So, about the movie…" He then started to talk about the film for a long time. There was no mention of the kiss, and her chest was struck with disappointment. It was as though her Phantom had left her. But she wasn't brave enough to bring it up.

Maisie's eye flew open, and she was now fully awake. The memory-turned-dream played over and over in her head.

She'd been only fourteen, and she'd never had a crush on anyone before. Even after that day, neither one ever brought up the kiss, not for the rest of ninth grade or the following year. It was as if it had never happened. Not even Perrie knew about it.

Maisie couldn't tell Perrie how she'd felt about him—he'd been her cousin's best friend.

Then the summer Neven's dad passed away, Maisie had been in Turkey visiting her family. Perrie had been there for him when Maisie wasn't. Perrie was the one who'd made him better, not Maisie, and then they fell in love. Maisie had selfishly wished it had been her who'd been there for him, because maybe he would've fallen in love with her instead. But then she'd seen Perrie and Neven together. She'd known then that it was right, *they* were right, so that was when Maisie brushed everything under the rug.

Maisie closed her eye with Neven's arm still tightly wrapped around her, pretending for a moment that she'd told him back then how she'd felt, before *everything*. She was about to drift back to sleep, when an ear-piercing scream roared through the street from outside. Neven and Maisie jerked up at the same time, and she could see the fear in his face.

Another wail tore through the dawn, accompanied by thunderous crackling. Lunging for the door, Maisie ran out into the morning light and discovered the source of the noise.

It was *Perrie*.

FOURTEEN

Vale

Vale woke to the blank space of a white wall and a throbbing headache. His eyes focused in and out, the pain in his head blurring his vision. This was something new and entirely unwelcome. He wanted to rip his brain out and slam it against the wall, if only that were possible.

He couldn't remember anything from last night after falling asleep—it was almost as if he had woken from hibernation. After he blinked a few times, the pain faded.

The day was new, yet something did not feel right. He rolled over to wake his lovely Bride, but found she was not there beside him. The covers were pulled back, revealing a cold and empty spot.

She normally woke him by nibbling on his neck. What the fuck was going on? He forcefully slapped the empty spot when a thought crossed his mind. Elise Rodriguez had come back to herself. What if…

No. Impossible.

He pushed himself out of the bed, throwing the door open

so hard it crashed and broke into the wall. Without a pause, he raced down the steps and called, "Bride?"

Nothing. No answer.

Vale brought a hand to his chest. If his heart could beat, it would have exploded with fury—this could not be happening. It *was not* happening.

He searched everywhere, including the front and backyard. Then he thought maybe she had gone downstairs to the basement, to relive the bloodshed. Opening the door, he hurried down the steps and found nothing except burned down candles.

Vale rushed to the living room where Red was sprawled across the couch, snoring quietly with a line of drool trailing down her cheek. *What an insignificant waste of space.* He could not understand what his father ever found in her that was worth saving.

"Red!" he roared as he approached her.

The immortal's eyes burst open and almost popped out of their sockets. He then slammed his hand around her throat, tightening his grip. Red's eyelids fluttered as the air in her lungs cut off. She clawed at his chest, but he only squeezed harder.

"Where is she?" he demanded, his voice low, frenzied.

She only shook her head and gripped the couch cushions, those filthy nails of hers digging in. Lifting her by the neck with one hand, he flung her to the floor.

Red brought her hands to her throat and lurched forward. "What was *that* for?" she seethed.

Vale sauntered toward her, prepared to rip her apart in the slowest way possible. She was no innocent—after her mortal death, she had come to the Underworld after all. He knelt beside her, fastening his gaze on hers. "Now, where is she?"

"The Bride?"

"Who the fuck else would I be talking about?" Vale growled.

Red had to go soon—she had irritated him since day one. She was a tick that would not go away, a parasite that had found its way into his father's bedroom. If he could dispose of her without consequence, he would do it in an instant.

"I don't know. I saw her earlier this morning when I was heading to the basement," she stuttered, running her hands through her hair, trying to press it down. "I assumed she went back upstairs with *you*." He could sense by the way she said the last word, she was not as nervous as she was pretending to be. In fact, she seemed elated to find out the Bride was gone.

Fiery flames coursed within his veins, sewing their way throughout his entirety. His anger wanted to come out and play a vicious little game with Red.

"Where did she go?" His voice was a calm, deadly whisper.

Her mouth hung open, and he could see her tongue stroking the inside of her cheek. If she did not come up with a good answer, he was going to cut it out and make her choke on it.

"I don't know." She shrugged. "I warned you that you were becoming too attached to her, *didn't I*?"

Running a finger through one of Fannie's curls, he gave it a hard yank and she yelped. "If I do not find her, I am going to rip this red hair, you so dearly cherish, out piece by piece and then move on to different body parts. Isn't that the way you like to torture your victims out here?"

"I understand."

"If you find her before I do, your punishment will be lessened a fraction." Vale whirled away from Red, then stopped and glanced over his shoulder. "And clean those nails of yours, you disgust me."

Fists tightened, he burst through the front door and out into the daylight. The sun's rays beamed down on him as he ground his teeth. The answer he did not want to think about earlier was there once again. He knew without a doubt his Bride was gone and replaced with Perrie Madeline.

The anger inside him needed to be released. Vale threw his fist into the first thing he came into contact with—the tree cracked under the powerful blow. He smacked his fist against the trunk over and over, watching bright crimson leak from his knuckles. Chest heaving, he lifted his hand and studied the red liquid as it trickled to the ground. The sight of his blood relaxed him for a moment. He swore to himself then and there that he would find Perrie Madeline.

The Glass Vault would have enough souls very soon, giving him the power to locate her. He would rip Perrie Madeline apart, then put her back together again and again, until she became his Bride once more.

It was impossible for him to love, but what he felt for the Bride, what he did not know he could feel, was stronger than anything he had ever experienced. She was his and *only* his, and he knew with everything in himself that he belonged to her.

FIFTEEN

Maisie

$\mathcal{A}$ few houses down the street, Perrie stood, her wild hair blowing in the wind, her white gown swishing around her. She released scream after scream, hurling bolts of lightning toward anything and everything. A stream of sparks struck a long, thick tree branch above Maisie's head, snapping it off. It crashed to the ground, missing her by an inch. Perrie's face looked pale with fear written in her expression. Maisie tried to take a step forward, but Neven tugged her back.

"How do we know it's actually her, Maisie?"

"It's her. I know it." She inhaled a deep breath, got in a runner's stance, and prepared to lunge toward her cousin.

"We're both going to get her. Just don't try to army crawl after her." He sighed, raking a scarred hand through his hair.

"That would be a better idea, but I wouldn't be quick enough." Before he could say another word, she sprung forward, thrashing her arms in the air. "Perrie! Perrie, it's me! It's Maisie and Neven!"

Neven shouted something at Maisie, the sounds of his feet

pounding right behind her. Between Neven's shouting and her running, Maisie saw the horror of recognition cross Perrie's face just as she released a bolt of power. Pure white light slammed into Maisie's stomach, sending her flying backward. Her body smacked against the pavement, her spine cracking into two.

"Maisie!" Neven yelled, falling to her side in an instant. His arm looped behind her neck, and one of his comforting hands clasped hers. "You're going to be okay."

As the world spun, she peered up at his perfect face and smiled. "Of course I am. I'm immortal, remember?"

"Oh my god! Fuck!" Perrie screeched, her voice filled with panic. "I'm so sorry, Maisie. I'm so, so sorry!"

Maisie could feel her spine fuse back together, each fiber connecting. Chest heaving, she sat up with Neven's help. Perrie stood frozen in place just a few feet away, her brown hair wilder, matching the expression on her face. Her cousin's shoulders relaxed, relief seeming to hit her once she found Maisie sitting, no longer harmed.

"See? I'm good as new." Maisie grinned.

Perrie's lower lip quivered as her eyes filled with tears. Her legs buckled and she collapsed to her knees, gripping the white strands of her hair as she sobbed. The sound of her agony pierced Maisie straight to her heart—it was worse than anything she'd ever experienced, even her own deaths with the Huntsman.

Neven pulled Maisie to her feet and they ran to her. Perrie rocked back and forth on her knees, her hands covering her face. They needed to get her inside before someone found them.

Neven made it to Perrie first and scooped her up in his arms, her tears spilling onto his shirt. "I've got you, Perrie," he said in a soft, soothing voice. "I've always got you."

Maisie touched Neven's shoulder and ran her hand through her cousin's curls. "No, Perrie, *we've* got you."

Perrie turned into his chest, racked with sobs, as they walked back inside the house. Neven took her to the couch, lowering himself as carefully as possible, so as not to disturb her. Maisie closed the door and locked it back up before joining them on the floor. She stroked her cousin's hair again to calm her.

She'd hoped Perrie would be her usual smiling self when they found her, but her cousin remained in this position for a long while, crying, not looking up at either of them. Maisie could only imagine how this must be for her, to know that August wasn't ever real. The word devastated wasn't strong enough to describe it.

Maisie didn't know how much time had passed when her cousin finally lifted her head, her tears slowing as she looked at them. "I'm so glad you two are all right," Perrie said with a ragged breath.

Neven moved Perrie from his lap and set her on the couch beside him. She took his hands in both of hers, squeezing them tightly. Maisie studied those joined hands, and her heart raced in her chest, singing louder. She couldn't make it stop, so she kept her gaze trained on her cousin's face.

"Hi, Perrie." Neven's voice was low, gentle.

"Oh, Nev," Perrie stuttered, tears sliding down her cheeks, "this is all my fault, I'm so sorry."

Neven wrapped the blanket he and Maisie had been sharing around Perrie's shoulders. It wasn't Neven and Maisie. It was Nev and Perrie. Maisie had to remember that. She stepped back and swallowed the tainted feeling stirring within her.

"I'm going to take a quick lap around the neighborhood to make sure it's clear," Neven started. "It will give you two some time to talk."

Perrie reached for Maisie and drew her down beside her. All Maisie wanted was for her cousin to be okay, inside and out.

"We were coming for you, Perrie. We've been looking for you this whole time and you found us!" Maisie squeezed her cousin's shoulder, breathless with relief.

"It must have been our blood oath." Perrie smiled, then it slipped from her tired face. "I've done terrible things, Maisie."

They both had.

"I did bad things, too, but we can't hold onto that. You've got this. You have to be strong here. I know the world is a wild carnival ride at the moment, but it could all be worse. There is *always* worse."

"How can it be any worse than it already is? There's a demon that basically murdered people and turned them into things that can't die, who by the way, are now wreaking havoc on Earth. Then to top it off, this fucker pretended to be someone I'm in love with. I killed a lot of people."

"Were in love with," Maisie pointed out.

"*What?*" She jerked, the color draining from her face.

"You just said *I'm in love with.* You meant were, right?" Maisie ran her thumbnail along the edges of her front teeth as she awaited Perrie's answer.

"That's what I meant," she said in a rush.

Was it? Maisie wasn't in Perrie's position, so she didn't quite understand. But she believed she would've been thinking of all the ways to kill the demon instead of crying over him.

She took Perrie's hands in hers and gently squeezed them. "Do you remember what you said to me back in Snow White's cottage? You told me Crazy Maisie wasn't me, and we were pretty much two separate people. So you're going to have to look at it like that in this situation, too. The Bride isn't you— it's your alter. She's not who you really are, nor the actions you would've chosen."

Perrie sighed heavily. "I didn't really understand the situation then, and now that I see the memories are all mine, I was still the one out there doing everything."

"You're going to have to separate them. That's what I've

been doing, or you're not going to be able to live with yourself." Her cousin could do this. Maisie knew she could.

"You're always so smart with things, you know that, Maisie? But everyone we know is dead. Dad, Uncle Jaron, and Aunt Krista." Perrie let out another rack of sobs, and Maisie circled her arms around her cousin.

Perrie's grief felt as though it was transported to Maisie when she thought about what had happened to her parents and uncle. "I know they're gone, Perrie, but are they really? All we know is their souls got sent to the Glass Vault, but their glass statues are still here. Maybe there's a way to bring the souls back to their statue?" She desperately wanted that to be true, but she didn't know if they were really lost forever.

Perrie shook her head. "I don't know, Maisie. You haven't been with Vale this entire time. I don't think there's a way to defeat him."

That might be true, but Perrie would know better than anyone if there could be a way. "Um, Neven told me you crossed paths with him in the Glass Vault."

Perrie's body hunched forward, but not a single tear escaped her this time. "As you probably know, August is Vale. I confessed to August that I loved him, gave him everything I had, and I've never felt that way about anyone. Then he dragged me naked by my hair and tossed me in the cage with Neven. And the outcome was this." She trailed a hand across the scar at her throat.

A rush of anger rolled through Maisie, and she wanted to find a pickaxe like she had back in the Snow White display. She would slam it through Vale's darkened heart when she crossed paths with him again. Her fingers fidgeted with her dress as she thought about something else, almost too afraid to ask, but she pushed herself to do so. "How bad did he hurt you outside the Glass Vault?"

Perrie lowered her head and avoided Maisie's stare. "He—he didn't."

Maisie's nose wrinkled and her eyebrows became one long caterpillar. "What?"

"He treated *her* much differently than he did with me. When he had me in that tower and in the cage with Neven..." She blew out a breath, then hurriedly changed the subject. "Anyway, all Vale's trying to do is fill the museum with more souls so his powers grow stronger. I don't know a way to stop him."

"Yet. But we will." Maisie would fight in every way she knew how to come up with something. Her thoughts turned to Neven outside, and all Vale put him and Perrie through just to break them apart. The feelings of wanting him as more than a friend had resurfaced back to the correct setting like a Rubik's Cube. But no matter how much she wanted them to, they couldn't stay, so like before, Maisie twisted them inside her head so the colors were mixed up once more.

This was the moment for Perrie to get her happy ending. Defeat Vale, Perrie and Neven together, and Maisie joyous for everyone.

Maisie nudged her cousin's elbow. "You know, you can be happy again once we get the world back to normal. Neven's right there. You two would still be together if it wasn't for Vale. Now's your chance to make things right."

Perrie lifted her brows and fought a small smile. "So, it's like one of those action movies where the world is practically destroyed, but people still kiss and make up at the end as if nothing ever happened?"

"Why yes, yes it is." Maisie silently pleaded for Perrie not to sink back in her hole, but she would always be there to help dig her out if she did. Before the Glass Vault, sometimes it took people longer to heal over things, but in this new world, there wasn't time for that.

"Look, Maisie, I'm not going back to Nev. I know you have some plan brewing to bring down Vale, and I'll help you, but we'll only ever be friends."

"I don't understand." Why wouldn't she want him back?

Perrie wrapped her arms around her stomach, tears beading her lashes. "This isn't going to make sense. It doesn't even make sense to me. Technically, August is Vale, but if I have to admit it now, I will. I'm still in love with August who doesn't exist, yet the way I felt for him was deeper than it ever was with Nev. So it wouldn't be fair to Nev. Our relationship was rooted with friendship more than anything else. With August, those roots flourished into a beautiful blooming tree, so I wouldn't go back to anything that offered less. In fact, I wouldn't go to anyone."

Maisie cupped Perrie's warm cheek and brought her cousin's head to her shoulder.

"As horrible as this situation is," Perrie whispered, "I know if you're with me, things will be better."

"Does that mean you're ready to plot?"

"I'm ready to plot." Perrie said, lifting her head from Maisie's shoulder. And as Perrie smiled, determination radiated from every inch of her cousin.

The door creaked open and Neven walked in, unscathed by his brief journey. He grabbed the box of breakfast bars from the pantry and tossed one to each of them.

Opening up a bar, he said, "Don't worry, we're all alone. No trolls and no crazy girls shooting lightning at pedestrians."

Maisie held her breath, waiting for Perrie to cry, but she didn't. Her laugh filled the air, and it was the sound Maisie had been missing.

"Time to plot." Maisie looked to Neven, giving him a wide grin, when Perrie stopped laughing.

"Ah, yes, more plotting," he said sarcastically and settled in a seat at the kitchen table.

Perrie sank down across from him, and Maisie took the chair in between them. Maisie peeled off the top paper of her notes and stuck it to the back of the sticky pad. She then wrote down a question.

Maisie was about to open her mouth when Neven held up his hand. "Before we begin on a long journey of plotting as Maisie would call it, the most important question is, where is Vale now?"

She lifted the pad directly in front of Neven's face. "As I will have you know, that's the first question I have on my list."

"It's also the *only* question you have on your list."

"Don't worry, I have more coming your way." Maisie peeled the sheet she'd stuck to the back, wadded it up, and tossed it at Neven's head, hitting the bullseye.

He reached for it and tossed it back, but she dodged out of the way, laughing. Maisie glanced at Perrie, her lips parted while her gaze shot between Neven and Maisie.

Neven cleared his throat and focused back on Perrie. "How did you escape?"

"I just ran. I woke up, remembered who I was, and I ran away." She frowned, burying her hands into the skirt of her dress. "He was still asleep."

"Do you know where he is now?" Maisie asked, not wanting to dig too much into their sleeping arrangement.

"He could be anywhere if he knows I'm gone."

"Then we should keep moving." Maisie stood from the table and threw the notepad in her borrowed bag. "Hopefully, he doesn't know which direction you ran in and we can stay ahead."

"Never eat her cheese." Neven rolled his eyes while they trekked through a wooded area.

Perrie arched a brow. "I could've told you that, Nev."

Speaking of food, Maisie needed to find more breakfast bars. Immortals may not have to eat, but her taste buds were yearning for something.

Neven filled Perrie in on mostly everything. Perrie didn't go into great detail when she spoke next, but she did give them bits and pieces of what happened while they'd been separated. The things she'd done were ruthless, but again, it could've been much worse.

"Remember Ben Johnston?" Maisie asked Perrie.

"Troll display. Yes."

"We ran into him a few days ago. I tried to get him to join our team, but that didn't pan out. However, he did have his memories back."

"You know who else did? Officer Rodriguez. She—she…" Perrie covered her mouth with her hand and took a deep breath. Maisie placed her arm around Perrie's waist and Neven wrapped his around her shoulders. "She did, too. But me and Vale … we murdered her. She's gone."

"An immortal?"

Perrie straightened, wiping a few tears away before explaining to them how an immortal could die at Vale's hands. If he could make them, then he could break them too. Sooner or later, Maisie believed everyone would have their memories back—if they were still alive anyway.

"After I finished with Officer Rodriguez, Vale sent her soul back to the Glass Vault," Perrie said.

"How does that work?" Neven sounded confused—looked it too.

"We're bound to the Glass Vault, same as Vale," Perrie started. "That's why he wants the souls. It makes him stronger. It's like—"

"The Glass Vault is a battery?" Maisie interrupted.

Perrie nodded, and the skeleton of a plan took shape in Maisie's mind. They *could* set the Glass Vault on fire. If they destroyed his source of power, then maybe it would make him weak—maybe it would kill him altogether. And maybe Vale wasn't as invincible as he believed he was.

"I think I know what to do. Originally, I was going to have

all the immortals gang up on Vale. Bind, gag, and bring him to the Glass Vault," Maisie said, striking her fist against the open palm of her other hand. "They would only be going up against a demon from the Underworld. No big deal."

"If everyone is like Ben, that wouldn't have worked," Neven pointed out.

"Precisely, but I think if that big museum is Vale's main generator, burning it may actually work. I just—"

Before she had a chance to finish her plan, Maisie's feet were ripped out from beneath her. She landed flat on her face, a sharp pain throbbing in her nose and cheek. Something took hold of her leg and yanked her backward. A powerful scream tore from Maisie's throat, vibrating violently in her ears. Neven and Perrie latched onto her arms, their teeth clenched, unwilling to let go.

An excruciating pain radiated through her abdomen as both sides of her body were pulled. It felt as if her stomach was going to be ripped apart. All she could think of in that bizarre moment was what a way to go. She at least hoped Perrie and Neven would be left with the upper portion, so she wouldn't have to watch herself be eaten or torn to shreds.

Neven gave one hard tug, saving Maisie from the unknown's hand. She flew straight into him and landed on his chest with a forceful blow, knocking him to the ground. His fingers dug into her waist as she sat up, her knees cradling his hips. Taking a quick swallow, she didn't have time to focus on the position she was in on top of him—she sprang to her feet.

"Maisie!" Perrie screamed. "Look out!"

A flash of Perrie's white light struck the dirt a step away from Maisie's feet, rumbling the ground. Then a scream pierced the air, a foreign voice, as Maisie searched for her attacker. And there she was, the mermaid sloth who'd slowly crept her way down the street the other night. *How did she make it the same distance we have without falling apart?*

Then Maisie's gaze fell to a sparkling pond behind Perrie.

Oh, that's how.

The mermaid recovered quickly enough and shot forward, not at a snail's pace any longer. Unhinging her jaw, revealing a set of needle-sharp teeth, the immortal screeched and launched her body at Perrie. The lightning bolt didn't release from Perrie's fingers in time as the mermaid hit, burying her pointy teeth into Perrie's shoulder. Perrie wailed, struggling to yank the mermaid's head away by her blue hair.

Half the mermaid's blue tail still dangled from her upper body like it had the other day. Maisie jolted for it, grasping her tail in both hands and pulling on it, hard. The immortal howled, tossing her head back, Perrie's blood fresh on her dark lips.

The mermaid lunged for Maisie and sank her teeth into her neck. Maisie released a shrill scream. With all her strength, she pushed roughly at the immortal's chest, but the mermaid was glued to her throat. As Maisie wriggled, she wasn't quite sure if this creature was trying to be a vampire or a zombie.

Her flesh throbbed even more as the mermaid began sucking. Blood pulsed beneath Maisie's skin, leaving her veins as it entered the immortal's mouth. She needed to get this leech off of her, and as she shoved, the immortal was ripped away. The creature was in Neven's grip on the ground while he tried to wrestle her down. But she continued to screech and whip her body and tail about.

"A little help would be lovely!" he called.

"Team effort!" Maisie yelled as she and Perrie rushed to his aid, each taking an arm while Neven put his weight on the mermaid's tail. With half of the creature's body dangling, she still showed no sign of weakness.

"Do it," Maisie said, remembering what helped them the last time. "Just like with Pinocchio." The mermaid seethed at them, speaking in a language Maisie didn't understand. "Sorry, I can't hear you, little mermaid." It probably wasn't worth hearing anyway—she doubted the immortal was begging for her life.

Neven pulled, his face turning red, until a loud bone-crunching sound drowned out the mermaid's voice entirely. The blue tail thrashed in his grasp and he tossed it aside.

Next came the arms, then finally Neven removed the head. Green blood leaked from the missing appendages, surprising Maisie. She figured it would've been blue.

Perrie held a mermaid arm, staring at the still-wiggling fingers and asked, "Now what?"

"Bury time," Maisie yelled.

"Déjà vu?" Neven cracked a smile at Maisie as he went to dig the first grave.

"Déjà vu," she said back.

"You two have done this before?" Perrie asked.

"Oh, I forgot to tell you"—Maisie grinned, clapping the dirt from her hands—"Neven and I had a run in with creepy Pinocchio in the woods recently."

"It got pretty fucking ugly," he said.

"Neven kicked his little wooden behind, though."

"I'm glad I wasn't there for that one." Perrie tilted Maisie's head to inspect her neck wound, but it no longer ached.

"You didn't want to try *singing* again?" Neven gave Maisie a teasing shove.

She pushed him back playfully. "I really do have the worst power. You can still rip immortals apart, and Perrie's power knocked the mermaid down." Maisie hadn't tried singing to the mermaid, though. Maybe this time it would've worked if she had. She would have to try it again when they encountered another wicked soul. That was what she should've been calling them all along.

Neven looped his arm around Maisie's waist and pulled her in close, surprising her. She breathed in his minty scent, and her heart fluttered.

"Like you said, Mais"—Neven leaned in close—"team effort."

Laughing, Maisie glanced up and her gaze met Perrie's, who must've been watching them this whole time. A sinking feeling dropped to the pit of her stomach and she left Neven's warmth.

SIXTEEN

Perrie

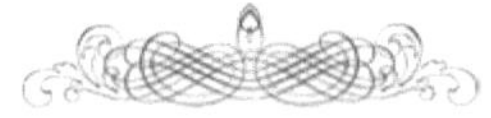

After their encounter with the mermaid, Perrie was even more exhausted. Every single part of her body and mind was.

She, Neven, and Maisie stumbled upon a, hopefully safe, place to sleep, far away from the fresh burial plots. There hadn't been any other sign of life along the way, only more and more glass statues. *Would this ever fucking end?*

They each took a shower, and Perrie curled up in bed beside Maisie in the abandoned room. Worry poured through her thoughts, almost all of it about Vale. Throughout the day, she'd wondered where he was, how damn close he could be. Maisie and Neven weren't overly concerned—they were too confident he wouldn't find them. Perrie knew better, though. Her gut told her he would find her, and that it would be before they were prepared to fight him. Yet, she didn't think they could prepare for him at all. Tomorrow they were going to continue toward the Glass Vault. It would be days before they got there, but they would attempt to destroy the museum as soon as they reached it. Maybe Vale wouldn't expect them to return to that hell.

She felt so … lost.

There were moments between Vale and the Bride that she wouldn't think about, that she *couldn't* think about. Perrie would rather hold on to the time in the tower when he'd snatched her by her hair and dragged her down the hall. That drive was what would help them win.

Maisie rested beside Perrie, fast asleep, her chest rising and falling. Most likely dreaming about sunshine and rainbows. Her cousin almost wouldn't sleep in the bed, until they'd found a spare set of sheets in the linen closet. Maisie was so lucky. Perrie wished she could borrow her damn optimism, even just for a little while. After all her cousin had been through, she was still just as strong as she was before the Glass Vault.

Much more than Perrie was. But she was going to force herself to push forward, like she'd done when she was inside the Glass Vault's displays.

As Perrie listened to Maisie's soft snoring, relief filled her again that she'd found her cousin. If she hadn't, Perrie didn't know where her dark thoughts would've taken her if she'd still been alone and on the run from Vale. She honestly didn't know if she could've survived. Even if they defeat him, Perrie wasn't sure if she would ever truly be free of him.

He was the reason she wasn't asleep, snoring softly like Maisie. When Perrie closed her eyes, she was back there in his bed, or on the metal table, bleeding out. She could see his green eyes, dancing in the shadows, following her wherever she went. Eyes she longed to gaze into, and eyes she wanted to run from. She saw his image in the faces of the people she'd let down—her dad, Aunt Krista, Uncle Jaron, and Neven.

Maisie.

Herself.

Gritting her teeth, Perrie pushed the covers away and padded quietly across the room. Maisie fidgeted, readjusted, then went back to snoring. Careful not to wake her, Perrie closed the door and headed into the living room. A dull lantern illuminated the room, casting shadows on the wall. Nev glanced up from the couch and offered her a small smile. The light lent itself to his pinkish scars, reminding her of another time, in another cell. And guilt seeped its way into her once more—she was the reason he went to the museum that day.

"Can't sleep?" he asked.

"No." She shook her head. "Why don't you get some rest? I'll take watch. Shouldn't let a good night's rest escape the both of us. It's better if someone gets some sleep while they can."

A loud whinny broke the silence from outside, followed by the hard thumps of hooves beating the ground. Perrie stilled as a rush of memories hit her of the time she'd spent in Sleepy Hollow—Josselyn as Katrina, bloodied severed heads in the graveyard, the Headless Horseman. Nev raced to the door, pulling Perrie out of her frozen state. She hurried to the window and peered out into the night. It was dark outside but she could see just enough to catch the alabaster fur coat of a horse as it passed by.

Not the Headless Horseman.

Perrie sighed, her body relaxing. *Am I going to get this worked up every time I hear a horse for the rest of my fucking life?*

"Get some rest?" Neven lifted a brow as they sank back on the couch. "I don't think I could sleep if I wanted to. I'm a mess, you're a mess, and the world is a mess."

"Maisie's not a mess." At least ninety-percent of her didn't seem to be.

"Well, Maisie's special," Neven said quietly. He could barely bring himself to look her in the eye as he'd said it too. Perrie knew what was going on—she'd heard it in his banter with her cousin only hours ago.

He could hide it from Maisie, but he couldn't hide it from

Perrie.

"You like her!" Perrie whisper-shouted, fighting a smile.

He opened his mouth to say something, but no words slipped out.

"Don't lie to me."

Nev pursed his lips, as if he'd eaten something sour. "I haven't ever lied to you, and I told you I never lie about anything."

Perrie jabbed a finger at his chest. "No, but I can tell you want to now, don't you?"

"It doesn't matter." Nev sighed, hanging his head after a few seconds passed. "The world has too many fucked up things going on, and nothing else matters except figuring shit out that doesn't make sense. None of this makes sense."

Perrie grabbed his hand and intertwined his fingers with hers. The gesture didn't stir that rush of butterflies like it used to, just the comforting thought that he was her friend. A friend she hadn't talked to in a long time. It was like coming home, and everything was the same as before, only this time, they really were only friends.

"I'm sorry about your mom," Perrie whispered. "I know if anyone loved someone more than life itself, it was you."

"Me too." A few tears slid down his cheeks, and he wiped them away.

"It's okay to cry. Cry as much as you need to, I know I did. I'm right here, and I promise I'll always be your friend, no matter what." Perrie pulled him into a hug, holding him tight as he cried.

After his tears subsided, Neven sat up and concealed his face as if he'd never needed that moment.

"Now, tell me the truth. You like Maisie, don't you?"

His mask finally broke, and he was as relaxed as she'd seen him in the last few hours. Then he nodded.

"Since when?" she asked.

He shrugged. "Since forever ago. Since recently."

"When we were *together*?" Perrie hissed. "What's fucking wrong with you?" *Okay, maybe our rekindled friendship is back to being dead.* She started to stand, when Nev tugged her back down by the wrist.

"No, Perrie. It was never like that, I swear." He threw his hands up cautiously, as if that could stop her from punching him in the face. "When I was with you, it was only ever *you.* Even after you broke up with me." He closed his eyes and stayed silent for several seconds. "But I liked her before *us.*"

The hell? "What? What do you mean?"

"Back in ninth grade, and most of tenth too."

Perrie's eyes shifted side to side as she thought back. That was when they'd all met, when they first started hanging out together. He'd never told her any of this. How did she *not* see it? "Why didn't you tell me? Why didn't you tell *her*? Is this why you were weird around her sometimes? I assumed that was because you thought she was odd."

He stayed quiet, not giving any damn answers, so Perrie elbowed him.

"Ow." He chuckled and rubbed his arm.

"Shut up, that didn't hurt. Tell me."

"Okay, but please don't be mad if I tell you this, and don't run off and tell Maisie. I know how you like to tell her everything."

"I swear. I won't say anything. Scout's honor." She held up two fingers, fighting a smile, anxious to hear about this new side of Nev.

He rolled his eyes and lifted another one of her fingers. "It's three fingers."

"What the fuck ever." Perrie smiled.

He bit his lip and gripped the back of his neck, appearing nervous. "You remember that time you got sick back in ninth grade? It was pretty bad, you were out for a few days."

"Yeah?" Where was he going with this?

"We were going to watch a movie, then after you left I

stayed with Maisie." He took a deep breath. "That's when I knew I liked her, for real. I had a crush on her before then, back when she would make those crazy bracelets before the eye patches became her thing." A shy smile played at the corner of his lips as he touched his wrist.

Perrie had almost forgotten about those. Maisie would take slap bracelets and place little pom balls in the center to make a design, whether it was a face, fruit, or something else. They'd been really cute and Perrie used to have a ton of them in her top dresser drawer.

"You never said anything to me. Or to her?" Perrie flicked his hand hard.

"Ow. Quit doing stuff like that." Neven rubbed at the spot dramatically. "I never told you because she was your cousin, and you were my friend. I didn't want it to mess up our friendship and make it too weird. But…" His voice faded, and he stopped talking.

"Go on." Before she got the chance to pinch him again, he continued.

"We were watching the Phantom—while wearing masks—and after the movie I sort of kissed her, sneak attack."

Perrie's jaw fell open, and she softly shouted, "You did not!" She then snorted because she remembered those masks. One time she and Maisie even made Aunt Krista and Uncle Jaron wear them during the movie.

"I did." He cringed. "She was wearing this really awesome perfume. I got a whiff of it when she helped me with my mask." Maisie didn't wear perfume, but Perrie knew what he was talking about.

"Banana berry bread," she stated simply. Neven cocked his head, seeming to not understand. "It's her shampoo. She uses that stuff religiously. Sorry, go on."

"Right." His brows creased together. "It was right after the movie ended. I kissed her, she screamed, then ran away."

"Shut up." Perrie laughed. "She ran away?"

"She came back out after a while."

"Then what?"

"Then, nothing. We didn't talk about it." He shrugged.

"That's the stupidest shit I've ever heard. You kissed her, and both of you pretended like nothing happened?" Perrie couldn't hide her shock. Neither of them had said a word to each other or to her. Maisie wasn't especially good at keeping secrets, and Perrie was surprised her cousin had held onto this one for so long. She was tempted to wake Maisie up right then and ask her about it, but she'd made a promise to Nev.

"Yep."

"If you ever do make another move, you have my approval, Nev."

"Thanks," he muttered, his expression becoming serious again. "But don't ever think I settled for you. I wouldn't take it back—I wouldn't take any of it back."

Perrie folded her arms around him again, remembering their first kiss, their first time together, and all their special moments. Their chapter had ended a long time ago, and a new one, though different, would begin. "Me neither, Nev. You should try talking to Maisie about how you feel since you never know what's going to happen."

"I don't think I want to make her scream and run away again." He chuckled.

Perrie didn't have an answer for him because this time she didn't know what Maisie would think of this. Her cousin hadn't ever liked anyone that she knew of.

They then talked for a while and their friendship felt as it always had, before Vale came into the picture. As Perrie's thoughts drifted back to Vale, a light shuffling came from the room behind them.

She released her hold around Nev, and they both looked behind them to find Maisie's shadow standing at the now half-open door. Maisie slid to the side out of view and didn't come out. Perrie rolled her eyes. *Does she think she's invisible*? Nev frowned at the doorway then turned back around.

"I better go see what that was about," Perrie said.

"Goodnight. Also, ask Maisie if she army-crawled back to bed." He smiled.

Perrie headed into the bedroom and glanced to her left where Maisie had slid to. But she was already gone, lying in bed like they hadn't just spotted her. Perrie crawled into bed beside Maisie, her cousin's body already cocooned into the blanket. Maisie didn't just wrap herself up into an angry burrito for no reason.

"Psst." She poked Maisie in the side.

Her usual response would've been a laugh. Instead, she didn't move and only whispered, "I'm sleeping."

"No, you're not," Perrie said to Maisie's back. "We saw you in the doorway. Look at me." Maisie finally rolled over, still bundled in the blankets. "What's going on with this attitude?"

"Nothing. Sorry I interrupted you and Neven."

Then it hit her. Perrie should've seen it earlier, but she'd only been seeing how Nev felt about Maisie. Her cousin was friendly with everyone, so it was harder to notice it. But it all made sense now. "You like Nev, don't you?" Perrie murmured.

"What? No, I don't," she answered hurriedly.

"I told you already we weren't getting back together."

"You should get back together. Plus, you were already cuddling," Maisie snapped. Perrie could hear the jealousy in her voice.

"We're just friends. You know, if you ever decide to get with Nev, you have my approval." Perrie smiled. Maisie may not see it, but Perrie knew she heard the smile in her voice.

"Wouldn't that be incestuous, though?"

"Maisie, how would that be incestuous? You aren't related to Nev," Perrie said, incredulous.

"No, but I'm related to you, and you've had sex with him."

"I think there are stranger things going on in the world than that right now." Perrie had more things to be worried and angry about, and she would never be upset with Maisie about this. She was her cousin, her best friend, and she wanted her happy.

"Thank you for the approval if I ever decide to go in that direction." Maisie unraveled herself from the blanket and spread it across the both of them. Her cousin liked him, more than liked. This was odd to Perrie because she didn't think Maisie ever crushed on anyone. She kind of liked that her cousin did have a few hidden secrets. Perrie had promised Nev she wouldn't say anything and she would keep that damn promise, but that didn't mean she wouldn't give Maisie a nudge in his direction.

SEVENTEEN

Perrie

*P*errie sat on the edge of the Galveston Seawall—her feet dangled and swung back and forth, lightly tapping the stone as they came down.

The night had already fallen, but lampposts lit the unbusy street behind her and August. They'd settled on a portion of the Seawall that wasn't too high from the ground, yet still enough to make her stomach flutter.

Waves crashed into the sand, and each time gravity hauled them back, it felt like her life. The sounds relaxed her as she closed her eyes. It was almost as unwinding as when she and August played cello together. August's leg pressed against hers, and he leaned back with his palms propping him up—his blond curls scattered in all directions.

Perrie watched him for a moment, something she didn't normally do, but he really was beautiful. He was more than that, though. August looked off in the distance, and if she could read his mind right now, she would want to know every minuscule detail that was there.

"What are you thinking about?" she asked.

"Hmm?" He lazily slid his eyes from the darkness toward her. "Oh, I was just thinking about things."

Perrie lightly kicked her foot against his. "Like what?"

"The world." He smiled.

Perrie thought about the world all the time, too. The future. How when she was younger, she knew what direction her life would go in, but a child's mind was a dangerous one. Thoughts were innocent, and life wasn't. "The world is a pretty damn big place, August."

"Then we will conquer it." His smile grew wide, and he leapt from the wall.

"August!" Perrie shouted as he fell through the air.

His feet slapped the sand, and he spun to face her, laughing as he said, "Your turn."

She peered down at the long distance. It wasn't far enough where she would break anything, but a dizzy feeling still swam through her. "No way."

August chuckled, then jogged over to the stairs and went up them. Perrie watched as he rounded the rail and strode up to her. He hovered above her while she gazed up at him, and she shook her head. She knew he wanted her to leap, but she wasn't going to.

"Come on, doll face. Just do it."

"Is this peer pressure, August? You know I stay away from those situations," she teased.

"Give me your hand." He reached his out for her to take, and she hesitantly put hers in his, feeling the comforting warmth.

Pulling her feet from the edge of the Seawall, she faced him, and he helped her to stand. They walked right to the edge, and she gazed over. "I don't know about this. It's still a rough landing."

He turned her face to his and murmured, "Together?"

Chest heaving, Perrie looked back down. It didn't seem as

daunting with his hand in hers. "Fine. Together," she agreed. Then they jumped.

Perrie shot up in bed, her chest tightening. "August? We have to leave." She turned to August to tell him they needed to find a way out of the Glass Vault, but no one was beside her.

Maisie crashed through the door with Nev at her heels.

"What are you shouting about?" Maisie asked as she hurried to Perrie's side of the bed.

Perrie's heart slammed against her rib cage, beating on overdrive. She didn't know if she could get it to slow down. Maisie crawled next to her and pulled Perrie to her chest. August wasn't here. August didn't exist. Perrie wanted to rip out the memory—all the memories of him, and bury them somewhere in concrete.

"Nothing. It was only a dream."

Nev watched them with his arms crossed, then moved toward her. "It sounded like more than a dream to me."

"It's okay. I'm okay," Perrie told herself more than them. The dreams or nightmares she could handle, because that was what they were. She could separate the two—she had to think about it in a different way. It was as though August was dead, and Vale would be fucking dead, too. And Perrie was the one who was going to end this, end *him.*

"Do we need to stay here a little longer?" Maisie asked.

"No," Perrie said. "We're going to head to the Glass Vault now." She would shatter every inch of it until it was completely destroyed.

"Let's go then." Nev unfolded his arms and waited for Perrie and Maisie to follow him into the living room.

As Perrie went to hand Maisie her purse, a loud knock at the door rumbled through the house, shaking her bones. She froze, Maisie's eye bulged so wide it might pop out, and Nev scowled at the door.

Maisie was the first one to shake off her shock and tiptoed

toward the door.

"What are you doing?" Perrie hissed.

Maisie threw her head to the side to look at Perrie. "I'm going to see who it is." When she turned back around toward the door, Nev was already there, peering through the peephole.

He whirled around to face them, his expression bewildered. "No one's at the door."

"Don't open it," Perrie whispered. The hairs on her arms rose as the electricity inside her crackled to life. Something wasn't right. And that something may have to do with a certain vicious demon from the Underworld.

"I wasn't planning on it," he replied.

Maisie pushed past Nev and glanced through the peephole. Perrie rushed to her, sliding Maisie away so she could look. From what she could see, no one was there, only a brick porch with potted plants.

Perrie wasn't going to linger around, and Nev and Maisie seemed to have the same thought as her.

"Backdoor," Maisie and Perrie said simultaneously.

"Start running now," Nev whispered.

They booked it to the door. Maisie reached it first, throwing it open and leaping over the patio. Nev passed through next with Perrie right behind him.

Maisie and Nev were a few feet ahead of her, and she was trying to keep up. Nev had his running experience with basketball, and Maisie was just ridiculously fast. The two of them swiftly leapt over the short iron fence. Perrie's hands gripped the top bar roughly and she hopped across, but part of her dress snagged on something sharp. Heart in her throat, she gave it a hard tug and ripped the material free.

They entered a lush green field, and not a single soul seemed to be in sight. Perrie chanted silently to herself, *Don't look back at the house. Don't look back at the house.* But she did. No one was behind them. She smiled to herself in relief and continued to run.

After close to a minute of hauling ass, Perrie must've been lagging, because Maisie yelled, "Keep going!"

Nev slowed his pace and glanced back over his shoulder at her to make sure she hadn't fallen too far behind. The Glass Vault hadn't improved her running skills by much because cramps were already churning in her stomach. Nev's determined expression switched to one of horror.

"What are—" Perrie started.

A hand jerked her back by the hair, wrenching her body to a hard chest. A raspy cry of pain escaped her throat. Perrie knew this particular type of hair pulling. An image of her being dragged down a hall by only her hair flashed through her head. This time she bucked her head as hard as she could, not caring how much pain shot through her scalp.

"Ah, you didn't think you could hide forever, did you?" Vale's hot breath struck her ear.

Despite his rough grip, Perrie kicked her feet at the demon and attempted to elbow his ribs. She focused on her power, unable to summon a single spark to electrocute this monster.

Nev and Maisie darted their way, but Vale didn't move an inch. He only grabbed her by the jaw, squeezing with enough pressure that she feared he would rip it off. "Oh, you did? How sweet." He smiled, baring his teeth.

"Let her fucking go!" Nev charged full force, and with his strength, he could tear Perrie away from Vale's clutches. It would give her enough time to try and gather her electricity.

Vale lazily tossed up a hand. Nev flew back about fifty feet, landing in the grass with a heavy smack.

Maisie looked at Nev, concerned, then dashed toward Perrie, her expression turning fierce as she tried to sing with her immortal ability. Vale's amused laughter echoed around Perrie as he threw up his hand again, flinging Maisie farther back than Nev.

"Stop!" Perrie shouted.

Maisie and Nev were off the ground, once again rushing

toward them, but then Vale lifted that fucking hand of his once more. This time, they still raced in her direction, yet they were going no farther, as though running in place.

Vale spun Perrie around, a murderous gleam dancing in his emerald eyes. "Listen to me, *now*."

Perrie didn't listen. She didn't want to listen. She would never listen to him. Not now. Not again. Not ever. If he wanted to slit her throat a hundred times, a *thousand* times, then so be it. She would *always* try to escape.

"You will return my Bride to me!" He shook her roughly, and her head bobbled, sending a jolt of sharp pain shooting through her neck.

Perrie peered into his green eyes, holding herself steady, remembering him and his Bride. The way he touched her, tasted her, made her shout his name in pleasure, how he'd done the same with hers. She would never give her back to him again. "No."

"What was that?" He crushed Perrie's arms and tilted his head, bringing his ear closer to her, as if the fucker didn't believe what he was hearing. As his fingers dug into her flesh, her eyes fluttered, but she held them open.

"I said, *no*," Perrie said, gritting her teeth. "I made sure she's gone, and she's never coming back. I killed her."

He then gripped the sides of her skull in between his hands—his nose rubbed against hers. "Then I will make it so you can't come back, and she does. We both know she wants to stay here with me."

With those words, he took a step back and slammed her head to the ground. It bounced slightly, hit again, then she fell to her stomach. Perrie's skull rattled, her brain shook, and the veins throbbed. She was dead. She had to be dead. This was what death would feel like, even worse than having her throat slit.

Before she could stand to spit in his face, Vale yanked Perrie forward by her hair. *Can he quit with the fucking hair already*? She wanted to stop him, retaliate, but her entire body was weak, exhausted.

"We are going inside to tuck you away, by any means necessary." The grass prickled her arms as he dragged her through the field. He began to hum, a soft melody, and Perrie recognized the tune—they'd always played it together on their cellos, back when she thought he was August.

A roar rumbled through her veins, and she gathered that inner strength, letting the anger fill her. As her head pieced back together, she geared up to make a move. With his casual strides, she could do this. Perrie's gaze became predatory while watching each leisurely step he took. He moved as if he had an eternity with her. *Well, he doesn't.*

She quietly brought her arms up from her sides, attempting to block out the pain at her scalp. Thanking the grass that he had her on her stomach and not on her back, Perrie picked her body up by her hands, lifted herself to her knees, and shot forward. Perrie's body collided with Vale's back, and she knocked his ass to the ground.

He released a loud grunt, and she beamed with satisfaction as she leapt onto his back. She raised her hands and tried to ignite the spark, but her electricity still wouldn't come, so she pummeled her fists against his muscles. Hard, harder, wanting to tear him apart like he'd done to Nev.

Vale moved with his inhuman speed, flinging her from him. Perrie landed on her backside, and she ignored the throbbing. But before she could jump to her feet, he pushed her back down, holding her by the arms.

"Enough!" he roared as heavy breaths hit her cheek, his voice seeming to shake the entire field. Rage filled his eyes and his mouth twisted into a harsh sneer. "You don't want to go inside? Fine! I'll break you apart right here with my bare hands. I need her and she needs me! Give her to me!"

He took hold of Perrie's left arm tightly and with one swift, forceful pull, she howled in agony at the loud snap. Her arm had to be gone. Numbness and burning soared through her. Perrie's head fell to the side, finding her arm there but out of the socket. Tears pricked at her eyes at the pain of it all.

Then Vale grasped her arm and brutally shoved it back into place—hot tears streamed down her cheeks as she screamed. And then, the masochist did it again to her same arm—nausea swirled in her stomach and bubbled up her throat. She was going to vomit—she was going to puke all over his damn face. More powerful than before, he shoved it in place, and she didn't think she would ever stop screaming. She *would not* become *her* again, no matter how many times he did this. He would never accept that his Bride was gone.

"That was only practice. Now, I'm ready to truly begin." *Please no.* Perrie didn't even want to think about what he would do to her next. So she focused, harder than before, letting determination fill her more than she ever had. His grip on her right arm loosened. *Please work damn it.*

Yanking her arm away, Perrie pushed her palm against Vale's chest and prayed the electricity would come. In answer, a flash of white light shot out, igniting the world around her in sparks. The explosion of her power barreled into his chest, sending him backward.

As he stumbled, Vale's gaze fastened on hers, a true look of pain on his face, before slumping to the ground. Perrie believed the pain wasn't even from the spark, it was because he knew his Bride was gone forever.

She shakily stood, inhaling deeply as the throbbing lessened in her arm. Perrie frantically searched for Maisie and Nev, then sighed in relief when she saw they'd escaped Vale's invisible hold and were headed her way.

Perrie's body relaxed as she studied Vale resting on his side, his eyes shut. Did her electricity work? Was he dying? When she stepped closer, a loud piercing shriek escaped him and she jumped back. Vale's hands cradled his head and his body curled into a tight ball. Fat tears rained down his cheeks while he howled in desperation. She should've moved forward to do to him what they'd done to Catherine, but she took another trembling step back. Maisie and Nev halted beside Perrie. She sparked up as Nev tightened his fists.

With Vale's hands still pressed against his skull, he slowly peeled open his lids. He settled his bright green irises on *her*. One word softly slipped from his lips, and it wasn't Bride. "Perrie?"

EIGHTEEN

Before-Vale

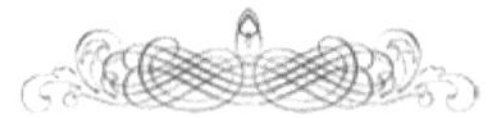

Vale was born in a damp room in the caverns of the Underworld. After hours of labor, his mother, Yorna, gave birth to a beautiful demon male—the first and only with a live heartbeat. That steady beat thrummed up and down the dark halls of the Underworld. She could not hold him with her wrists bound to her ankles, but she lay beside him, whispering words in his ear.

After unlocking the cell, Vale's father charged into the room, scooped up the little infant and tossed him to the ground away from Yorna.

"What have you done?" he yelled at her.

Yorna quaked and shook violently from the sound of her master's voice. "I did nothing. Please, don't take him away." She attempted to crawl to her child, but the chains held her back.

Yorna wouldn't call herself good. She lived her life destroying and tearing apart souls by any means necessary, obeying her master's orders. Things became different for her when she discovered she was with child. Her master's child.

She reveled in each passing moment as her belly grew, until the day was bestowed upon her that she knew she had to leave. The child could not be raised by her master—so she ran.

Yorna attempted to escape out of the realm but failed before being dragged back to her master in thick and heavy chains, binding her wrists to her ankles. The remainder of her pregnancy was spent with clangs of her metal chains echoing through the cell.

Yanking her chin in his large hand, Master narrowed his ebony eyes at her. With the sneer on his face, she knew this would not end well. "Please, Master. Don't separate Vale from me," she pleaded. Yorna had known a demon should never beg, yet she had done it anyway.

His sneer turned into a devious smile that warned Yorna what would become of her. She would not see Vale again. Yorna's dead heart grew frantic as her eyes slid to where her little Vale rested. Master now watched the baby with a curious expression. Curled on his side in a snug ball, Vale did not wail, even after being slung to the ground. His heartbeats were miraculous music, singing to her his lovely song.

Master released Yorna's chin and thrust her face to the side. As her black hair flung into her eyes, all she could do was watch. Lifting the baby off the freezing floor, he stared into the peaceful, unconscious face. Then his gaze shifted back to Yorna. "You did this, you made him this way with your witchery."

Yorna loathed her master, wished flames would burn him until he was nothing. She wanted to gut him to pieces, take the baby and run, but it was useless. He always got what he wanted.

Master lifted his hand and placed it over the tiny infant's chest. A current popped and crackled until Vale's heartbeat quieted. No other sound could be heard, except for the continuous soft breaths of the child.

He gingerly set Vale back on the ground as though he hadn't taken away the one beautiful thing here. With no time to react, Master ran at Yorna with speed quicker than a flash of light. "The child is only mine, Yorna." Then he twisted her neck with a loud snap before vanquishing her soul.

Nine-year-old Vale's eyelids bolted open. He knew exactly where he was—his cage. Father made him sleep in one at night when he could not keep an eye on him.

Vale brought his frail hand to his chest and felt the beat that had come back to life. Letting out a small sigh of relief, he left his palm over his heart, absorbing the *thump, thump*. With the organ's movement, he was able to remember his mother. Despite how short their time together had been, he had loved her. But then he remembered his father, and what he would do once he heard Vale's heartbeat had restarted.

At that moment, he thought maybe it would have been better if his heartbeat had never come back at all because he knew what his father would do next—to him.

Vale leaned forward, pressing his small chest against the cool floor, trying to conceal the vibrato as long as he could.

There was no escaping the iron bars, so he relished his new thoughts and shoved out the memories of his father— imagining perhaps one day, he would have enough strength to leave his prison.

His thoughts were interrupted when he heard loud, heavy footsteps—the sound of anger, of hate.

Vale didn't rise, though. He remained on the floor with his eyes hidden behind the darkness of his lids, attempting to summon a power that would make his father disappear. But he didn't have the strength to bring forth any energy. The gate wrenched open and slammed against the wall. He still did not open his eyes as he tried to hold on to wishes and hopes.

Two hands lifted him by his shirt and shoved him against the wall, his lids flicking open. Vale then met the two darkened irises of his father.

"Vale? Is it already time for a lesson?" His father's lip curled, his eyes gleaming with a hidden thrill.

"No, Father." There was no use pleading or begging because as Vale had learned, it only made him more vulnerable and his father more pleased that he was at his mercy.

"Oh, I think it is." Father dropped him, and Vale's small arm roughly hit the ground.

As soon as he lifted his head, Vale gazed toward the open door, ready to try and make an escape. His father waved a hand in the air, slamming the gate shut, and locking it, as though he had read every one of Vale's thoughts of desertion.

His father pulled out a long brown whip hidden behind his back, the edges lined with sharp metal spikes. Father would give Vale his lesson before snuffing out his heart once more.

Vale did not cry, did not scream as the whip cracked down upon him, time and time again. Thick blood poured out from his wounds, and before they would heal, the whip would snap down again, harder than before. With each heavy crack, Vale tried to hold onto his hope of the possibility of one day escaping. As much as Vale wished for his father to stop his heart and the pain, he wanted to keep all his memories more, so he could eventually find a way out. One day he would be happy because he knew it did exist, even if for the time being it was only hidden in his dreams. Always, he would try to find it.

As Vale grew, there were moments when his heartbeat would

return on its own, and he would remember every detail from the instant he was born. When the memories would strike through him like lightning, he wanted to run, tried to run, but his father could always hear the heartbeat when he drew close enough. Then, all of himself, including his wishes and hopes, was buried back into the depths of his mind where there would be no remembering.

Vale's father had taught the dark part of him well. He'd shown him everything there was to the Underworld, including the souls he would one day torture.

That time was now.

"Vale, grab the scalpel." His father pointed to a tray lined with a variety of sharp objects. A thrill flowed through Vale's limbs at his father's trust in him to help perform his duties.

"Yes, Father." Vale padded to the tray and lifted the cool steel into his palm, rolling it delicately back and forth. He absorbed the moment.

Rows of cages filled the room—in one sat a woman, bright red hair falling past her shoulders. She crouched on all fours and stared at him, smirking. "I want that one." Vale pointed in her direction and sauntered toward the cage.

A strange tightness formed in Vale's chest, as if something was knocking at his ribs. Something sparked in his head, an image of an emerald-eyed female he had forgotten existed, who he would have called mother, followed by a rush of wrongness for all these souls in cages. He needed to escape the Underworld as his mother had whispered in his ear when he was first born.

Vale would get out. He would leave this place. Hastily, he turned toward his father, ignoring the surprise crossing his face, and thrust the scalpel into his chest and ran.

He was quicker than his father. Endless times Vale had done this but was always found and dragged back. This time would be different. The burn in his chest felt good, and he did not want it to go away again.

He passed by the darkened stone halls where souls endlessly wandered, others locked in more cages, and none remembering who they were. With certainty, he knew he could not become like them again. Not now and not for all eternity.

Vale reached the dim black hall, where a bitter, salty smell invaded his nose. Everyone there might be dead, but they still bled. Again and again and again.

The barrier was not far away, and he believed he would make it out this time. His father would not be able to get through, but Vale could. Hurling himself at the obsidian stone wall, he was roughly tossed back. Vale lunged toward it four more times before the pounding of his father's heavy footsteps slapping against the ground drew near.

"You cannot get through with a heartbeat, and when I shut it off again, you won't remember." His father's lips curled into a calculated smile as his dark gaze penetrated Vale's.

Father cocked his head. "I will tell you something, Vale. I figured a way to shut it off so it does not come back easily this time. You will do as I say, and you will come up with a plan to serve as I do down here, except you will do it up there with the humans." Vale's hands trembled as he planted himself against the wall. He tried to back up farther, even though there was nowhere left to go.

"I will not perform what you tell me to, Father. I'll remember. I always do." Vale lifted his chin in defiance at his father, even with fear coursing through his veins.

His father savagely arched an eyebrow. "Not this time." Vale felt a hit to his head and blackness darkened to nothing.

Vale awoke in the same room with the rows of cages from earlier. The tray of torturous devices rested across from him, prepped for his choosing. Swallowing deeply, he blinked several times to rid the blurriness of his surroundings.

It was near impossible to push himself up to a sitting position as he found his wrists were chained at his ankles. He was not surprised. This was the same tactic his father used endlessly. But he finally managed to bring himself up to a sitting position.

Vale turned his head side to side, and there was nothing to see. All he could do was listen to the screams reverberating from the hallways. His father was not there, but he knew he would be back. His father would shut him down again, but it was temporary. It would always be temporary, and he was strong enough to find his way back. He had to.

When Vale looked back at the rows of cages, his gaze stopped on the one with the redheaded female. Without fear and only confidence, she watched him. He slid his eyes away from her—something was not right with the female, more than the other corrupt souls there.

"I ripped them to shreds up there," she cried out.

Vale chose to neglect the mad creature and peered down at his knees. At that moment, he desperately yearned to be out of the chains and away from her. But she continued to speak, seeming not to care that he was not listening to her.

"You will, too."

He turned to her then. "Listen. I do not care what you are talking about. I am not going to tear apart *anyone*—up there or down here."

Her expression turned smug. "I may be the first for you to torture once you turn back into your better self, but I will get your father on my side. Since you are special and are able to bring souls with you, I will help. I heard what your father had to say about you."

Vale ignored the mad female, but her words continued to tap at him. She rambled on about how everyone believed Jack to have been a male and that made the situation easier for her.

Why was she the only one down here who remembered

their past life? Vale thought.

The redhead's words were cut off by his father's entrance. "Vale, it's time. You are to begin on these souls, *now*." Before Vale could protest, his father held up a new device he must have crafted himself. As it pulsated with an electric current, Vale tried to move away, but his chains only caused him to stumble to the ground.

In an instant, his father's instrument was now pressed at Vale's chest. As his body vibrated from the instrument, Vale wondered if maybe this time he would not wake again. And in a moment of weakness, he decided he would be fine with that. But no, he shook that awful thought away because that would mean his father would have won.

Vale's memories gradually faded as his heart slowed, but he fought to keep them from escaping. He held his eyelids tightly together, not looking at his father, the strange female, or the instruments he knew he would be picking up if he let the memories vanish. His heart barely pumped, taking two more sluggish beats before ceasing.

He unclenched his eyelids and studied the male in front of him with black eyes, blond curls, and his jaw grinding. His father, his master.

"What do you remember?" the male asked.

Frowning, Vale tried to touch his head, but his wrists were chained. *Remember?* An eagerness stormed through him until he grinned with pleasure. "I was about to get started." Vale's dark gaze fell on the corrupt souls in their cages.

His father smiled a wicked grin in return. "Good. Now let us begin. You are master to all these souls." His father, glowing with pride, held his arm up and dragged it across the air in front of the cages.

Father unlocked the chains binding Vale's wrists and ankles. As they clacked to the ground, Vale rose to full height and walked to where his father motioned at a tray of instruments.

"Now, as we were before. Pick one," his father demanded.

Vale ran his tongue across his teeth while staring at the shiny instruments with longing. He lifted a scalpel from the middle and focused on the cages. His father was already moving to the one with the redheaded female covered in filth. She crawled out, and a smile tugged the edges of her lips that Vale did not understand.

He did not care, though—he was going to slice her up in ways that would make her never stop screaming.

NINETEEN

Perrie

Tears continued to pour down Vale's face, and the lightning crackled in Perrie's palms as she prepared to strike him with her power again.

"Perrie," he gasped for the second time, releasing his hold from the sides of his head. "I am sorry." He pushed to his knees and dropped his hands to the ground, his fingers gripping blades of grass.

A desperation crawled onto his face, in his eyes, while Perrie's heart thundered, conflicted. She stared at her feet so she could think, concentrate. An image slid into her mind—the night she escaped from Vale. A kiss. Him calling her Perrie instead of Bride. A heartbeat. Her sparking him.

Realization struck, and she lifted her gaze to meet his, her entire being pleading. Perrie took off running toward him with hope blossoming in her chest.

"Perrie!" Neven shouted.

"Stockholm Syndrome," Maisie yelled behind her. "Stockholm Syndrome! Don't!"

Ignoring Maisie, she came to a stop in front of him, falling to her knees as he peered up at her with those green eyes that called to her. She pressed a trembling hand to his warm cheek, her lips mere inches from brushing his. "August?" Perrie whispered.

The expression in his face fell, no longer appearing desperate. Something like empathy stirred within his eyes while they moved side to side, as if he was trying to keep up with a metronome.

"August does not exist," he said softly. "I am Vale."

Perrie jerked her hand back, her entire body recoiling from him. Maisie pulled her out of her shocked state, tugging Perrie to her side. Nev yanked Vale up by the collar of his white shirt, holding him in the air, his toes scraping the grass. Curling his other hand in a fist, Nev delivered a hard blow to Vale's face—a loud cracking sounded as his head was thrown to the side.

Vale held up his hand, and Nev released him. Nev floated backward through the grass, punching air, and slowly dropped to his knees.

"Stop," Vale whispered, his voice calm as he hovered above Nev.

Perrie now had a clear shot, and she hurled a whip of light at Vale's chest. But he was too fast, swinging his other hand up, her lightning dissolving to small sparks that fell to the ground. She tried to launch another, yet she couldn't do anything. Couldn't move her legs, only her upper body, but no ability would come. *Shit.*

A humming drifted through the air, coming from Maisie who seemed to be immobilized too. Vale cocked his head. "You can stop. That isn't going to work on me."

Blood trailed down the side of Vale's mouth from Nev's hit, and he swiped it with the tip of his tongue. Then he brought the sleeve of his shirt to his mouth to wipe the rest away, marring the white silk.

"I'm going to tear you apart this time, you fucking

asshole," Nev threatened, spewing out all the ways he was going to do it. Perrie shook her head at him, telling him to stop talking.

Lines creased Vale's forehead as he lifted his hand and snapped.

Perrie's heart hammered, panicked, expecting the world to split into two. But Nev remained whole, except no words spilled from him as he still tried to shout.

Maisie was also at a standstill, attempting to sing again, but only silence escaped her mouth.

With what appeared to be hesitation, Vale stepped toward Perrie.

"One more step and you're dead," she threatened, hiding the fear pumping through her veins.

His gaze dropped from her face, to her feet firmly planted in place, then drifted back up to her eyes. "I do not think so."

"Your Bride is already gone. I'm not going back with you, and I'll find a way out. We all will." Perrie would claw and claw at him forever, until he decided to rip her hands off if he wished. The Bride may have treasured the earth Vale walked on, but she sure as fuck didn't.

Sighing in defeat, Vale shook his head and ran a hand through his blond curls. "Look, Perrie."

"So what, you're fine with me being Perrie now? Not *Bride*?" she spat.

Vale frowned, wounded, like he was the one who'd been torturing the world as someone else. "I—I don't want the Bride. Can you listen to me without talking for a moment? You need to hear this."

Perrie shook her head. "More lies?"

"No. Not more lies. Only truths." He held up his empty hands showing no weapons, but the fucker must've forgotten he was full of invisible ones. Dirt covered his hands and fingernails, and she was surprised he hadn't taken out that damn file to pick at those stupid nails of his.

"Don't you need to clean your nails first?" Perrie hissed.

Vale blinked. Blinked again. Then a rumble of laughter poured from his mouth. The sound reminded her of her partner back in the Glass Vault. But that wasn't a real friend, a real lover, it was an enemy.

Vale stopped laughing and studied his filthy hands. "That is what I am trying to talk to you about if you will drop the stubbornness and listen closely to what I have to say. *All of you*." He exchanged a glance between the three of them.

Maisie no longer tried to fight and watched him intently, as if she might be considering being on Team Vale. Perrie waved her hand to get her cousin's attention, then Maisie turned to her to speak. Nothing came out, but she nodded, pointing from Perrie to her ear. She wanted Perrie to listen to what Vale had to say…

Perrie threw her hands in the air, while Maisie kept tapping at her ear. Maybe she knew something Perrie didn't? When she turned to Nev, he shook his head *no*.

But they were glued to the ground with really no other choice except to hear what Vale wanted to say. Perrie folded her arms. "If you let Maisie and Nev speak, then I'll listen."

Vale bit the edge of his lip. "Only Maisie for now. Neven will continue to interrupt."

"Fine, but after, you will release him," Perrie demanded, though her heart still thundered. She was sure he wasn't worried since she couldn't even move her useless legs.

Vale snapped his fingers, releasing Maisie, her breathing making the lightest of sounds.

Maisie's eye stayed open wide as she spoke, "Perrie, I have a theory, but first you need to listen to him."

A *theory*? Perrie shot her cousin a surprised look before turning to Vale. "Go ahead."

He continued to chew on the side of his lip for a moment, and he looked more human than the demon he was.

"As I was trying to explain to you earlier, Perrie, I am not

August. He does not exist and never has. I am Vale.”

Perrie could feel her anger rising, her hands shaking as she narrowed her eyes.

He hurried on, “But I am not *that* Vale.”

What? Perrie took a deep swallow, her tongue thick in her mouth. He had to be lying. But she would play along until he unrooted her from the ground, then she would make a move. “I—I don’t understand.”

He blinked at her several times like he didn’t understand why she couldn’t grasp the concept. “You had your emotions disassembled, but your heart still beat in your chest. My father completely shut my heart off, causing me to no longer be myself. I was like the Bride, Snow White, Frankenstein’s Monster.” He paused, his lips set in a thin line. “Except I was more vicious with my emotions completely shut off. I couldn’t escape my prison the way you did”—he pressed a hand to his heart—“and I was locked inside this body.”

“I knew it! You have an alter too!” Maisie shouted.

Maisie’s voice drew her attention away from Vale. “You believe this shit?” Perrie asked. “Vale may not have had many emotions, but he sure as hell could pretend to have some when he was August.”

She lifted a shoulder and shrugged, apologetic. “I believe him. What would be the point of him saying all this when he could just as easily take you away again?”

“I don’t know! What was the point of him acting like August, if he could easily have just thrown me into one of those displays like you were in? And by the way, you didn’t think August was a demon either.” Perrie glared.

Maisie ran her palms against one another. “That’s true, but Vale also wanted to unleash havoc on the world at a rapid pace once we were out. What would be the point of him slowing down now, only to pretend he’s good?”

“Let’s say this Vale is actually the real Vale,” Perrie started, “what makes you think he’s a ‘good guy?’”

Maisie wiggled her finger side to side. "This Vale…" Her words faltered mid-sentence as she looked at Vale, who watched them with wide eyes. "Why doesn't your alter have a different name? This is getting confusing even for me, since you're both named Vale."

He cocked his head, his arms folded in front of him. "Because *my father* continued to call me Vale."

"Okay, well we will refer to him as Bad Vale from now on." Maisie slid her gaze suspiciously to Vale once again. "And what do you mean *me,* if you're not him?"

He exhaled slowly and said, "You may sit here and call these sides of yourselves whatever you want, but they are still you, only a darker version of you. A deadlier individual."

"Why do we have memories from the displays, then?" Maisie asked.

"I was going to get to that. The images of Snow White having her eye ripped out by the dwarves was all a game to 'Bad Vale' to toy with you." He brought his fingers up to quote.

"Did you just *air quote*?" Perrie asked, taken aback by the movement.

His hands gripped the sides of his head. Perrie's chest tightened, her body still. In a moment, she knew he was going to laugh, then say how this was all just a game of him toying with them. After that, he would continue to play with her arm sockets, demanding his precious Bride be returned to him.

But then Vale released his hold on his head.

"I remember all of Bad Vale's memories as if they are my own, including the human things from when he pretended to be August, and they are my images now. I know all Vale has done." He stopped and stared her in the eye, and something like sorrow flickered in his gaze. "I know all August has done."

Perrie pinched the inside of her wrist to keep from looking down. She didn't know which parts he was thinking about.

She'd tried not to think about Vale and the Bride's relationship. Besides them both being sadistic, there was something between them that was pure. She hated it. Hated that they could've been so happy together after what they were doing. If he was thinking about her and August in that tower, then he knew Perrie at her most vulnerable. And she hated that too. Instead of anger stirring, her cheeks heated with embarrassment and she couldn't stop herself from looking down. But if what he said was true … then he was a prisoner, just as they were.

It took a moment, but Perrie gathered her courage and lifted her chin high to face Vale. She still saw the sadness he held for her in his eyes, and she didn't want it.

He snapped his fingers—her knees collapsed, and she fell to the grass. Perrie swallowed hard, past the lump in her throat, then rushed to Maisie.

"You really believe this bullshit?" Nev shouted after Vale released him.

"Yes," Maisie said simply before Perrie could get a word out. Perrie thought about Vale's words again. She needed to be sure, but something nudged her to agree with Maisie. And a part of her was irritated at herself for it.

"You would." Nev glowered, pissed. Perrie completely understood why he would be.

"Then why did he free you?" Maisie asked. "And why is nothing happening now?"

Vale observed them, but didn't make a deceitful move. He only stood there, quietly, patiently.

"Damn it, Mais." Nev's nostrils flared. "You've been right a lot so far, but so help me if you're wrong about this and something happens to either one of you, I'm going to find your ghost and shake you."

A wide grin spread across her face. "I'm not wrong."

Nev palmed his face.

As for Perrie, her emotions were being pulled in every

direction imaginable. She studied Vale, his face the exact replica of August's, and she wished it were different. But it was never August's face to begin with—it was Vale's.

Perrie thought about something he'd voiced earlier, and she took a few hesitant steps in his direction. "What's this about your father? Even back with Fannie, you mentioned him several times."

Vale clasped his hands together, then rested them right below his bottom lip. "My father is the one who concocted this plan to begin with, and Bad Vale was the one who grew the seed into this nightmare. I think Red has a hidden agenda with him, but I am not sure what it is."

"Where's your father now?" she asked.

"He cannot come here—he is down in the Underworld, ruling it."

Maisie slipped up right behind her, craning her neck over Perrie's shoulder. "Like a king? So, that makes you a prince?" *Is she fucking serious*?

Nev rolled his eyes, and Perrie didn't think he would ever stop. He then said, "Next, you're going to ask if we should bow down to him, and I really don't think you need to be bowing down to evil."

Maisie stepped around Nev until she stood right in front of Vale and poked the demon in the arm. "He's not evil, but he's still a prince."

"It is not quite like that." Vale's brows drew together, seeming confused.

This whole conversation has gotten too strange and too damn odd. I mean, people are dead here. There were creatures from the displays and souls turned immortal out in the world killing people.

"What about serious matters here?" Perrie focused on Vale. "What are we going to do about what's happening? What are *you* going to do about it?"

He rubbed at his chin and held her gaze for a long moment

before he finally nodded. "Follow me."

TWENTY

Perrie

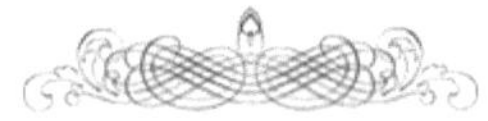

Follow him? Perrie wasn't sure where in hell Vale wanted to lead them. She hadn't budged, and neither had Nev. But then Maisie took the first steps forward.

Vale's powers were much stronger than any of theirs, and Perrie wouldn't let Maisie go with him alone. Nev seemed to have the same thought as her as they both followed them back to the house they'd started in.

Perrie came to a stop on the front sidewalk beside Vale and looked up and down the street. "This is where you wanted us to come?" she asked. "A *damaged street*?" A deep, crooked crack ran up the pavement, seeming as though the earth was being pulled in two different directions. Small craters, resembling pockmarks, were scattered throughout.

Vale searched across the street farther down, his gaze focused on a brick house with all its windows broken. "We are not alone."

Perrie stiffened.

"Come out," he called, a light breeze rumpling his hair.

Perrie wasn't sure if they'd made the right choice in following him. She didn't know who or *what* was going to slither out from his call.

A loud swooshing sounded, cracking like thunder from the direction of the brick house. Perrie threw her hand up, trying to get her electricity to stir—it didn't. After his little paralyzing spell, he'd never returned her power.

The heavy beating turned louder as a shadow took shape, rounding the corner and heading straight in their direction. Not slithering, but *flying*.

"What the hell is that?" Nev asked, his chest heaving.

A strong gray body with cracks marring its flesh, as if it were made of stone, stormed toward them. Paper thin wings, covered in thin veins so dark they looked black, beat heavily against the wind. The creature's face appeared human except for its pointed ears and flat nose. *Gargoyle*.

Maisie, Nev, and Perrie backed up as the creature came closer. Vale lifted his hand and the gargoyle froze midair, its wings continuing to crank.

Perrie squinted her eyes to get a better view of the male gargoyle, her heart beating erratically. Bright blood caked its chin and razor-sharp teeth jutted out from its mouth. A protruding spine detailed the middle of its back so tightly that if the gargoyle bent any farther, the thin skin looked like it would rip.

If Vale held any fear, his nonchalant persona did a fucking good job at covering it up. "It is only a gargoyle."

"You mean a wicked soul inside the gargoyle," Maisie pointed out.

"Yes." As though bringing two long-lost lovers together, Vale gracefully clapped his hands in front of his chest, their sound almost musical.

The gargoyle was there one moment and gone the next.

With wide eyes, Perrie scanned the street, not seeing any sign of the gargoyle. "Where the hell did it go?"

A hint of a smile touched Vale's mouth. "Back in a display at the Glass Vault."

"And what about the rest of them?" Nev asked, glowering.

This time when Vale slammed his palms together, a loud boom pierced her ears. Her hands automatically covered them, but nothing seemed to change.

"What did that do?" Perrie narrowed her eyes with suspicion.

His smile grew a tad bit more. "All the corrupt souls are back at the museum now."

Maisie's mouth was open in awe, while an inner battle on what to think stirred inside Perrie.

Nev didn't appear to buy it. "You're telling me all you had to do was clap your fucking hands together, and everyone returned back to that shit hole? How are we still here, then?"

Oh, he has a damn good point. Why didn't they return there too? A chill ran down her spine, and she silently pleaded for Vale not to clap his hands and send them back to the Glass Vault. Nev should've kept his mouth shut.

Vale's smile slipped. "As Perrie knows, Bad Vale didn't have all his powers earlier because the Glass Vault hadn't consumed enough souls, but as more have gone in, the stronger he got—I got. That is how he was able to locate you. I cannot do everything, but since they are connected to the Underworld, I could send them back." He slammed his hands together in another explosive clap. "And I can do this."

Perrie panicked for a moment, feeling her arms and chest to make sure she was still whole, then to see if she'd been transported somewhere else. But she was still here. Her stunned gaze remained on Vale, words trapped in her throat. Maisie and Nev stood quietly beside her.

"No questions?" Vale asked, sarcasm dripping from his voice.

A part of her wanted to laugh, but she didn't. "Well?" she finally said.

"I took away everyone's powers and restored their memories." His smile this time was only for her, and it was a captivating one. She felt drawn to it for a moment but shook her head to clear it. Did he want her to thank him? Bow down to the demonicness?

"Again. How do we know you aren't making this shit up?" Nev folded his arms across his chest. "You already took away our abilities, and we already remember everything."

Maisie perked up, pulling back her shoulders. "I believe him. So is everyone not immortal anymore?"

Perrie couldn't manage to think straight. Too much was going on, *way* too much had happened, and too much had changed in the last few days.

Vale grimaced. "Now, that is the problem. There won't be any more destruction, but since all of you died within the Glass Vault, it is not something that can be reversed."

"What's the real answer?" Perrie asked, tightening her grip on the skirt of her silk dress. Maisie chewed on her thumbnail. Nev just looked confused and pissed. Her heart kicked up again, her nostrils flaring.

Vale rubbed the back of his neck, then gripped it. "You can stay here and remain immortal, or I can deliver your soul to the Glass Vault. When I return to send the souls from the Underworld back to their rightful place, yours can go where it would have eventually gone when you died."

Horror hit Perrie, and her hand slammed over her mouth. Maisie gnawed harder on that nail of hers.

"So, we *are* dead." Nev moved toward Vale, his face inches from the demon. "This is all your damn fault!"

"Sorry I was born." Vale stared him down, even though Nev hovered above him.

Maisie pushed forward, splitting the guys up while Perrie silently thought about what Vale had said. She knew they'd been slaughtered in the displays like it was their own personal horror movie. But she'd thought that maybe since she felt real and still had a heartbeat, she wasn't technically totally dead. *I mean, I suppose immortal isn't dead, but it's not something I'm sure I want.* They still had a heartbeat when they came out…

"Wait!" Perrie shouted. "Why did we still have heartbeats? When yours came back, your memories returned to you, but our hearts never turned off. They still continued to pump as they always have. Why?"

Vale stepped away from Nev's glare, and Maisie tugged Nev to her side. "I am a demon." He shrugged. "Demons normally do not have heartbeats. You, on the other hand, were born human, even though you are immortal now. Without a heartbeat, you would perish, your existence snuffed, and that is why I believe you all were able to remember. With no way to turn off your hearts, the loss of emotion was only temporary."

Perrie let his words seep through her, trying to analyze them. It made sense … even though it also didn't. This was a damn disaster—a horror movie gone more than wrong. She peered out at the glass statues lining the street and raced toward them. Maybe their souls could be returned too.

She slowed to a stop, placing a hand to her chest. A glass child who was maybe about five with hair just below her shoulders, her mouth open in a scream, stood before her.

"What about them?" Perrie asked when Vale pulled up beside her in a split second.

In answer, he clapped his hands together once more. She expected nothing to happen. Or she didn't know? Maybe the clear glass would morph into human skin, a live little girl appearing in its place.

Something did change, though, and it wasn't what Perrie was hoping for. Like snow on a blazing hot day, the glass turned to water, crashing down to the concrete, where the clear liquid pooled around them.

"What happened?" Perrie shrieked, searching the street.

The other statues were no longer standing either, only puddles of water soaked the cement in their places. They'd become nothing but liquid, too.

Vale said nothing.

"What did you *do*?" she screamed. All she could feel was the little girl's warm water brushing her bare feet.

"I had to send them away," he answered, his voice soft, sad.

"Away where? Back home?" Perrie pushed at his chest once. She shoved at it again. Then she bulldozed him to the cement. She straddled his hips, and pinned his shoulders to the ground. He gave no resistance, only stayed lying there, watching her. His defenselessness only made the anger within her roar.

Perrie got right up in his face, her nose a centimeter from his. Her heavy breaths struck his skin, and he still didn't say anything. "Where. Did. They. Go?"

Vale's gaze drifted down to her mouth, holding there for a moment before sliding back up to meet her eyes. "The souls were taken. The bodies turned to glass. It is not how it was in the Glass Vault where glass can turn to skin. This happened outside of it, so they are only glass. That is all of them that was left."

Before he could say another word, Perrie slapped him across his cheek. The sound echoed throughout the broken neighborhood. She pulled her hand back to strike him again, but before she could contact his face, Vale managed to roll her to her back. He held Perrie's arms above her head against the cement, his body on top of hers.

"Stop," he said gently, his expression pleading.

Perrie thrashed and tried to kick, but he didn't budge. She was going to murder him. It didn't matter if he was Bad Vale or Good Vale. She needed to know what happened to her family. "Tell me!"

"I am *trying* to, but you keep lashing out. Allow me to

finish. *Please.*"

"Fine," she said between clenched teeth.

He released her arms and took a deep breath. "The souls were sent to the Glass Vault and were prisoners there, feeding their energy to me. They cannot return here, but they are no longer trapped there either. Before you start kicking me again, they are not in the Underworld either unless that is where they were meant to go. Otherwise, they have moved on."

Tears pricked at her eyes. She hadn't known if they'd be able to come back, but she had *hoped* since the glass was left behind. Now her dad really was gone forever.

Vale furrowed his brow. "Did you want them to stay trapped? Now they are not hurting anymore. I can guarantee you, your family is okay where they are now."

Perrie understood what he meant, but she still wanted them here with her. Her dad, Aunt Krista, and Uncle Jaron. Aunt Krista's huge birthday celebrations with all the leftover food would no longer happen. Uncle Jaron with his laid back and funny personality wouldn't joke anymore. Perrie's dad, who was always there for her, with the power of being two parents after her mom left, would never hug her again. *All gone.*

"Do you think I *wanted* this?" Vale paused, his eyes glassy. "You aren't the only one who has lost something here."

Perrie was unable to hold back the sob—it started out small but then she couldn't control it. Vale hauled her into his lap in an instant, letting her cry against his chest. She helped do this, destroy the world. The one thing keeping her from breaking and falling to pieces was the fact that she wasn't the one who'd killed her family. If that had been her, she wouldn't have been able to live with herself.

Perrie circled her arms around Vale's waist, latching onto his warmth. The guilt of everything clawed at her, making it hard to breathe. The tears wouldn't stop—they sang their own melody … for him, for her. Their alters had destroyed life around them, shattering the world as they knew it. And somehow, despite everything, they were meant to go on, to continue breathing.

At that moment, she realized survivor's guilt was a true thing.

Vale's arms held her tight as his chin rested on top of her head. Perrie remembered a time with August, back in an orchestra closet that felt so long ago—the day she'd thought a real friendship had started. Vale tenderly lifted her chin so their eyes met. His soft fingertips brushed across her cheek, wiping her tears away.

Perrie's breath hitched, and she leapt out of his arms, on the verge of running away. She stopped herself, and only stepped back a few paces. Heat flooded her cheeks, embarrassed, for crying in his lap when she didn't really know this Vale at all.

"I'm sorry. I didn't mean to do all that." The words came out in a rush.

He nodded and smiled shyly. "It is okay. I know you do not understand or truly know me, but through it all, I was there with you, just tucked away. I do not want to see you hurt ever again."

"Thanks." Perrie turned away from him, not wanting to hear any more. And yet…

She then froze when she spotted Maisie and Nev. How had she forgotten about them? She'd been too lost in her damn emotions.

Maisie flung herself toward Perrie, and Nev seemed to fight against an invisible barrier.

It took Perrie a split second to realize what was going on. She spun to Vale, who was already snapping Nev out of his temporary state.

"Why did you do that again? Please don't do that anymore," Perrie said. It was too weird.

"I wouldn't have, but I needed to tell you everything, and he was already trying to come and hit me again."

"Damn right," Nev seethed as he strolled up beside Perrie.

"Why didn't you run over, Maisie?" she asked, keeping her gaze on her cousin's solo eye.

Maisie smiled sadly. "I knew there was nothing to fear, except what he needed to tell you, and we all had to listen."

Perrie pulled her into an embrace and rested her head on Maisie's shoulder. "They're gone. They're really gone."

"I know." A lone tear slid down Maisie's cheek, and her cousin reached out, grabbing for Nev.

He inched closer, drawing them both into him. Maisie looped her arm around his waist and Perrie's, so they were all cocooned together—they were all they had left.

They stood there for a long while, just the three of them, before breaking apart. At first, Perrie didn't see Vale, and her stomach plummeted, thinking he may have left them without a goodbye.

But then she found him, sitting nearby, his back against a tree and his knees drawn inward. With his elbows propped on top of his knees, he gripped his hair while studying the grass.

Perrie wasn't sure what to do or say because everything was so fucked up. She still walked up to him anyway.

"Are you all right?" she asked, biting the inside of her cheek. "I know it's a stupid question."

He lifted his head, quickly masking his haunted expression by putting on a smile. But she'd caught the switch. From the memories Perrie had of Vale, she could only wonder how horrific all his past memories must be. She couldn't even imagine what had taken place. She didn't know if she wanted to either.

"Not completely, but I feel better with all my emotions back on." He pushed himself up and fished out something from his back pocket. A silver file.

Her shoulders stiffened, but then he tossed it to the grass. She immediately relaxed—the other Vale worshiped that stupid file. *Good riddance.*

They stared at each other, neither one saying anything. He was the first to break the silence. "I have got to leave."

"Where are you going?" Perrie grabbed his arm, then dropped it when he peered down at her hand.

"Back to the Glass Vault. I need to send it back."

"I'm coming with you." There was no way he could go by himself and not because she didn't believe him, but because she needed to see it disappear with her own eyes.

"No," Maisie piped in. "*We're* coming with you."

Vale chewed on the side of his lip and nodded. "I cannot poof us back there, though, so it will be a few days' journey."

Her electricity had started his heartbeat... "That's fine. But can you give me my power back? In case something happens to your heart again." Otherwise, they'd be fucked.

The crackle of energy lit up within her, igniting each nerve, flooding through her veins. Sparks sizzled at her fingertips as Vale gave her another warm smile.

TWENTY-ONE

Before-Vale

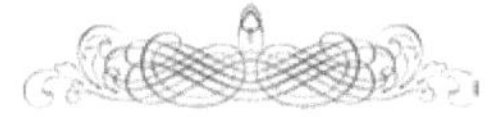

Vale inserted the scalpel in between the male's collarbone. The corrupt soul screamed, pleading for mercy. Closing his eyes, Vale sniffed the air with a greedy suction, as if the sound itself smelled delicious.

Hot blood spilled out from the fresh wound, and Vale purposefully dragged the instrument down the male's fleshy chest. When the metal connected with the soul's navel, Vale lifted the scalpel and set it to the side, gazing at the red liquid as it spilled out. The soul continued to howl in agony and the sound pleased Vale.

Not quite finished yet, Vale dug his index finger inside the collarbone where the wound began. He then glided his digit through the incision until it reached the navel, all while watching the man buck and chew on his tongue.

Lifting his finger, Vale sucked off the excess blood. He inspected his nail and digit, confirming they were now clean, even though they would only become messy again.

A pair of forceps would need to be used next. He clamped

them on one side of the incision and tugged gracefully. As the skin slowly peeled back, he licked his lips in anticipation, then repeated his movements on the other side.

Vale waved his fingers in the air as he gazed at what instrument would take priority. The large knife became his top choice. He picked it up from the tray, then shaking his head, he set the blade back down and reached for a long and thin metal baton. First, he wanted to play a little with the intestines.

Vale bared his teeth into a grin and jabbed the baton into the soul's stomach, digging around the organ so the instrument wound through to the other side. Then he gave it a violent yank, and the man screamed in torment, the soul's eyelids fluttering.

Now, it was time for the knife. Vale picked up the sharp instrument from the table, and admired the blade, captivated by how clean, strong, and beautiful it was before bringing it to his mouth. Slowly, he made contact at the hilt with his tongue and licked his way up the sharp side with firm pressure, until he reached the pointed tip. A metallic flavor burst onto his taste buds, and it may have been his own blood, but he still shut his eyes and felt the rush of ecstasy flow through him.

Now it's time to really play.

The knife hovered in the air over the open stomach, when a female's voice called from the doorway, "Master?"

Fury sewed its way through him, and he slammed the knife into the soul's stomach, ignoring the man's endless, agonizing moans.

"What?" he roared as he turned to Red.

"Your father wants to see you," she crooned.

His anger snuffed as quickly as it had appeared and turned into boredom. "How come he is not here to fetch me himself, then? Why is it you are freely walking around instead of back in your cage?"

Red's lips curved into a seductive smile. "He requested pleasure, and I gave it to him. He's still recovering from it."

She sauntered closer to him, and he hastily brushed past her to find his father.

Vale headed down the long dark hallway, the click of heels echoing behind him. He stopped and calmly turned around. "Why are you following me?"

"Your father never said he was done with me. On the contrary, he demanded I return." She grinned, twisting her finger around a red curl.

He frowned before turning to continue his pace. Red's fucks were not good enough to let her roam around on her own, but it was his father's decision.

Vale entered his father's room—lit candles, casting their glow, filled the three brass chandeliers that hung from the vaulted ceiling. His father, still naked, sat up in bed with his hands laced behind his neck, his blond hair tugged in all directions. The silky black blankets rested in a clump on the floor.

Vale did not care about his father's disheveled state—he only wanted to return to his plaything. "Yes, Father?"

His father did not move from his position as he tilted his head in Red's direction. "The little slave mentioned you have been growing bored with your duties and are constantly trying to figure out new torturous activities."

"Yes." Vale's appetite was always curious for more.

"I think you should go up there." His father pointed to the obsidian ceiling and Vale peered up in confusion. "You can prey on humans instead of the corrupt souls here."

"None of us are able to leave." There had never been a way of escape for anyone.

His father flashed a secret smile. "That is not true. *You* can, and you may choose who to bring with you. I am unable to leave, but I can live vicariously through your actions. And I feel you are ready, my son."

Son. He had never called him that. Vale felt nothing, only cocked his head.

"She will explain to you the plan." His father barely glanced in Red's direction.

Vale nodded. "Let me clean up my work first."

"Very well."

Vale strode from the room, already obsessing about what his father had said.

Red clicked her heels behind him as he walked back down the stone hall to his plaything. The soul still lay in his place. Vale snapped his fingers to light a small fire and began cleaning his work, but only after first pricking a few places on the soul with the blade.

Humming to himself as he worked, Vale watched Red lift the soul, then she returned him to the cage across the room. Vale picked at his nails with a smaller instrument and thought to himself how this was not as delightful as it could be. And that would change.

Surrounded by boredom, Vale wanted those new souls, *needed* those new souls, lusted to feed on them in miraculous ways.

Red stood before him as he turned to her and asked, "What is my father's plan?"

TWENTY-TWO

Perrie

How could so many cars have been destroyed? It amazed Perrie how every car they'd found had the same problem, the engine fried. So, running during the day was their only option.

The new Vale situation had started to finally hit Perrie, and it struck her hard. She didn't show how she felt on the outside—not a single tear was shed. On the inside, however, she was *screaming*. She couldn't look at Vale most of the time because it confused her more than ever—his beautiful face reminded her of August, but then she would think of the other Vale. And it wasn't the Vale from up in the tower as one would think. It was the Vale, who in his own way, treated the Bride as his queen, his equal.

But this Vale was like neither—he was quiet, calm, and offered her apples he'd plucked from a tree. It sent a strange feeling to her chest. Needless to say, she refused the damn apples.

As they turned down a curving road, the sky above dark with flecks of stars shining, she could barely hold her eyes open. Farther up the long and narrow road sat a small wooden cabin.

"Let's stop for the night," Vale said, seeming to notice her tiredness. Relief washed over her when Maisie and Nev both agreed.

After breaking inside, they searched through the tiny home for something to give off light. There was only one bedroom, one bathroom, a living room, and a small nook that would be considered a kitchen. Vale stumbled on two flashlights in a kitchen drawer, which would be good enough.

Perrie's body was too drained to shower, so she crashed on an old, cloth couch, curling on her side.

Vale plopped down on the floor beside her. Perrie's eyes widened at him, unsure about what he thought he was doing.

"What the fuck do you think you're doing?" Nev angrily demanded, stomping to Vale. Apparently, Nev thought the same thing.

Vale stared Nev down with a calm expression. "I am protecting Perrie."

Perrie arched a brow. She didn't think she needed any protecting now that the souls from the Underworld had been sent back to the Glass Vault, and she sure didn't know if she felt comfortable with Vale lying on the floor beside her. It was fine during the day, but the night was a different matter altogether. Night was when the Bride and Vale slept in the same bed, when she rode him to bliss, when he thrust inside her until he brought her over the edge. It was when sexual desire was their only conversation. That, more than anything, scared Perrie because she could still feel that lingering chemistry between them. And she could lie to herself all she wanted, but the fact remained that she wasn't indifferent to it.

"I don't think so," Nev said, taking another step toward Vale.

Vale didn't move a muscle, not even to toss up his hand and freeze Nev in place.

"He's fine, Neven." Maisie tugged Nev back by the elbow.

Nev whirled around and scowled at Maisie. "What do you mean he's *fine*?"

Maisie brought her thumb to her mouth and chewed on her nail, then shrugged.

Perrie didn't have the strength to argue about any of this. "He's fine, Nev. I have the electricity if I need to use it."

Vale bit the side of his lip, seeming surprised by her willingness. But after being through hell after hell, she needed to face things for herself.

"We can all have a slumber party out here if it'll make you feel better, Neven," Maisie suggested.

"No thanks. I'm not sleeping anywhere near that bastard." Stomping away to the single bedroom, Nev slammed the door behind him. Maisie shook her head and studied the door, frowning.

"You should probably go in there to calm him down," Perrie said, hoping they'd have a chance to talk about their feelings for each other. "I'll be fine." *Fine* was probably exaggerating, but it was a word that had to get her through this.

Maisie nodded and exchanged a glance between them, as if she was completely *fine* with Vale. "If you need me, just scream. I'll be out here in a jiffy."

"Okay," Perrie drawled.

Maisie closed the door to the bedroom behind her. So, she really did leave her alone with Vale. He'd been nothing but *fine*, so why was she worried now?

Slowly, Perrie turned and Vale met her gaze. A comforting smile crossed his lips, which provided her no comfort. Not when the image of Vale's face between Bride's legs slipped into her mind.

"Apple?" he asked, offering her one of those absurd ripe red ones he still had left.

"Apple." She huffed but stretched forward and took it from his hand. She didn't want to deny him this *sacred* act he'd continuously been offering her.

When Perrie bit into the apple's suppleness, it reminded her for a second of the same damn fruit in Rapunzel's castle back in the Glass Vault. Hurriedly, she shut the recollection out and chewed determinedly, trying to create a new memory of the fruit, as ridiculous as it might be. But it seemed to work.

"Thanks, Vale." Perrie meant those two simple words—he may not realize the small gesture helped, but it did. Vale had faced cruel things too, and she needed to remember that.

"You are welcome." His green gaze locked onto hers, and she studied the red apple.

Perrie finished half the fruit and glanced up at Vale, who hadn't stopped watching her eat. But he wasn't staring at her, he was staring at the *apple*.

"Next time, just let me know if you want to eat it." She let out a small laugh that surprised her and handed over the half-eaten apple.

Eyes practically twinkling, Vale bit right into the thin skin. "This is a new experience for me—eating fruit first hand."

"*What*?" Perrie slapped the couch and lurched forward. "You've never had fruit?"

"I have never had anything. When I lived in the Underworld, there was nothing. We do not have to eat, remember?" He winked.

Did he just wink at me? Okay, I think I need to sleep now. "Well, I guess we'll have to find more fruit for you to try." Perrie lay back down so he'd get the hint that she was done talking for now. But a part of her wanted to keep the conversation going.

"Good night, Perrie," he murmured, his voice sad.

"Good night," she said, fingers twitching at her sides. Closing her eyes, Perrie listened to each crunch as Vale chewed the fruit, until the sound stopped. She heard rustling as he nestled onto the hardwood flooring, his breathing turning slow and deep.

Perrie rolled to her side and opened her eyes, unable to sleep. She couldn't relax. Her heart thundered. She held out her hand defensively in case Bad Vale crept out and she needed to electrocute his heart to a crisp. Another part of her sang inside her head that he was *fine*. *Is that Maisie singing in my brain?*

After a while of lying there restless with her newly-acquired paranoia, Vale began tossing and turning. Perrie started to reach out to wake him, but decided not to as soon as he settled into a curled ball. He looked … helpless. Taking a deep swallow, she pulled her hand back but still left it open, just in case, as she fell asleep.

The day had been a blur of feelings. With the absence of glass statues out in the open, it only reminded Perrie that those people weren't coming back. *Her family* wasn't coming back. It was going to haunt her for a long time, but when she looked at Maisie and Nev, she held hope. When she looked at Vale, on the other hand, her emotions were scattered, especially when she thought about that morning.

Something poked Perrie's arm and she groggily peeled open her eyes. Her gaze settled on Vale and she smiled.

She should've been terrified when she'd woken, but oddly enough, that emotion hadn't stirred in that moment. As the day went on, she constantly caught herself glancing in Vale's direction, then she got irritated at herself for staring. His movements were strong, graceful, and the way his eyes took in the world was as if he recognized it yet found a newness there.

As the night unfolded, they stopped at an empty house with a musky odor. Nev and Maisie claimed a set of bunk beds in a kids' room, leaving only one bed remaining.

"Do you need new sheets?" Perrie asked with a grin.

Maisie waved her off. "I'll make due. Might have to take them off like last night though."

Nev rolled his gaze toward the ceiling and Perrie shook her head as she left to go and get cleaned up.

"You can take the other bed," Vale whispered as she passed him in the hall. She was about to argue when he'd already gone into the living room.

After a long, cold shower, involving too much damn thinking, she headed down the hall to the master bedroom. She halted when she stepped into the room and found Vale with his eyes open, curled up in a snug ball on the floor. Her heart beat with a familiar thump as she stared at him, and she pushed it away.

"You know you can sleep on the bed or the couch if you want?" She didn't mind sleeping on the couch. In her opinion, it was just as good as a bed.

Vale lifted his blond head to look at her, his lids half-closed. "I am fine right here, and I want to make sure you are safe." A tired smile crossed his lips.

That again? Hesitating for a moment, Perrie decided to ask if he wanted to share the bed. It was a king-size mattress with plenty of room, as strange as it still would be. After the night before, she wasn't scared to sleep beside him. If for some reason his heartbeat shut off, she would be ready to flip the switch.

"Um, you can sleep up here if you want, Vale. You don't have to sleep on the floor. There's plenty of room." Perrie hopped onto the bed and lightly tapped the mattress.

He shook his head. "I am already used to the ground, no need to worry."

Used to the ground? How often *had* he slept on the floor? But she didn't ask as she slipped beneath the covers and shut her eyes.

Perrie laid there for what felt like a fucking month, staring up at the darkness above, her head spinning with too many thoughts. She wondered if anyone would ever return to these cities she'd helped destroy, or if they would always remain empty.

A cool breeze drifted through the cracked-open window. Perrie rolled to her side and pulled the thick blanket up higher, thinking about what Vale had said. They could either remain immortal or move on to the other side ... wherever souls go. After all she'd done, she hoped she didn't get shoved down into the Underworld, but she wasn't willing to go anywhere yet.

A tiny whimper interrupted her thoughts, and Perrie jerked up in bed. She scanned the dark room, thinking she'd imagined it, when the sound came again ... from Vale on the floor.

Last night, he'd tossed and turned for hours. He hadn't been moaning like this, though.

With a heavy sigh, Perrie threw off the blanket and left the comfort of the bed. She shut the window, then rubbed her own arms to warm them. Her gaze dropped to the floor where Vale's otherworldly face seemed to glow beneath the moon's silvery light, as if it was giving him his own spotlight. Should she let him continue sleeping, or wake him? He shivered, and another soft sound of pain slipped out from his mouth. *Wake him, it is.*

Perrie gently nudged his leg with her foot, waiting for him to stir. Vale didn't, so she nudged him again, a bit firmer this time. A small sob escaped him, yet his eyes stayed tightly sealed. Her chest tightened as she studied him, something akin to sympathy taking root inside her. He looked so helpless, just like the night before. Why couldn't she shut off her feelings?

Then she thought of the Bride, and she wouldn't ever want to turn that emotion or any other one off ever again. She wanted to feel *everything*.

Perrie didn't know why she did it, but maybe because the human side of her ached to come out. Or maybe, because Vale had comforted her the other day in the street, or maybe it was just the familiarity of him.

Either way, she took a deep breath and lowered herself behind him on the carpet. She shifted closer and draped her arm around his waist. Her breathing hitched as he took her hand and slid it to his chest over his own heartbeat, like she was his salvation. Maybe she was? Did he even have anyone? Perrie still had Maisie and Nev, but she didn't know who he had.

Vale's heart increased against her palm, and she lifted her head to peer down at his sleeping face. He wasn't asleep though—he was smiling, his eyes almost fully open. Perrie yanked her hand back.

"Did you just fake all that to get me down here?" She frowned while hovering over him. If he did, she would kick him outside.

"Pretend to do what?" His expression turned serious as his eyes met hers. Maybe he wasn't pretending...

Her frown left her face and she bit the inside of her cheek. "You were crying in your sleep."

"Oh. I was having a nightmare." He rolled over to face her.

Perrie studied the loose lock of hair that fell over his eye, but she left it where it was. Even though her fingers ached to push it back. She adjusted herself on the floor and propped her head in her hand. "Demons can have nightmares?"

A dark blond eyebrow drew up. "Well, I do sleep, don't I?"

"I find that odd too." Before, she wouldn't have imagined a demon could sleep, let alone have a bad dream.

"That I sleep?" He let out a low chuckle.

"Yes!" Perrie whisper-shouted and threw her other hand up.

"You're immortal and *you* still sleep."

"But that's completely different." It was way different. She'd at least been born on Earth, so if she slept here before, it made sense that she still would.

The edges of Vale's lips tugged to the side. "Not really."

"Um, yeah it is."

"We both don't age and live forever. It's the same." They could argue about this all night, but he did have a point.

"So, you were born this size?" *I mean, was he even born like humans are?*

He chewed on his lip. "No, I was born a baby, like you."

"Before this gets any more weird, how old are you really?" she prodded. "You aren't eighteen, are you?"

"No." He adjusted himself so his head was propped up too.

"Please don't tell me you're like five-hundred years old." It was already fucked up that she'd had sex with a demon, but if he was some ancient age, she'd be nauseous.

His grin grew wide. "I am nineteen."

"You could've said that right away instead of just saying 'no.'" Perrie smacked his arm and laughed. Realizing she so flippantly hit him, she tucked her hand between her waist and the floor to prevent *that* from happening again.

"What about family? Friends?" She thought about Fannie who'd followed him around endlessly, but she didn't want to bring that bitch up. The thought of Fannie made her want to find her, then electrocute her over and over. Perrie supposed she did have that aspect in common with the Bride.

The half-smile faded away, and he shook his head. "I've never had any. My father murdered my mother after he found out she had given birth to a demon with a heartbeat. It had never happened before, but with how powerful I could become, he wouldn't have her whispering ways to turn me against him. Father would shut my heartbeat down every time it would emerge, until finally, he found a way to turn it off permanently, or at least he thought he did."

"No friends ever?" Her jaw dropped, taken aback that he was nineteen and never had a single friend, regardless of where he was from. She didn't know much about his father, but he already sounded like an asshole.

"None."

"Oh." Her chest felt as though it had been punctured, the air slowly leaking.

He lifted his shoulder and shrugged. "It is okay. I have the memories of you, so I know what it is like to have a friend."

Perrie didn't feel like that was the same thing at all, not in the slightest. "Well, I'll be your friend." She was surprised by her suggestion, but she believed he needed one.

"I will take what I can get." He chuckled and rolled over.

Perrie started to push off the floor and return to bed, but he wrapped her arm back around his waist.

"What are you doing?" she asked, not sure if she should be feeling uncomfortable about this whole situation, but she didn't.

"Friends help friends, so you can stay holding onto me to keep the nightmares at bay."

"I think this is just a way to keep me down here holding onto you." A laugh forced its way out from her throat.

"Perhaps," he said, giving her a smug look. Maybe he could help keep *her* nightmares from making an appearance too. She thought of Officer Rodriguez and what they'd both done to her. She closed her eyes to escape the woman's frightened face. Perrie and Vale had been through the evilest of things together, and they both needed those memories to stay away.

As soon as her forehead pressed into his warm neck, she drifted to sleep. All her thoughts eroded not into a nightmare, but a dream.

Something tapped Perrie's bare foot, and she drowsily kicked at it. Then the quick pressure came again, and she blinked her eyes open. Maisie hovered over her, smiling, while Perrie was still clamped onto Vale. His lids were already open like he'd been lying there a long time.

Perrie quickly removed her arm, and, with a smile, focused on Maisie. "Did you really have to tap my foot to wake me?"

Maisie gave her a sheepish look. "Neven said you were taking too long, and we need to get moving." Perrie glanced toward the door, finding Nev staring at her and Vale with his brows up his forehead. *You would think he just found Vale and me naked together.*

Then Perrie remembered how they'd been like that in the past, in every which way possible. The breath in her lungs seemed to constrict, and she pressed a palm to her chest, the memories playing over and over. The sex. The blood. The glass. The deaths. Their *romance...*

Vale's expression turned concerned, and Maisie knelt beside Perrie, taking hold of her hand. Perrie didn't rip it away, even though she wanted to melt to the floor like the glass statues had done the other day. She wanted to vanish from everything and everyone.

"Can I have a few minutes with Perrie before we leave?" Vale asked. "Please?"

"It's fine," Perrie rushed out.

Maisie pursed her lips and nodded, while Nev narrowed his eyes at Vale before following her cousin out of the room.

"What is wrong? And do not try to tell me everything is okay." Vale propped his back against the bed, leaving her enough room to breathe.

Perrie was going to be honest with him. The way she was with everyone, especially her friends. "I was thinking about before. With August—with you."

She didn't have to say anymore—he knew exactly what she'd meant as his throat bobbed with a hard swallow. "I am sorry about that. He—he did a terrible thing in the tower. It feels like my fault, if only I had found a way to have not let my father shut off my heart." Terrible wasn't quite the word she would use, but it hadn't been him.

"It's not your fault." Perrie took a few shallow breaths before continuing. "The first time with August, I wanted to, but the outcome afterward wasn't the best." She could've used a more descriptive sentence of how she really felt, like how she'd been hollow and powerless as she was dragged naked across the floor. Then when her throat was slit, and she was still inside, she only wanted death. He knew this. And she didn't want to make him feel any more self-loathing than he already did because he knew what *that* Vale did.

"The other times as the Bride..." Perrie trailed off.

But she needed to talk to him about this because he was the only one who knew how she felt. Maisie might say she understood, but she really wouldn't because she wasn't in Perrie's head. And Nev? He would just threaten Vale even more. They wouldn't understand. She knew it wasn't just the Perrie show here—they'd all been through horrific things. But she couldn't get past her damn emotions as easily as Maisie and Nev.

"Vale? Can I ask you a question?"

"Of course."

"When we were um, together, as the Bride and Bad Vale … I know with every fiber in me that we both wanted each other, every single time. It was never a one-way street. I wanted you and you wanted me. It was like the darkest parts of ourselves chose it, so it wasn't ever a violation. Or was it? Since we didn't choose to have our emotions taken away. *You* didn't choose to have your heart shut off." She paused. "How do you feel about it?"

Vale ran his hands through his hair and avoided her gaze. "I don't really know. I have never had intimacies with anyone when I was me, but I have all these memories and feelings of being with others—with you. Most of my life has been without anything being *my* choice."

Perrie inhaled sharply. She might've been through hell herself, but he'd really gone through it. He had *lived* there.

"And, maybe it is wrong," Vale continued, "but I am glad I have the memories of you. Not the ones after the Glass Vault, but all the ones leading up to it, including when we were together inside the museum getting through all of it side by side. Even the simplest ones where we sat on the couch in your home watching old movies together. I know it wasn't me with you, but those memories ... those memories are holding me together. It is the one thing I have that is good. I may not be someone you would like to be around, but I want to do the same for you. If you need it, I want to help hold you together with new memories. Although, I know you don't need me. You are strong enough to do it without anyone."

Perrie remained quiet, but she managed to give him a small smile. His words sank in and she wanted to be brave for herself, but she wasn't sure if her pieces would stay glued together.

Earlier that day, everyone remained mostly silent while they covered a great distance. As they got closer to the Glass Vault, the world appeared even more broken, catastrophic. Every tree was ripped from the ground and thrown like twigs—not a single trunk still stood. Power lines were scattered all around, and almost every house and building lay in shambles.

Perrie stayed focused, quiet, just to make it through the day.

They stopped at a house for the night with several outer walls torn off, but it still stood, so that was good enough. After two more nights, they would be at the Glass Vault.

Maisie went into the bathroom to take a shower, while Vale headed into a bedroom. Nev still hadn't come inside, so

Perrie opened the door to find him sitting outside on a porch step. He hadn't even tried to speak to her that day.

She shut the door behind her and asked, "What's going on?"

Nev stared at a hummingbird yard decoration and watched its spinning wings before turning to her with a frown. "No. What's going on with you? You and Vale were cuddled up together on the floor this morning. You do realize this is *all* his fault, and everything we've suffered through is because of *him*."

With a sigh, she sat beside him on the porch. "Vale isn't the Vale you hate. He may still be a demon, but I'm starting to trust him."

"Like you trusted August?"

It felt as though she'd just been slapped. "That's not fair, Nev. He has no one."

"But how do you even know he's not worse than before?" His stare became hard, as if the answers would all pour out from her soul, but she didn't have them. If he was going to accuse Vale, then he would have to blame her and Maisie, too. They were all a part of this, whether they'd known it or not.

"I don't. The thing is, I've been through a lot. You and Maisie have been through just as much, but I can't live my life wondering if Bad Vale will come back or if things may get worse. I'm giving him this one chance, but believe me, if a third Vale pops out or if this one goes hostile, there will be no more chances."

"I just can't see you get hurt again. I don't want him to do that to you." Nev fidgeted with his hands as he studied her.

"It isn't like that, Nev."

He cocked his head and lifted a brow.

She mirrored his movement right back at him. "It isn't!"

"Maisie and I have your back no matter what, Perrie."

Her heartbeat sped up. The two of them meant everything to her—they were her family. "I know you guys do." She wrapped her arms around his waist and held him tight while he ran his hand through her hair, comforting her.

"But I still don't trust him."

"You don't have to, Nev."

They sat on the porch and stared up at the night sky for a long time, just shooting the shit, until Perrie finally decided to head back into the house. She found Vale still in the bedroom, curled on his side on the floor. His apparent routine shouldn't have surprised her, but it still did. *I'm only staying in here with him in case he needs my electricity to revive him.* Or that was what she told herself anyway.

After maybe two minutes of resting in the bed, Perrie sighed and dragged her pillow down beside him. "Okay, so tell me what the deal is with the floor? Why do you insist on sleeping like this?"

The wooden floor was hard against her back, so she wasn't quite sure why the hell anyone would want to sleep on it versus a soft bed.

Vale rolled over to face her with a weak smile. "It is what I am used to. I have always slept on the ground. I remember *him* sleeping on mattresses outside the Underworld, but I never have."

Perrie's heart sank to the pit of her stomach as she thought about what he'd just confessed.

"Do you want to now? Everyone needs a chance to melt into a mattress." She tugged lightly on his shirt. "You can test it out for yourself. I'll even stay down here while you sleep."

"That would be a stupid idea. Down here is where all the fun happens." He softly patted the wood several times.

"What fun? Bad back fun?" Perrie laughed.

He chewed on his lip in thought. "Re-energized fun."

"That doesn't even make sense. You can get re-energized even better on a soft mattress." Perrie motioned at the bed.

"You can go back up there if you want." Something in his voice seemed to yearn for her to stay.

"No. I think I'll stay down here and keep you company." She rubbed a hand across the wood as if it was her new best friend.

"Roll over."

"Why?" Perrie blinked, twice.

"Do you question everything? Roll over."

She wrinkled her nose, then awkwardly rolled to her side. He folded his arm around her waist, and she melted into his warmth.

Time slowed, and Perrie flipped back over to face Vale as she recalled a moment she'd had with him when she was Bride. "It was you that night, wasn't it? The kiss. Your heartbeat fainter, but it was still *you*."

He didn't answer, and she thought he may not, until he did. "It was. I thought I was hallucinating—I wasn't fully aware of everything because my heart was sluggish." His gaze dropped to her lips, becoming hooded, before focusing back on her eyes. "Now, roll over, I'm going to keep your nightmares away tonight."

Perrie wanted to forget about that sweet moment with his mouth against hers, tasting, caressing. But it continued to linger as it was now her turn for her gaze to fall to his mouth. So, she rolled over.

After they woke this morning, it was another uneventful journey with no sign of life anywhere. Not even a bird, stray cat, or dog. Only emptiness. An ugly quiet that Perrie could feel down to her bones. Chill after chill slithered up her spine, and it felt more and more like a movie she'd seen that she never would've expected to be real.

As night started to fall, and their bodies grew tired, they stopped for their final night at an old apartment complex with half the building still intact.

"You can have the bedroom," Maisie said, not taking no for an answer. Nev stayed with her cousin while Perrie headed into the room.

It was small with band posters covering every inch of the walls. She ignored the smoky odor lingering in the room as she peered around. A vintage stereo system took up the corner and hundreds of vinyl rested in blue plastic crates. Plaid sheets sat in a heap at the end of the bed.

Before Vale could be the first to achieve floor status, Perrie positioned herself on the carpet as he got out of the shower, his soft steps sounding down the hallway. He came to a stop in the doorway when his gaze fell to her, amusement dancing in his eyes. Instead of meeting her on the carpet, Vale closed the door and dove straight onto the twin-size bed. The springs squeaked with the bounce from his weight.

"I think I will take the bed tonight." He peered over the edge, and a grin spread across his face.

Shrugging, Perrie smiled back. "That means the floor is all mine." She stretched her body against the thick carpet.

"We may have to switch positions." In a flash, Vale leapt from the bed, swooped her off the floor, and tossed her on the mattress, her body bouncing two full times before she could process what the hell had just happened.

Perrie laughed a real laugh and rolled to the edge of the bed. She found Vale already on his side with his arm up, ready for her to crawl in. As she hopped off the mattress and curled up beside him on the floor, she told herself the main reason she was indulging him was because this had been keeping her nightmares at bay. But she knew deep down that wasn't the only reason...

After she was cozily tucked into his side, a low muffle escaped Vale's throat. She stilled, then flipped around to face him. "What's wrong?"

"I'm sorry," he rasped. Tears streamed down his face as he

sat up, then turned away from her.

Perrie's shoulders slumped, and she didn't want to tell him it was okay because nothing was okay. She scooted beside him as he brought his hands to his face and sobbed into them. Tears pricked at her eyes and streamed down her cheeks when she thought about what he'd done, what she'd done, what they'd done together. It may not have been them, but it hurt like it was.

"Do you want to talk about it?" Perrie pulled him toward her and lay his head in her lap, letting him cry while she stroked his rumpled hair. Everything was catastrophic and nothing was their fault, but it was. His hand squeezed her knee as his warm tears fell harder.

"I am so messed up. I did such terrible things while I was in the Underworld with my father—when I was *him*. I keep hearing the screams down there when he would perform unmentionable acts of cruelty on the corrupt souls. I hear your scream, too. I—I do not know how to repair myself."

"Look at me." Perrie gently lifted his chin. "I hear screams too from when I was the Bride. I may not know everything about you, but we have been through a lot together, and we are going to get through this together. Maisie will help you, too. Nev might need a lot more time."

Vale's laugh was half sob because they both knew how Nev felt about him.

"If it comforts you at all, the Bride would've loathed this version of Vale. She would've fought to have her Vale back by any means necessary, far worse than anything he'd ever done." Perrie continued to stroke his hair, and with her free hand, she brushed the scar at her throat. The raised skin reminded her every day of a time in her life she ached to forget, but it was also something she needed to remind her how she could overcome anything.

Vale's gaze found hers. "He was going to tell her, you know. He was going to tell her every single thing he had ever done in order to bring her to life."

"I know. She told him to tell her in the morning, but I had already gotten my memories back."

Vale stayed silent.

"She wouldn't have hated him," Perrie said softly. "She would've thanked him and loved him even more because if he hadn't done it, she wouldn't have existed. And together they could be even stronger."

A palpable instant passed between Perrie and Vale as he murmured, "He loved her. That emotion may not have been possible for either one of them, but somehow it existed in its own way."

Perrie looked out the window at the night sky, and it was just as dark as their alters' hearts had been. "Everything in the world could burn except for the two of them and that would be perfect. A twisted romance that would be a superb movie. Now, roll over. I think you need to be held tonight more than I do."

"And in the end, they could both be happy," Vale whispered quietly, so quietly that she wasn't sure if he'd meant for her to hear him. But she knew he was no longer talking about Bad Vale or Bride, he was talking about *them*.

Tomorrow they would reach the Glass Vault, and once the museum was gone, maybe they could start to truly heal.

TWENTY-THREE

Perrie

Perrie woke this morning to Vale robotically poking her arm, and she kept swatting him away, trying to fall back to sleep. Then she shot up when she realized they would be at the Glass Vault that day.

Maisie was already jogging in place at the doorway while Nev stared at her with, Perrie's guess was, longing.

Even though the city was in shambles, the weather was perfect with the sun shining high up in the sky. Maybe the world was trying to tell her that everything would be all right.

They took off on a heavy sprint, running the entire way without stopping once. Perrie's bare feet slapped against the ground and after each step, she felt freer. With how good the earth felt against her feet, she may never wear shoes again.

As they went down Oak Street, a pit formed in Perrie's stomach as the Glass Vault loomed before them. It appeared just the same as the last time she'd walked out from it. They slowed to a stop in front of the building, and she gazed up at its outer shell. She thought that maybe it would've vanished, like it had all those weeks ago when she'd come with Aunt Krista and Uncle Jaron. But no, here the piece of shit was now—existing before them with its tall wooden door, no windows, and gray-colored stones that wrapped around its entirety.

Vale's curls swayed as the warm breeze blew through the strands, a lock fluttering right at his brow. "Let's get this over with and put the Glass Vault back where it belongs," he said, his jaw clenched, determined. No worry sounded in his voice, and that helped to trigger a new-found confidence to bloom in her chest. He stared at the stone museum, barely blinking— the first time he was seeing it in person as his true self.

Perrie reached out and squeezed his hand to give him support, even if he didn't think he needed it. "Let's send it back," she whispered.

The three of them waited for Vale to make it disappear, but instead, he said, "I am going to go inside, and I will be back out in a moment."

Perrie's heart felt as though it stopped beating before plummeting to her toes.

"What do you mean go in?" Nev demanded.

"I mean, I have to walk inside, stroll down each of the halls, make it to the circular room, look at each display properly, return through the hallways, and then appear back out here." Vale cocked his head and stared at Nev.

Nev narrowed his eyes at Vale's sarcasm. "I didn't need all that info. The point is, why do you have to go inside at all?"

"I did not say *you* had to follow me inside."

"Yeah, I'm not following you inside that shit show again."

"I'll come with you." Maisie raised her hand, and Nev shot her a dirty look.

Perrie's stomach was more than tied in knots at the thought of entering this building again. It was bound together by ropes, chains, and locks—all squeezing at her intestines. She didn't want to go back in there, and she couldn't believe Maisie would volunteer to. But it was Maisie.

As much as Perrie would rather have a tea party in the forest, she wasn't going to let her cousin traipse inside by herself. Perrie didn't think Vale would do anything, but it *was* the Glass Vault—who knew if it would trigger some magical slap of brainwash once inside. Then they would be back to square one.

"Me too," Perrie sighed, and reluctantly raised her hand.

"That means we're all going, apparently," Nev huffed, "but you're leading the way this time, Vale. None of that walking behind us shit."

"Fine." Vale shrugged and started for the door, followed by Maisie, while Perrie and Nev watched. She reassured herself by knowing that if they got rid of the museum of horrors, then maybe the world could be semi-okay. Swallowing her fear, Perrie grabbed onto the back of Maisie's dress. Maisie gave her a quick pat on the hand, letting Perrie know everything was all rainbows and roses. *Yeah, maybe black decaying roses and rainbows leading to evil leprechauns.*

Vale opened the door, and they stepped into the long hallway. The lanterns lining the walls were still lit with what must be a magical fire that never dissipated. Not surprising. As soon as they were halfway down the red wallpaper hall, that now reminded her of dark blood, the door slammed shut.

Everyone froze except for Vale who continued walking. *Maybe we should've waited outside.* Vale halted and peered back at them, then rolled his eyes harder than Nev ever had. "It is only an effect. Now, come on." He motioned them all forward to the torture chamber.

A need burned through her veins to help end this, so she hurried and jogged up behind Vale.

They completed their walk through hallway number one and turned down the next, where the chandeliers were practically waiting to drop and crush them below. Perrie wondered about the halls, but she would ask questions about them later. The walls were drenched in blue, like an ocean, but then an image came to mind of blue lips on a bloated dead body.

Perrie gripped the back of Vale's silky shirt, and he offered her an encouraging small smile. Maisie then latched onto the back of Perrie's dress, and Nev fastened onto her cousin's. End of hallway number two was now complete. One more.

"Hallway of doom," Maisie whispered.

Perrie focused on the white of Vale's shirt instead of the green walls as they continued walking in a line that connected like a train. Sparks of lightning crackled within her as her heart thundered.

Once they reached the opening leading to the displays, Perrie lifted her chin, holding her head high, and took slow breaths.

Vale glanced over his shoulder at her. "Here we are."

"Yes, here we are," Perrie said sarcastically. Then she yanked on his shirt, his back meeting her chest. "If we walk in there, we aren't getting sucked into the displays, right?" Sparks sizzled inside her, prepared in case something fucked went down.

"No. You will only be able to go back in if I allow you to."

Vale placed his hand in hers, and she stepped beside him. Perrie remembered the moment he'd taken her hand when she'd awoken as the Bride. But the way he looked at their entwined fingers now, the same way she was looking at them, like it was familiar yet unfamiliar, made her feel strange. But not in a bad way—she couldn't even explain it to herself at that moment.

At the center of the circular room, the displays all still remained, except this time, some of the glass figures were missing. Perrie came across the werewolf scene—the wolf stood in a new position, but Little Red Riding Hood was gone. The wolf's glass fur was the color of tree bark, and a pile of human skin surrounded its clawed feet. She peered at the Frankenstein's Monster scene, finding it empty.

"Why isn't there a statue in that one?" Perrie nodded to the empty display.

Vale bit his lip as he studied the scene. "Because that one is mine, but I do not have to be in it." *Victor Frankenstein. Fair enough.*

"What are you doing?" Perrie watched as Vale walked away, scanning the displays.

"I am making sure they are all here."

Perrie's gaze followed him and stopped on Sleepy Hollow. Glass heads, drenched in bright blood, surrounded the hooves of the rider's horse. The Headless Horseman's blackened buttoned-up coat shone under the light as did his dark brown boots that appeared as though they could crush anyone. If it wasn't for the transparency of the glass, she would think the horse could leap out of the display. *Maybe it still can…* She brushed the thought away and glanced at the other scenes—the victims were all missing, but the villains looked the same. Only they stood in different poses than before.

Vale focused on the Jack the Ripper display, squinting his eyes like he was trying to read the scene. The box held no one. Perrie's heart unfolded like paper origami with stress lines practically tearing it apart.

"She is not there," Vale whispered. He finished searching the rest of the displays as Maisie and Nev watched him closely, but Perrie's eyes lingered on the empty display. She should've known that bitch would be tricky. Fannie seemed to be tamed by Vale, like she was his personal mannequin to do with as he saw fit. But there was always something off about her.

The sound of Vale's heavy feet echoed through the room as he ran to the first display, then studied each one with precision again.

"If only I had a magnifying glass," Maisie grunted as she inspected the scenes.

Perrie rushed to the opposite side and examined slowly. She wasn't sure what she was looking for exactly—if it was supposed to be a glass figure of Fannie in her normal attire or a top hat and cloak, so Perrie searched for both. But she found neither.

Vale scratched his head and turned to face them. "Well, she is not in her display."

"I knew something fucked was going to happen here." Nev struck his leg with his fist, seeming to want to break every statue in this place.

As anger shot through Perrie, her power sparking, she might join him on that damn adventure.

Vale arched a brow at Nev like he was an idiot. "Fannie may not be there." He pointed both his hands like they were guns at the Jack the Ripper display. "But she is here." Then he took his gun-made hands and triggered them at the ceiling.

Perrie marched right up next to him as he lowered his pretend guns. Nev watched them as if actual bullets were going to appear. But in this place, anything was possible.

"How do you know?" She hadn't seen a sign of her anywhere.

Vale glanced at the empty hallway as if Fannie would pop out right there. "Because when I sent the souls from the Underworld back here, I put a barrier up. The front door is sealed, preventing their escape. There is also a seal keeping them from stepping out of the displays."

That couldn't be right because Perrie had seen Fannie with who she'd thought was Neven. "I don't understand. Fannie has been out of the Glass Vault before."

Vale chewed on his lip, as if thinking about the same thing, which he probably was with how fiercely he dug into that lip. "That was only when she was allowed out. At that time, the barrier was open to her, but now it is closed to all of them, including her."

Vale stretched his spine to his full length. "I am going to

have to go in."

"Go in where?" Perrie blurted. He couldn't be talking about what she thought he was.

"The displays. She is in one. But her statue is not appearing because she is not in the correct scene."

"How do you even know that?" Nev asked.

"Because while I may not know which display the corrupt souls are in without seeing their statue in their correct scene, I can still feel her inside the museum." He ticked his index finger back and forth at the Jack the Ripper scene.

"Which display do we all start in, then?" Maisie asked, stepping beside Vale.

Nev ran his hand agitatedly through his hair, seeming more pissed than he was earlier. "Maisie! Seriously! Enough of this. We already traveled through this death house to fulfill your investigation needs. But get real, there's no need to go traipsing through different horror shows here."

Maisie pointed between Nev and herself. "*We* are immortal. Therefore, we'll be fine."

Perrie arched a brow at her. Maisie might be all about venturing back into the displays, but she sure as fuck wasn't.

"If you want to begin at one end, I will start at the other," Vale said to Maisie, then paused. "But when you reach the Sleeping Beauty scene, you will have to stop there and wait for me. You are right about being immortal, but if you enter the Snow White display again, there is no escaping, and you will be heading back with the Glass Vault."

"To the Underworld?" Perrie gasped, taking a few steps back.

Vale slowly nodded, his lips pursed.

"Fuck that. Vale can go by himself," Nev hissed.

Perrie shut her eyes for a moment—she would face this. Opening her lids, she took a deep breath. "Maisie, you stay here. As the older one, I'll do it."

Maisie whipped her head to Perrie. "We're the same age.

You're only older than me by a few weeks.

"Exactly." Perrie smiled. "So you stay here."

Nev shook his head. "Wait a minute, what if Vale becomes 'Bad Vale' in the displays again."

Smart question. Before Perrie could respond, Maisie darted off to a display near the hallway. "Team effort. Perrie with Vale. Nev with me." She waved Nev to her, and he stared at Maisie with wide eyes.

"Two things," Vale started. "Good news, the souls listen to me and should not attack you. Bad news, you have no power inside the displays." He gripped the back of his neck as he looked at Perrie. "That means your electricity will be gone."

Fuck. "None of this is adding up. What if Fannie slips past us into one of the other displays, and we continuously run after her forever? Also, I won't be able to run through my scene."

Vale grinned. "The Bride is special, you can run through your display if you have to."

That's dumb. Then I should be able to use electricity if I'm so special.

Vale clapped his hands together. "Barriers are up."

Perrie wrinkled her nose, confused. "Sometimes you have to explain things a little more to us. I thought they were already up."

"I wasn't close enough to put that barrier up earlier. Whichever display Fannie is in, she won't be able to leave it now that they are up between each display."

"Then why can we walk through the barriers?" Maisie called over.

"Because I am allowing you to. Weapons will be at your waist in case you need them for Fannie."

That must've been answer enough because Maisie looked toward a display, where a glass pond rested in front of a greenish, fish-like creature. Maisie clasped Nev's hand tightly, seeming to wait for the wind, that had pulled them in before, to blow. Nothing happened.

Vale snapped his fingers, and a gust of wind stirred, blowing Perrie's hair around her head. But it didn't tug at her though, only dragged Nev and Maisie's feet across the floor.

"Meet you at Sleeping Beauty," Maisie shouted while waving like she was going on a damn vacation.

"See you then," Perrie yelled back. She tried to appear calm, but inside she was freaking out—she didn't want to be separated from Maisie again. *They'll be okay*, Perrie told herself once they were both gone.

"You know you can wait out here for us," Vale said. "You do not have to go."

Waiting out here would be easier, but Perrie didn't want to do easy. She wanted Fannie to be sent back to where she belonged, and she would help put her there.

"Let's do this." Perrie punched the air as Maisie would've, then followed Vale to a Hansel and Gretel display. She truly believed the world was laughing at her. But then she remembered all the fun times she'd had playing Hansel and Gretel with Maisie when they were kids. Vale did say the immortals wouldn't attack, but was he even sure about that?

Vale held his hand out to hers, and she peered into his emerald eyes. There wasn't fear she felt, only hope, so she gripped it tightly.

"Together?" he asked.

"Together." Perrie smiled.

TWENTY-FOUR

Before-Fannie Caldwell

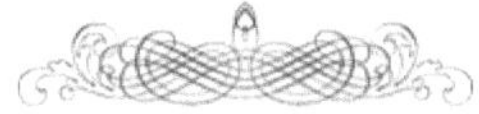

Fannie Caldwell was born Jaqueline Richards. She'd had entertainment while it lasted—murdering whores, slicing and dicing into their luscious flesh. She may have been a whore herself, but she'd yearned for the blood—the warm, red liquid that she loved to lick off her tools after a murder.

She would have never been found out. Her intelligence was beyond anyone's thinking capacity, and that laughable police force would never have been able to discover her.

A common cold turned into bronchitis that led to pneumonia was what had ended her killing spree. Something as simple as that. She would have preferred to be taken down with her skin peeled off—something painful, yet pleasurable. A simple cut was all it would take to light up all her nerve endings. Alas, Jack the Ripper was only a mortal.

Jaqueline had wanted a new name when she returned from the Underworld. She would become immortal, and nothing would take her down this time. Fannie Caldwell was the name that rolled off her tongue.

"I went over the plan with your son," Fannie said, focusing on her master—*her real master*. She only truly wanted him. Not Vale.

"Does he approve?" Vale's father still lay in bed naked, and Fannie thought of all the delicious things she had done with him earlier. Sucking him, riding him. The things she would do again once this conversation was over.

"Yes." She smiled, licking her lips. "With his abilities, he is going to build a barrier of sorts. It is to resemble a museum, and there will be different boxes that will trap individual souls. Those souls will be able to perish inside their box and become indestructible, and they *will* bring more souls into its walls once released."

Master ran his wet tongue across his white teeth, tempting Fannie to obliterate the conversation.

"You did not tell him I will eventually be released once enough souls are pulled from the earth, did you?" His black eyes narrowed into thin slits as if he believed she could be tempted by another. *Impossible.*

"No, Master." When she was pulled from her cage on her first day in the Underworld, after Vale cut into her repeatedly, Master found her. He could see she was not fearful like the others but enjoyed every minute of her torment, so he confiscated her. She told him about the days of her own joy above, and he was astonished she could remember. He relished it, relished her.

He knew she had a purpose, and Vale would be their personal little marionette. Master would hold the strings, but Fannie would keep them from unraveling. That frail, miserable young male she'd watched from her cage, her first day in the Underworld, had been undeserving of the powers he held in his possession. He still was. Those powers were waiting to be fully unleashed, and Fannie and her master would have it all.

"Good. His heart seems to have been permanently stopped, but if it ever beats again, he cannot know this." A deep crease settled in between Master's blond brows.

"As you wish." She took a sultry step toward him.

"Vale must believe you serve him up there." Master leaned forward, staring hard at her. "Do not make a single mistake for him to believe you want this for yourself. He can only believe I want this for him, to help him grow stronger, and he *will* grow stronger. But then his powers will come to me as my insides drain him of all he has."

Fannie nodded, peeling off her dress and letting it drop to the floor. She took another step in his direction, heat pooling at her core, lust filling her.

"When I'm released, you will stand by my side." He held up a finger. "But if this fails, I will find you, and the things you did above ground, the torture Vale presented to you, are minuscule to what I will do. I will shred every part of you there is." Master stuck the end of his index finger in between his teeth and lightly bit it.

Fannie closed her eyes and let those sentences flow through her. Those words were a delicacy she wished to taste. Either way sounded like a triumph to her. She wanted to be ripped into by her master with *her* weapon of choice. If they were above ground, she would still make him do so, with the new power he would possess. That was a true dessert she craved. Her nipples hardened at the thought.

She sauntered to the bed and closed the distance between them. Master's eyes roamed over her naked body hungrily, as if knowing what she wanted from him. And she was going to have him begin now.

TWENTY-FIVE

Maisie

The strong gust of wind flung Maisie to the hardened dirt, the graininess scratching at her forearms. Neven's hand was still firmly in her grasp as his head plummeted to the ground.

"Are you okay?" Maisie asked while Neven massaged his scalp.

"No."

She knew he was talking about more than the pain, but they both leapt to their feet and surveyed the area.

A small pond rested in front of them, blocking their path to the other side of the display. When Maisie glanced to her right, a certain fish man, with light green scales and razor-sharp needle claws, watched her. He was knelt to one knee and looked incredibly similar to the classic horror film character, Creature. But there was a little variance—eerier.

Tiny horns sprouted above each dark eye—eyebrows?—and his teeth were like sharpened sticks of charcoal. His gills oozed thick green slime onto slightly lifted scales. He studied them, but she eagle-eyed him right back. Maisie remembered this little deadly game with Pinocchio. She adjusted her patch to give off the warning vibe that she may only have one eye, but she could see every single movement he made. *I'm prepared for his bag of tricks.*

Neven hastily tapped her shoulder. "Are you going to stare at him all day, or do you want to try to move on to the next display?"

Maisie gave Neven a once over before doing the same to herself. Their clothing hadn't changed—unlike when they'd been here last and their outfits had matched their scenes. But, this time, Vale graciously gifted them knives at their hips, as promised. *No time for playing with these glorious weapons, though.*

The space in this display wasn't the same as in Snow White, or the ones Perrie had traveled through. Instead of going on for a good distance, the display seemed more similar to an extra-large living room—four walls painted like a forest with tall, thin trees and a bright blue sky. Maisie looked at Fish Man, his eyes following their every movement, but he remained immobile. She was ready to pounce if he tried anything sketchy, though—and she *would* fillet him.

"Run!" Maisie yelled as she dove into the freezing pond, ignoring the icicle sting. Slicing through the liquid, she kicked her legs hurriedly. Neven's arms beat at the water beside her, and they landed on the other side in no time. Maisie sprang to her feet, waiting for the wicked soul to follow. The creature's head was now tilted in their direction, his dark eyes focused on them, but he stayed planted across the pond.

"I guess Vale was right about them not coming after us," Neven said, shaking his head like a wet dog. A few drops splashed against her skin.

Squinting her eye, Maisie observed the stretch of land one more time. "I say Fannie isn't here unless she's hanging out at the bottom of the pond." They padded to the edge and gazed around the clear water, not seeing anything.

"Next one." Neven turned toward where their escape should be. Maisie grabbed his hand, and they easily walked through the barrier as the gust of wind sucked them through.

They hopped to their feet as soon as they hit the ground. Another small area. *Good.* It would be much easier to spot that red hair of Fannie's. No red hair, though. Only a vampire with razor-sharp canines in Maisie's line of vision. Long—at least three inches—alabaster claws lazily tapped from pinky to index finger across his knee—all while sitting on the edge of an empty bed covered in magenta satin sheets.

Transparent, chalky-white skin wrapped around his skeleton, a map of thin red veins pulsing through his flesh. He ran a thick black tongue across thorn-like canines.

Maisie wasn't sure if the vamp would stay there and obey Vale. So, she moved her hand to her belt of goodies. This time, wooden stakes of all sizes and varieties were attached at her hip. *This is what I'm talking about.*

Neven frowned, rubbing his jaw nervously. "I think we have to leap over the bed."

Her eye darted around the room. It was empty besides the too-long bed touching the walls to their left and right. Still no red hair or Jack the Ripper gear, but Maisie didn't know if the heathen was underneath the bed skirt. Diving to the floor, wooden stake in hand, Maisie lifted the edge of the bed skirt. Nothing.

Neven hauled her back with his arms wrapped around her waist. "Are you an idiot?" His voice cracked during his whisper-yell attempt.

"We can't very well move on before we search the area, right?"

Maisie received no response from Neven except for a puckering of the lips.

The vamp still sat in his same comfortable position, tapping that knee of his.

"Now!" Maisie screamed.

She took hold of Neven's hand, and they bounced a foot onto the bed, leapt to the floor, and ran for the wall. The heavy suction pulled them through with a clean sweep.

They landed on their feet this time.

Neven tugged her elbow. "Maybe I do want your plans, Mais, before you start getting all gung-ho and doing things without explaining."

"So, you do like my planning." Maisie grinned while searching the area. She didn't spot a wicked soul anywhere. *Oh wait, there it is.* Small bubbles popped within a mysterious green liquid, and two large violet eyeballs blinked in their direction. The slimy substance coasted from side to side, and Maisie just stared at the creation in awe.

"This one's too weird," Neven muttered. "No sign of Fannie—let's go." Grabbing her hand, Neven tugged her forward. They hopped over several toppled metal cans before the gust of wind yanked them to the next display.

Maisie somehow landed on top of Neven, and she gazed at his face. "I think you're the planner now." He didn't lift her off him as she examined the display. She didn't want to leave this position either until … she saw what was in the room with them.

"Run!" Maisie shouted.

Neven shoved himself from the floor in a second with her hauled to him. Before them, a person sat huddled on the ground—blackened limbs barely hung on to his torso, and thick black blood leaked out from the wound. And no Fannie. They barreled across the crow-colored grass, where the infection must've also spread, then they passed through the barrier.

"What was that about?" Neven asked as they crossed into a nursery rhyme nightmare. A woman leaned against a large boot, as tall as the ceiling, with tiny ivory skeletons of children on the ground surrounding her. She lightly smacked some sort of white stick against her palm.

"Black Plague. We had to avoid it." Maisie's chest heaved, trying to catch her breath. Having an arm chopped off would be one thing, but a rotting limb dangling about was a whole different ballgame.

Neven broke into a wide grin and tapped the side of his head, his dark hair swinging forward. "Immortal, remember?"

"I know, but it was still a risky situation. Some scientists believe the plague wasn't spread by fleas on rats. They believe it was airborne!" Maisie shuddered to herself.

"You know that immortal back there could've transferred venom into you and turned you into a vampire." Neven tugged one of her dark curls.

"But my ligaments would've still been intact." She could deal with vampirism but not *rotism*.

Neven rolled his eyes and studied the tall black boot. "I'm not sure what this display even is."

"There's a lady and a shoe."

"Okay?" he drawled, his expression bewildered.

"The nursery rhyme of the lady with too many kids that lived in a shoe." That rhyme was creepy even without it being converted into a horror display—living in a boot filled with kids and more kids was a nightmare in itself.

"Sorry, Mais. I must've missed that one." He shrugged and glanced back at the woman.

Maisie took a better look at the lady—the immortal's black hair was pulled into a raggedy bun, and something red was smeared on her chin. Maisie squinted at the immortal's tapping hand—it wasn't a white stick she was holding, it was a *bone*. One of her children's bones.

"What's coming from her mouth?" Neven should've already known the answer to his question.

"Blood! Time to run!"

The immortal's empty eyes bored into them as they leapt over the skeletons of her dead children. As they passed their surroundings, there was no sign of Fannie. Neven yanked the door to the boot open while Maisie clamped down on his arm. Then a tornado of wind unleashed and pulled them through.

As they stood in the next display, Neven pressed a fist to his mouth like he was about to gag. "I think I'm going to be sick. This was your bright idea, Maisie."

"It's all for the good of humanity," Maisie said and let go of his bicep.

"I think humanity needs to defend themselves." Neven's gaze drifted through the room, then paused.

"Well, we've gone past several wicked souls, so we pretty much have to keep doing the same thing." She followed his gaze until she halted on a woman with metal from wrist to fingertip, gripping her own bloody, fleshy hands.

"What? See sick shit and then run?" Neven watched the blood droplets splatter to the ground in a large puddle that took up almost the whole room. Blood dripping continued to echo throughout the space, sounding like a loud drumbeat.

"That's correct," Maisie sang and nodded as she kept rubbernecking Metal Hands on their sprint to the barrier.

Neven released a loud puff of breath. "Okay then. Let's hurry and make it to Sleeping Beauty."

With no sign of Fannie, they ran and kept on running through scenes. No wicked souls attempted to lunge at them, only staring contests with her and the immortal while Neven avoided this new sport.

Eventually, they were spit out into the Sleeping Beauty display, green walls surrounding them. Maisie should've counted from the beginning to know just how many wicked souls they'd had to bypass to get to this scene.

There weren't any big surprises here when Maisie spotted the dark fairy hovering in a corner. She wore a sleek black gown with a low v-neck reaching her belly button, the swells of her breasts exposed for all to see. Her horns were longer and thicker than Maisie would've imagined. Instead of coming to a single point, the horns looked more like tree branches with tiny limbs sprinkled across them. The dark fairy gripped a deep brown staff in one hand, beating it against the wooden floor with a slow repetitive thump.

Maisie didn't feel like sitting in a room, waiting for Perrie and Vale, with this immortal watching them the whole time. She darted toward the dark fairy and whirled her around, so she faced the corner of the wall. Her staff continued to pound the floor, so Maisie took it from her hand and laid it beside the fairy's feet. The wicked soul didn't move to reach for the staff or turn back around.

"Didn't I say to tell me your plans?" Neven said, seeming more impressed than irritated.

Maisie peered past Neven to look at the bed—it was huge and high off the floor. Large wooden posts with vines engraved in the wood stood at each corner of the bed, and green satin sheets covered the mattress.

Striding to the bed skirt, Maisie lifted the material and found no Fannie. Her heart sank. She hoped Perrie and Vale pinpointed her soon because she and Neven had failed their mission.

With nothing else to do, Maisie crawled underneath the bed as if it was a tent. It even felt like one since she could almost sit to full height.

Neven drew up the skirt from the other side. "What are you doing?"

"Waiting for Perrie and Vale, but I couldn't help but test this out." She stroked the wooden bedframe, her fingers trailing over the thin vines.

Neven rolled his eyes but crawled beside her. Even with his long body, he fit snugly under the bed. "This is weird as shit."

"Would it be weirder to sit on the bed and see the wicked soul?" Maisie asked, peeking through the front edge of the bed skirt. The fairy still held her soldier stance as she faced the wall.

“Point taken.”

Under here it was like she wasn’t in the room. The quietness felt a little strange, though. Even during the attacks with Pinocchio and the mermaid, there’d been other sounds.

“Do you think Perrie and Vale are going to find Fannie?” Neven ran a hand down the side of his face and rested it on a pale scar.

“I do. Vale is the one who brought the Glass Vault here. As soon as he finds her, this place can be tossed back to the Underworld.” Maisie had faith in both of them, no matter how slippery Fannie might try to be.

“I take it you’re all about Vale, too. Now that he isn’t evil or however you would word it.” Neven clenched his jaw while seeming to bore holes into the ruffled bed skirt.

“What do you mean *too*?” Maisie did like Vale. Over the past few days, he’d proven he was like them—controlled by the King of Darkness himself.

“Well, Perrie was instantly attracted to him again once it was revealed he isn’t ‘bad’ anymore.” He continued to stare straight ahead, so she couldn’t really see his expression.

Perrie hadn’t said anything to her, but Maisie had noticed how her cousin observed Vale. She’d thought Perrie had wanted him to be like August, but she was wrong about that. Perrie watched him differently. Maisie wasn’t sure if it was only a friendship situation, yet the cuddling at night made her question that aspect.

“So, you’re concerned with Perrie liking Vale?” Maybe he did still want Perrie back...

“No. I said *too*. As in, I’m concerned that you’re crushing on him, *too*.”

What? Maisie’s lips parted. “Why would you even think that?”

“Over the past several days, every time, you’re the first one to hop on the bandwagon of doing what Vale does.” Neven worked his jaw back and forth, frowning.

"That's only because I believe him." She couldn't explain it, but she somehow knew what he'd said was true.

"But why?"

"I could just feel it." Before Maisie had known August was an evil demon, she'd had no idea. But now that she knew Bad Vale pretended to be this person, she could see how they were connected. At times, August would have the same empty expression Vale had, except he would disguise it quickly. Now, even if there was a neutral expression, his eyes didn't feel empty.

"That's not logical."

What was he even getting at? She didn't like Vale in that way. She liked Neven, but she didn't want to shout it in his face.

"Every time Vale did something or said something, you were right—"

Maisie didn't want to scream how she felt, so she quickly pressed her lips to his. His mouth was like a fluffy pillow against hers, and she wanted to melt into the touch. Maybe now Neven would be quiet about the Vale stuff. His eyes opened wide, and his jaw dropped slightly when she drew her head back.

Heart racing, Maisie smiled at him mischievously. "I didn't run this time."

"Or scream." A nervous laugh escaped him, but then he turned serious.

Neven reached out and ran his hand across her cheek to the eye patch. She closed her lid and let him tenderly slide it off. He scooted closer to her, leaned forward, and softly kissed where the eye was missing. His lips then trailed kisses down her cheek, all the way down her neck, until his mouth was on hers once more.

Nev kissed her gently, a soft caress, and she mirrored his movements. He then rolled to his back, bringing her on top of him. The tip of his tongue traced the seam of her lips, and she parted them for him. His tongue danced with hers as his hand pressed on her back, drawing her closer. As their kiss deepened, grew bolder, and the warmth in Maisie's body became hotter, she had to pull back for now. She wanted desperately to continue the moment, but duty called. They needed to monitor the dark fairy in case she really did try to pull some sort of stunt.

"We have to keep an eye on the fairy, but we'll continue this later," Maisie said, kissing him deeply one more time before crawling out from underneath the bed.

Neven followed her and swooped her into his lap before leaning against the wall. While he circled his arms around her, she couldn't stop herself from smiling. Snow White didn't find a prince or a huntsman in the end, instead she found Frankenstein's beautiful monster.

TWENTY-SIX

Perrie

The strong gust of wind wrapped its invisible leash around Perrie and Vale, then easily glided them through the barrier. After their feet hit the ground with a slight stumble, Perrie anxiously scanned the small area with blue frosted and sprinkled walls. The room didn't have an odor, not even a sweet scent from the frosting. Her gaze connected with the plump witch sitting on top of an old-fashioned stove with her legs crossed at the ankles, leisurely swinging them up and down.

The witch's dark brown hair was styled in a long braid, and she appeared much younger than Perrie would've expected, not a single line creasing her beautiful face.

Chocolate chip cookies rested on a metal tray in her lap, and Perrie waited for the witch to try and shove a dessert down her throat. But she didn't, only observed them with a twitch of the lips.

"Why is the room so small?" She thought back to how most of the displays she'd been in held large forests and had felt like a real place.

"After everyone was released," Vale started, "the Glass Vault returned the displays to their normal size. The illusion of something larger is not needed any longer."

"Okay then." Perrie peered down and found a belt around her waist, loaded with a variety of tiny knives. When she'd come to the Glass Vault last, she'd only been given a small dagger in Billy Goats Gruff.

"She is not here," Vale said, scanning the space.

He took hold of her hand, and they moved to a frosted wall. The gust of air came to life, rumpling her hair and dress before sucking them through. This would be easier than Perrie had thought, since the displays were miniature versions of themselves. She only hoped finding Fannie was as simple.

Still clasping Vale's hand, she searched the new room. Old headstones, broken and cracked, covered the sparsely grassy area, but she didn't see anything else. And she didn't see a sign of Fannie anywhere either.

Something to Perrie's right moved, catching her attention like a flare in a night sky. She whirled to the side and pushed Vale out of the way, nearly knocking him down. He steadied them both before they crashed into the dirt of the cemetery.

A long arm with a slight greenish tint protruded from the ground. It had somehow managed to claw its way out from the dirt one way or another. The ring and pinky fingers were ivory bone, while a loose flap of flesh hung against the hand. A thick yellow liquid ran down the other digits, the skin there appearing as though it wouldn't stay attached much longer. That sight alone put *Night of the Living Dead* to shame, and it was only a damn hand.

"I told you they would not do anything." Vale watched the wiggling digits like he was confirming what he'd said.

"That doesn't make it any less creepy, Vale!" It wasn't as bad as the giant trolls ripping apart bodies and goats, though. She could easily stomp on a hand if she needed to.

They skirted around a few of the grave markers and rushed for the next scene. Their pace increased as she got used to seeing a sinister immortal studying them in each display. Still, Fannie wasn't in any of them—no bright red hair or Jack the Ripper clothing. They then traveled to the next scene, and then to the next, and then to the next after that.

As they continued crossing new world after new world, it felt like it would never end, that they would never find her. But when they stepped into the next display, Vale stiffened. "She is here."

Old stone cathedrals were painted on the walls in neutral shades. To Perrie's right rested the gray gargoyle that Vale had made disappear days ago. The beast sat crouched in a position that resembled a real statue. But as its broad chest heaved up and down, it clearly indicated the gargoyle wasn't one. Its large wings spread fully, the tips reaching toward the heavens. Black veins were set in a leafy pattern that throbbed against the appendages' thin skin.

The gargoyle's left wing twitched, and Perrie just happened to catch a glimpse of a lock of red hair behind it.

Perrie's hand reached for her belt, pulling out the longest knife there. Even though she couldn't spark up, she still tried to ignite her electricity. *Of course nothing, damn it.* She waited for Vale to make his move—possibly clap Fannie away, or telekinesis her to them so Perrie could stab the immortal in her devious heart. Something besides standing there with a crease between his eyebrows and looking lost.

"What is it?" she hissed, clenching the knife harder.

He snapped his fingers. "Something is off. My power is not working in this one."

"What do you mean?" Perrie screeched, glancing back at the gargoyle with its sharp protruding teeth.

"Stay here."

What the hell is he talking about?

Vale lunged for the gargoyle. Perrie waited for Fannie to

run at her and proudly held up her knife, ready for the bitch.

Fannie didn't pounce as Perrie expected, but the gargoyle did. The beast tore forward and rammed Vale to the floor, restraining him by the shoulders. The gargoyle then dug its clawed feet deep into Vale's thighs, blood seeping to the surface. Vale winced but didn't release a scream.

Movement came from where the gargoyle previously was. Fannie rose from her kneeled position, smirking. A beat of wings cracked behind Perrie, and she glanced back at Vale—the gargoyle's stone-like hand now squeezed Vale's throat. Her heart roared, louder and louder.

Should she try ripping the gargoyle off Vale? *No...* She couldn't do that because then Fannie would try to do something to her from behind. Perrie didn't think anymore—she charged at Fannie. But the immortal spun to the side, somehow ending up across the room. Thinking back to their Ripper times, Perrie remembered how fast Fannie was when she'd sliced Perrie's arm in the display. How sneaky she could be. She still was.

Perrie charged at her again, swinging her knife like crazy. Fannie bent backward like she was doing the fucking limbo, and Perrie missed her completely. Even mid-movement, Fannie still managed to turn around and slice the back of Perrie's arm. Perrie gasped at the sharp sting, warm blood oozing out from the wound. She'd had enough. Enough of this. And enough of her. Fannie was going to die.

"You know, little puppet, we can do this all day long." Fannie beamed, running the bloody scalpel across her lower lip. Perrie's chest heaved, but she was far from stopping. "We will be returning to my only master, *your* master." The immortal's gaze shifted to Vale, who choked as he attempted to speak. The veins at his temples looked like they would burst, his face turning a bright cherry red.

Perrie desperately tried to reach into herself, to somehow gather that spark, but she couldn't.

"Option one did not work out, so we are moving on to option two," Fannie said. "Vale is coming back with us to his father, and you, dear *Bride,* are coming along. I don't want your soul to travel anywhere except with us to the Underworld." Her smile was laced with pure venom.

Perrie was *not* going there, and Vale wasn't either. She couldn't let his heart be shut off again by some sadistic fuck, then have this whole process repeat. Vale didn't deserve that. With the knife still tight in her grip, she thrust herself at Fannie.

Perrie had the immortal's movements down. Just as Fannie was about to spin to the side and flip around, Perrie shot forward against her back. She lifted the blade and slammed it into Fannie's right side, piercing her lung, all while knocking her down.

Before Fannie started bucking, Perrie ripped the knife from the immortal's back with a sickening squish. Perrie straddled Fannie as the immortal began to lift. Without a pause, she yanked Fannie's head back by her red hair and sliced a half circle at her throat to match Perrie's. Blood poured out from the wound.

The gargoyle still had Vale pinned down, and Perrie needed to figure out how to get the beast off him. But first, without a care, Perrie flipped Fannie over to her back—she wasn't going to risk it, so she shoved the knife into the immortal's heart. As Fannie choked on her own blood, her hands desperately clawed to her throat.

Not satisfied yet, Perrie stabbed over and over and *over*— she didn't want Fannie or anyone else here to tarnish any more innocent people. She didn't want whatever humanity was left outside the Glass Vault to go through what she or any of the others had. Maisie had done this to the Huntsman back in the Snow White display, but Perrie stabbed Fannie even more.

The immortal's laborious breaths slowed before turning into nothing, her chest still. Perrie didn't know how long it would take before she woke again, so she needed to hurry. With her knife at the ready, Perrie leapt off Fannie and dove for the gargoyle. An odor of burnt feces struck her nose, the only thing she'd smelled thus far, coming from the beast. She yanked it by its paper-thin wings, but the gargoyle's hold on Vale's throat didn't release. Perrie lifted her knife high above her head and stabbed it in the back, ignoring its shrill shrieking as blood splattered the walls. The gargoyle's wing was next, and she sawed at it.

Vale managed to slide out and get to his feet, then hauled ass toward Fannie. The gargoyle flapped his wings, creating a large gust of wind that flung Perrie backward. It then whirled around and backhanded her in the shoulder with its thick skin. She went flying into the wall, her head slamming against it with a powerful bang. The room spun as she crumpled to the floor.

Perrie shakily rolled to her back, nausea bubbling up her throat. She prayed Vale was achieving something with Fannie. He had to.

When Perrie lifted her head, two massive gargoyles hovered over her, then her double vision cleared. Before she could make a move, the beast pounced on her and raised its knife-like claws. The gargoyle slashed them across her chest, her stomach. Again and again. Perrie screamed at the top of her lungs, pain, so much pain, roaring through her. She wished the first slash had killed her because, with each strike of a claw, the agony only became worse.

By now, her organs must be displayed for his choosing. Most likely to eat. If only she had her electricity… Perrie closed her eyes and blood seeped into her mouth. A cracking sound echoed when the gargoyle's hand plowed down into her chest where he would rip her heart out.

But then the slashing stopped.

Everything stopped.

Her eyes fluttered open, her gaze locking on an angel and

cloud-covered ceiling. She tried to lift her head, but it only stayed rooted to the floor. This pain was the worst she'd ever suffered, including her own death before.

Perrie was about to close her eyes again, beg to the heavens above for her body to either heal or let her die, but then a beautiful mess of blond hair and an angelic face leaned over her. *Am I hallucinating?*

"Hold on," Vale murmured as he scooped her into his arms. Perrie wanted to reassure him that she could walk, but all she tasted was blood on her numb tongue. His green irises stayed locked on hers, and she didn't look away. Those two emeralds were the only thing grounding her in this horrific moment.

Vale lay her on the hard marble, and an uncontrollable cough escaped her throat. She struggled to cover her mouth, but she managed, and her hand came away with droplets of blood.

"You are going to be okay, Perrie," Vale said softly as he stroked her hair, but worry shone in his eyes. Her hands trembled—her body wasn't mending, and she felt tattered and torn to pieces.

Vale leaned forward and pressed his lips gently against hers, and they came away with speckles of her blood. She was too numb to feel anything in the kiss. But she wished with everything that she had.

"Wait here. I'll be right back." And then he was gone.

Where is he going?

Everything faded, growing darker… Everything gone. Then she was gone too.

"Perrie?" She knew that voice. Her eyes were too heavy to open. "Perrie?" There it was again, that female voice.

Perrie finally jerked her eyes open. "Maisie?" Three heads awkwardly hovered above her face. She sat up as they shifted back.

The first thing she noticed was her dress, ripped and drenched in blood. It was practically saturated to where there was more red than white. Then it all hit her—Fannie and that monstrous gargoyle.

Vale sat beside her with his hand against her lower back, propping her up in case she fell. But she was okay now. No more pain.

"How are you feeling?" he asked.

Perrie swallowed, peering up at his concerned face, and she didn't want to look away. "Remember that hand we saw sticking out from the ground?"

He nodded but also looked confused. "Yes?"

"That's how I feel, except like I crawled out of the heavy dirt and am relieved I'm out. I thought I was gone."

"Immortal, remember?" Maisie piped in.

Perrie's attention stayed focused on Vale. "But Officer Rodriguez was immortal, and she still ended up dead."

"That is because after she died, *he* sent her soul away," Vale said in a weak voice.

"So, I did die." *Again.*

He slowly nodded, chewing the edge of his bottom lip. A much better habit of his than the compulsive nail picking. "Did you wish I would have sent your soul away?"

"No!" Perrie practically yelled. This immortality would take some getting used to, but she didn't want to die yet.

"Good. I kind of wish for you not to leave." Vale grinned.

She smiled back at him.

"Now we have to finish getting rid of the Glass Vault," he said, seriously.

"Okay, but what about Fannie and the gargoyle?"

"She is over there." He gestured toward the Jack the Ripper display. A panic flowed through her until her gaze settled on one lone glass form, hidden away beneath a black hat and cloak. She guessed that answered her earlier question—Fannie wasn't wearing the dress.

"How?" Perrie asked while Vale helped her stand.

"My abilities were off in the display with Fannie and the gargoyle, but after you killed her, they re-appeared. Before she came back to life, I transported her to the Ripper display. It took me longer than I liked, or I would have gotten to you sooner." He closed his eyes, clenching them tight.

"I'm glad you didn't, Vale," Perrie rushed out the words. "I mean, what if you went after the gargoyle first and then Fannie woke back up leaving you powerless again." She would've withstood any amount of pain, as long as Vale was able to send Fannie away.

"I know, but you still had to go through all that. I knew you would be okay, but I did not want to screw anything up for you any more than it already has been. If I did not get Fannie to her display, it would only have made your life worse, and I could not have her send you down there to my father."

"It's okay, Vale. I under—"

"Then," he interrupted, squeezing at his hair, "when I turned to you and saw what the gargoyle had done, I was so angry. I brought you out and went back into its display first, punching the gargoyle over and over until he told me everything. Fannie and my father were using the gargoyle as a spy when she was not around. She had a charm that would be able to shut my powers off in a display that wasn't her own, and Father was going to use me when I became fully charged. He wanted to drain my powers into him so he could rise. Then I dropped the gargoyle and immediately went and found Maisie and Neven because we have to close up the Glass Vault."

Perrie listened to everything he said while Maisie and Nev watched. Nev was the first to speak. "Then what the hell are we doing here still talking? We could've done all this after."

"Let's go," Perrie said, wondering what their next move would be. Vale waved them over, and they hurried down all three hallways. As soon as Vale touched the gold knob, the door opened.

Once outside, and even though it wasn't over, Perrie could truly breathe for a second. She inhaled the fresh air, peered up at the sky, and listened to the rustle of the wind through the trees.

Vale took a few steps forward in the direction of the Glass Vault and clapped. This time before he separated them, he slowly bent his knuckles, leaving the outer edges of his hands together, like he had something in between them. Where the museum once stood was now only a lot of land, as if the Glass Vault had never been there at all.

Perrie gasped. Maisie watched in wonder. Nev sighed in relief. With his fingertips still touching, Vale rotated his hands. One faced the grass, the other the sky—he lifted the top hand gracefully away. A miniature form of the Glass Vault now rested in his palm, and Perrie wished he would bring his other hand down to smash it.

"What are you going to do with it?" Maisie asked, tiptoeing up to the tiny building and inspecting the small structure.

"Crush it?" *Nev is in the same thinking boat I'm in.*

Vale shook his head. "I have to transport it back through the barrier that leads to the Underworld."

"How do we get to the barrier from here?" Perrie hoped it wasn't too far.

Vale gave her a sly look. "Right there." He walked to the spot where the Glass Vault once stood, tossed the little stone building into the grass, snapped his fingers, and poof, the small toy-like building vanished.

Fucking finally. "That's it?"

"That's it." He smiled.

"What now?" Perrie asked, her heart pounding. "You're

not going to go back, right?" She hoped he wasn't going to jump into the grass and disappear too.

"No. I cannot go back. Father would try the same thing, but this time maybe my heart would never beat again."

Perrie didn't want him to go, not only because she didn't want the Glass Vault to come back, but because she didn't want to see Vale hurt again either.

"But what if your father still tries to escape?" What would they do if this *king*, as Maisie would say, were to come up?

"I cannot dissolve the barrier, but it is sealed. I will only have to monitor it every now and then to make sure the seal remains strong."

This little portal reminded her of her dad's favorite 80s horror movie, *The Gate,* only it wasn't in her backyard. She wished with everything in her that her dad was here too, but he wasn't.

"So, what now?" Perrie asked.

"That is the question." Vale tilted his head. "What now?"

Perrie stepped out of the shower after thoroughly scrubbing away all the blood from what had happened in the Glass Vault, as well as the memories of everything the Bride had done. Her silk dress lay sprawled out on the floor, and Perrie kicked it aside—she was never putting that damn thing on ever again.

She was home now. Well, she wasn't sure how long it would be her home. It felt strange and heartbreaking to be there without her dad, and she caught herself before she could cry. Maisie had gone with Nev to get some of his possessions from his house before they went back to her place. Perrie had told them she'd meet them there in the morning, then they'd head off wherever they decided to go. Besides, she wanted to stay at her house for one night and pretend as if everything was normal. Even though it wasn't.

A noise penetrated through the crack under the bathroom door, and Perrie closed her eyes as she listened to the sweet, graceful strokes of a bow across four strings, intertwined with a mixture of chords being pressed. This melody from the cello fractured her heart with brutality and delicate sounds. He was good, better than anything she'd ever heard from August before, and that was saying a lot. Her ears drank in the notes as she wrapped a towel around her body.

Stepping to the mirror, Perrie drew a quick picture of a heart with broken vines on the glass. She thought about her mom and wondered if she was out there somewhere, but then stopped. Her mom wasn't real family after she'd abandoned Perrie. Even now, she still couldn't stop drawing the mirror doodles they'd always done together after bath time. It was their thing before her mom had left, but it was all Perrie's now.

Knowing what she was about to do, Perrie took a deep breath and padded down the hallway to her bedroom as the music continued to play.

She stepped into the room wearing only her towel, her wet hair brushing her skin. Vale faced away from the door, sitting in her desk chair. Perrie's heart thumped as she inched toward him, and he startled when her cheek met his warm one. Her right hand looped around to lay on top of his, ceasing the bow's movements, while her left rested atop his fingers on the strings.

"Show me?" she whispered, wanting to play this song with him.

Vale didn't speak, only began to play. Perrie lightly kept her fingers pressed against his and they moved together as if they were one. The music felt like his, like hers, like *theirs*.

The melody drifted for a long time, notes swaying in the air around them. And when he finished, they stayed there, breathing deeply together before she removed her cheek from his. His eyes were closed, then he finally opened them as she stepped back.

Without looking at her, Vale got up to set the cello against the wall. He then turned to face her and stilled. His eyes grew wide, and she just stood frozen in her towel, not saying anything. He didn't say anything either. Heat flooded her cheeks, and she felt ridiculous, stupid.

Perrie closed her eyes, reopened them, and shakily took a step forward. Vale's lips parted, and she continued to walk until she stood right before him. But he didn't move away. So she reached out and stroked his soft cheek, and those perfect green eyes of his closed as he leaned into her touch.

"Be with me," she whispered.

He lifted his head and bit his lip. "Why?"

Perrie brought her other hand to his chest and rested it against his rapid heartbeat. "I want to be with you knowing that *I'm* choosing this, not the Bride. I want to be with you because I'd like to see what can come from this. More than anything, I just want to be with you."

"I am not August." Vale said it in a way that made her believe he was envious of someone who never existed.

"I don't want you to be." She wanted him to be *this* Vale.

"You are not in love with me." His gaze shifted from her eyes to her lips and back up, seeming to search for an answer in her face.

"But one day I could be." And Perrie meant it. If he could care about her after seeing what the Bride did, even though it wasn't her, then why couldn't she feel the same way about him? She was already attracted to him and his kindness.

Vale's hand met hers at his chest, his thumb gently rubbing her skin. "I do not want to get hurt. Not anymore."

Perrie didn't know everything he'd been through, but she knew it was awful, and she wanted him to eventually confide in her—his entire story.

"I wouldn't hurt you." She took their hands from his chest and intertwined their fingers. "I've been through a lot. You've been through a lot. Maybe we can help mend each other. Both of us could cross a tunnel on our own, but together? Together we could be *stronger*."

Taking a deep swallow, Perrie unwrapped the towel at her chest until she was baring everything before him, including her emotions.

He reached out without any hesitation to bring her face to his, and his soft lips molded to hers. Vale's hand shook, and his kisses were gentle and sweet, like him, until they weren't anymore. He hauled her to his body as his back hit the wall, and they melted together to the floor. Vale pulled her to sit on top of him and she moved back, so he could yank off his shirt.

Vale watched her for a moment, deliberating about something he wanted to say. "Perrie, I—I love you. I fell in love with you through the memories, and the feeling has not gone away. It has only intensified. I choose to always be your strength in any way you need, even if you never feel the same way."

Perrie may not be there yet, but she knew she'd catch up. She had to do it before with August, when she'd thought Nev had cheated on her, and she wanted to do it again. She didn't think she would ever want to, but how quickly something could change. Her heart was already waiting to open up for him, but her head just needed to deal with everything that had happened in order to get her there. For now, she would give him all of her—at least, what was there for her to give.

Her mouth crashed to his from his lovely words, and their lips sailed across each other—he caught her bottom lip in between his teeth, giving the area a soft lick. Perrie kissed along his jaw to right behind his ear, and he pulled her tighter against him. As she tugged on his blond curls, she softly bit his earlobe.

He rocked her against him while they kissed for a long time, until they both needed him to remove his pants. "Do you want the bed?" he whispered against her ear as she helped him out of his clothing.

"I want the floor," she whispered back. They were already used to sleeping there anyway.

He gave her a beautiful smile that was all Vale, and with a smile in return, she drew him closer. His hands touched everywhere—she arched as his fingers trailed feather touches down to her breast, then ventured between her thighs, circling with beautiful movements that had her on the brink of shattering completely.

And Perrie wanted nothing but to show him how good he was making her feel. She grasped his length, stroking him as he groaned in the crook of her neck. His lips came to hers once more and she continued her pace until they both needed him inside her.

Vale carefully lay Perrie down on her back and kissed between her breasts. He then flicked a nipple with his tongue and brought it in between his teeth, making her moan. With a soothing suck, he released it and kissed his way back up to her lips.

She could feel him at her entrance, and she threaded her fingers through his curls. Her body was singing to his, and his was calling to hers. He pushed inside her, and she gasped in pleasure. His body trembled as they stared at one another.

"Are you all right?" she asked.

"With you, how could I not be?"

Her mouth collided with Vale's and his trembling subsided. Perrie gripped him tighter when he started to move inside her, holding onto him with everything she had. Then they showed each other how through the darkness that hibernated in them all, the light could always subdue it.

EPILOGUE

Six Months Later-Perrie

Trying to get back to normal hadn't been easy. There were moments when Perrie needed her dad, Aunt Krista, and Uncle Jaron. Other times, she was okay because she had Maisie, Vale, and Nev.

So many areas had been destroyed throughout the Americas. The first thing they'd decided to do was search for everyone who'd become immortal in the Glass Vault.

The main reason they did this was because Perrie had wanted the immortals to have the same option Maisie, Nev, and she had—whether they wanted to stay here or let their soul move on. It took a while to find them all, but they did.

Most of the immortals had wanted to stay, but if and when they changed their mind, they could search Vale out. A few of them had decided to move on, such as Josselyn. She was too haunted over the headless statues she'd created. There were times when Perrie couldn't cope with what she'd done, but then she forced herself to remember that the Bride wasn't her and if she'd been in her right mindset, none of this would've happened. Fannie, however, was a whole different story. As vicious as it may be, Perrie could honestly have stabbed her as many times as needed in order to save everyone.

Earlier, they'd found the last immortal—Ben Johnston. He'd chosen to stay immortal and was just glad he could take photographs for an eternity while not having to worry about sunscreen any longer. Then he'd ventured back out on his own.

"How do you feel now that our mission of finding lost souls, as Maisie would say, is accomplished?" Perrie asked, studying Vale as he watched Ben fade into the distance. They would have to let Maisie and Nev know they completed this final task. To search more quickly, they'd gone in one direction and Maisie and Nev in another.

"It was all for you." Vale looped his pinky with hers.

"That's a lie. You wanted to do this, too."

There were still nights when he woke up trembling, and Perrie wrapped her arms around him to let him know she was there. Sometimes his nightmares were about his father and the Underworld, other times they were about the people who had normal lives before and were left with no choice but immortality after.

Some nights it was him who held onto her, when the past crept into her mind.

"I could have found better ways to occupy my mind." Apparently, he could start joking for a bit since everyone had been found.

"Cello, right?" Perrie grinned.

"Definitely the cello." He ran a finger across his lower lip.

Something about his expression, the way the sun hit his blond curls, the glint in his eyes… She didn't know exactly what did it, but her heart filled with so much emotion, tears threatened to fall. Before she could talk herself out of it, she rushed to Vale, practically tackling him to the ground. Her arms wrapped around his waist, squeezing him with all she had.

"I love you," she murmured.

Vale froze, then sighed softly above her head, like everything had been set right with him. "I should have mentioned a long time ago how much I *love* that cello occupies my mind, then maybe you would have said those magical words sooner." He chuckled as he brushed a kiss right at her temple.

"That's totally what would've made me say it sooner." Perrie smiled, listening to the beautiful beat of his heart while it played its own symphony just for her.

Life wasn't always straightforward, and immortal life was even less clear, but with Vale, Maisie, and Nev, they would continue to hold each other together and make sure the barrier remained sealed.

If it ever broke, they'd be ready.

End of Book Two

Turn the page for a special epilogue scene from Maisie's POV

HEART OF GLASS

Maisie

Some immortals' hearts were like glass, easy to shatter.

But not Maisie's.

Maisie pedaled her old bike down the dusty abandoned road. This thing had been sitting in her garage for years before it helped her to venture across the country. Two months had passed since the world almost came to a dreadful end, when a demon prince and his wicked souls had run the show. *But hey, the world survived.* Just as Maisie had. Although, she was immortal. Forever and ever.

"I think I see her, Mais," Neven said as he pedaled faster, catching up beside her. The wind blew his shaggy hair back, exposing his perfect scars even more. Since they'd started dating, she couldn't get enough of him, couldn't believe the guy who she'd ran from after their first kiss, when she'd been fourteen, was now hers.

Vale and Perrie had separated from them for a while, so they could each track down the turned-immortals from the Glass Vault. It had been time to ask them a higher-power of a choice—live or die.

Maisie squinted her eye and found a lone woman curled up beneath the shade of a maple tree at the edge of the woods. Her gray dress was a raggedy mess and her blonde hair hung in knots down her back. *Yep, there's Josselyn.*

With a smile, Maisie hit the brake at the same time Neven did. Hopping off her bike, she released the kickstand and clapped her hands with a smile. *Another immortal down!*

Maisie held a finger over her lips, telling Neven to stay silent as they walked to her. She didn't want to frighten Josselyn and have to chase after her. They'd already had to do that twice now with two other immortals.

As she peered at Josselyn's form, she wasn't sure if she was dead. Then the immortal's chest rose and fell. *Nope, not dead.* Even if Josselyn had tried to pierce her own heart or something less messy, she wouldn't have died anyway. Vale, who was no longer Bad Vale, but Good Vale, was needed to perform that duty.

Maisie crouched down at the sleeping woman's side and shook her arm. "Josselyn," she whispered.

The Immortal's lids jerked open and she screamed when her gaze met Maisie's.

"It's okay." Maisie tightened her grip on Josselyn's arm, while Neven grasped her other one. "It's just us. We were once part of the same wicked club, remember?"

Josselyn's body trembled, her eyes widening in fear. *Maybe I shouldn't have brought up the club just yet.*

"No one's going to hurt you anymore," Neven said softly. Josselyn seemed to relax a fraction at his words.

"Vale is good now," Maisie started. "Bad Vale is gone. He's giving you a choice if you want to live or die." And then she explained the rest to Josselyn, everything that had occurred in the Glass Vault, all that had happened between Vale and his father, how he was hurt as much as they'd been, and how he was willing to look for every last immortal, no matter how long it took. To give them this choice.

When Maisie finished, Josselyn pressed her hands to her face and sobbed.

Maisie patted Josselyn's back. "There. There. It isn't so bad."

"Isn't so bad?" Josselyn glanced up at her as though she were back to being Crazy Maisie. "Look at the world. Look at *us*."

Neven shrugged. "I mean, it's better than it was a few months ago."

"I can't do this," Josselyn cried, tears streaming down her cheeks. "I just can't."

And she wouldn't have to. Maisie understood the immortal life wasn't meant for everyone. She pulled her backpack off her shoulder and fished out her notepad and pencil from the front pocket. Josselyn's brow furrowed while she watched Maisie write down the address to where she could wait for Vale and Perrie.

Tearing off the note, she handed it to Josselyn. "Meet them here and your wish shall come true. No more tears."

"I don't know if I trust this." Josselyn's lip quivered while taking the note. "But it can't be worse than what's already happened."

Things could always be worse, but Maisie kept her lips zipped as not to upset the immortal more.

Josselyn rose and slowly walked down the dusty road, her shoulders slumped and her head lowered.

"Wait," Maisie called after her. She jogged to her bike and pushed it toward the immortal. You don't have to walk there. Take this." It was the least she could do.

"Thanks." Josselyn smiled warmly, placing her palms on the handlebars. She pulled her dress up a bit to take a seat on the bike, then took off down the road to get her happily ever after somewhere else.

"Now"—Maisie whirled to face Neven, a huge grin on her

face—"I have a surprise for you."

He arched a brow.

"I swear it's a good one this time." She laughed, remembering the last time she'd taken him to a cave and they couldn't find their way out for days. Before he could reply, Maisie yanked him by the hand into the woods. She hadn't planned to do this here, but spontaneity was the answer.

The leaves crunched beneath their feet as she drew him a bit deeper into the trees. She whirled around and grasped both his hands in hers. "Today's your birthday."

"Yes?" The edges of his lips curved up as if he was still unsure about what she was planning. At nineteen, Neven should've started college with his basketball scholarship already, but maybe he still could once the world was healed. He would have to be hush-hush about the immortal thing, though.

Maisie released his hands and set her backpack on the ground, then drew out two cans of spray cheese and placed them next to her backpack.

"Are you sure you don't want them both?" He grinned, watching as she pulled out a box of crackers and put it beside the spray cheese.

"Hey"—she stood and poked his chest—"I won't deny that, but I at least share."

He rolled his eyes. "I don't think you'll ever let me live that one down."

"Before our little picnic, I have something else for you first." She held his hands once more, his calluses beautifully rough against her skin. "We're going to have sex."

Neven coughed, choking. Then laughter poured out from his mouth, his body practically convulsing. He grabbed her by the hips and drew her to his chest, then pressed his head to hers. "I love how you're so fucking forward. But are you sure you want your first time to be here?"

It didn't matter where she took him at, and out here, in the woods, with the wind blowing and the sun shining, was the right choice. "Yes, unless you're not ready."

"Oh, I've been ready." His fingers dug into her hips. "Are you sure?"

Maisie had been ready since their kiss in the Sleeping Beauty display, but she figured they'd needed to go slow. By that, she meant do almost everything but sex. "I want it more than the cans of cheese." She grinned and bopped his nose before taking a step back to peel off her eye patch. "So let's get undressed."

"Yes, ma'am." She could tell he wanted to laugh again, but he only smiled and lifted his shirt over his head.

They removed their clothing, item by item, their eyes locked all the while, until they stood naked before each other. To the majority of the world, it may not be the most romantic concept to talk about sex before having it, then study each other's naked forms before crashing into one another. But it was to her.

Maisie looked at Neven as she would an art sculpture, taking in each one of his pale pink scars, his tan skin, his charming face, his strong hands, and the part of him that was no longer soft.

"You're beautiful," he whispered, his gaze traveling across her body like he was studying a map, wanting to take in each line, each curve.

And then, Maisie closed the distance, drawing his head to hers. She brought her mouth to his, and he lifted her so her legs wrapped around his waist. Neven carefully lowered her to the grass as though she were made of glass.

"You won't break me, Neven," she said as his body hovered above hers, the heat of his skin warming her perfectly.

He rolled his eyes, then kissed the tip of her nose. "I love you, Mais."

"I love you, Neven." Heart pounding, she trailed her fingers across a light scar on his cheek. She then cradled his face and brought his mouth to hers. "We can do foreplay later. I just want you right now. Then break for the cheese and go into round two after."

Neven brushed a lock of hair away from her face. "You may hate round one."

"Then that's what round two will be for. Good or bad, I don't care." It wouldn't matter—it was him, her Frankenstein's Monster, and that was all she needed.

"Here goes round one then," he murmured. His gaze trained on hers, his expression turning serious. "Let me know if I need to stop or slow down, all right?"

Maisie nodded, her fingers entwining with his hair as anticipation coursed through her. His lips softly pressed to hers, then he slowly pushed into her. A sharp ache filled her and she gasped. She'd been through worse, felt worse. Still, was this what everyone liked feeling? But then, the pain subsided and it was just Neven inside her, them peering at one another. Neven and Maisie.

"I'm still good," she whispered.

In answer, he pulled back slightly and rolled his hips forward. Her heart sang at the movement and the new magical thrum pulsing within her. Neven then did it again … and again. Maisie needed more, needed to feel him everywhere. She pulled his mouth to hers—kissing, nipping, tasting. His hand trailed to her breast and cupped it, his thumb softly circling her nipple, sending wonderful shivers through her body. She skimmed her fingers down his spine to his backside, then gripped it as he moved. Neven's pace picked up as she held him tighter. She felt him down to her bones, in her mind, *everywhere*.

Her heart sang higher as a pleasureful feeling rose within her, peaking out of its hidden depths. She'd felt this before from his fingers, his tongue, but this time, it was more powerful. A roaring, an explosion, spread through her as her heart continued to sing. Maisie didn't release a scream or moan, just as she always did when he touched her, tasted her, only heavy puffs of blissful breaths. But when Neven followed down her path, he was much, much louder, same as he always was when she touched him, tasted him. Yet this, this was different, and it was oh so heavenly.

Both their chests heaved, Neven's gorgeous face slick with sweat. He peered down at her with a smile and ran his thumb across her bottom lip.

"That was fun." Maisie grinned, softly nipping his thumb. "Now we can eat, then do it again."

He wrapped his arms around her, laughing as he rolled over, tucking her into the crook of his arm. "I fucking love you."

Did you enjoy Bride of Glass?

Authors always appreciate reviews, whether long or short. If you enjoyed the Wicked Souls Duology, then you may want to check out **Clouded By Envy**, Boon One in the Cruel Curses Trilogy!

He only ever wanted to be human. She only ever wanted to save him. Sometimes the very thing you wish for, is your undoing...

Brenik has always been envious of his twin sister, Bray. Everything always came naturally to Bray, even after crossing through a portal from their fae world, while Brenik spent his time in her shadow. So, when Brenik discovers a way to get what he has always desired—to become human—he takes it. However, the gift turns out to be a curse that alters him in ways he never saw coming.

Bray can't help but be concerned for her brother, more so when he vanishes. While waiting for Brenik to return, she meets two brothers who realize she isn't human. Her dark bat-like wings are proof of that. But somehow, an aching bond forms between Bray and the hot older brother, Wes.

When Bray reunites with Brenik, she finds he has an overpowering need for blood stirring within him. If Bray doesn't help Brenik put an end to his curse, it will not only damage those who get close to him, but it could also destroy the steamy romance blooming between her and Wes.

Check out Candace's books!

Wicked Souls Duology
Vault of Glass
Bride of Glass

Marked by Magic
The Bone Valley
Merciless Stars

Cruel Curses Trilogy
Clouded By Envy
Veiled By Desire
Shadowed By Despair

Faeries of Oz Series
Lion (Short Story Prequel)
Tin
Crow
Ozma
Tik-Tok

Cursed Hearts Duology
Lyrics & Curses
Music & Mirrors

Immortal Letters Duology
Dearest Clementine: Dark and Romantic Monstrous Tales
Dearest Dorin: A Romantic Ghostly Tale

Campfire Fantasy Tales Series
Lullaby of Flames
A Layer Hidden
The Celebration Game
Mirror, Mirror

These Vicious Thorns: Tales of the Lovely Grim
Between the Quiet
Hearts Are Like Balloons
Bacon Pie
Avocado Bliss

Vampires in Wonderland Series
Rav (Short Story Prequel)
Maddie
Chess
Knave

Demons of Frosteria Series
Frost Mate (Prequel Novella)
Frost Claim

Once Upon A Wicked Villain Series
Spindle of Sin

Acknowledgements

I really want to thank the readers first, especially since most likely you read the first book and continued to want to read the second. I knew where I wanted the story to go after book one, but I didn't know if I could pull it together, but then all of a sudden it came. So, thanks for being part of this journey.

My big helpers! Amber Hodges for being amazing and going through this story multiple times! Elle Beaumont, Victoria Robinson, Donna Weiss, Gerardo Delgadillo, Alexa Whitewolf, Rebecca Ayala, and Amanda Wright. You guys rock!

My husband who let me write another book while he works incredibly hard, my daughter who continues to be fabulous, and my mom who is always there when I need her.

This book was about making a different sort of fairy tale, and I had a blast while working on it.

About the Author

Candace Robinson spends her days consumed by words and hoping to one day find her own DeLorean time machine. Her life consists of avoiding migraines, admiring Bonsai trees, watching classic movies, and living with her husband and daughter in Texas—where it can be forty degrees one day and eighty the next.

Connect with Candace:

Website: https://authorcandacerobinson.wordpress.com/
Facebook: https://www.facebook.com/literarydust
Twitter: https://twitter.com/literarydust
Instagram:
https://www.instagram.com/candacerobinsonbooks/
Goodreads:
https://www.goodreads.com/author/show/16541001.Candace
_Robinson or ignore that and just try searching for Candace Robinson!